TONGUES OF THE MONTE

BOOKS BY
J. FRANK DOBIE

TONGUES OF THE MONTE
A VAQUERO OF THE BRUSH COUNTRY
CORONADO'S CHILDREN
ON THE OPEN RANGE

J. FRANK DOBIE

TONGUES

OF THE

MONTE

DOUBLEDAY, DORAN & COMPANY, INC.

Garden City, New York

1935

PRINTED AT THE *Country Life Press*, GARDEN CITY, N. Y., U. S. A.

The Things Which Are Cæsar's

Despite conflicting claims of patronage, aids, esteem, friendship, love, policy, some books require to be dedicated to the sources of their life. This one is such. Yet life is so riddlesome and its intricate courses flow from springs so far removed that any author resolved on such a just dedication might, not to be metaphysical, make it to "some old lover's ghost who died before the god of love was born." Or, with justice equally direct, he might inscribe it with the legend etched on a Mexican machete: "Viva Yo!" (Long Live I!) Looking between the extremes of these sources, I with much pleasure of remembrance dedicate my book:

First, to Don Federico Graves, whose only home for many years was in camps amid Mexican sierras, whose endless accounts of "what happened unto me," had he transferred them to writing as he charmed me with them during a long association, would have made a far more delightful book than I can ever write, and whose ex-

v

periences—even to the use of his name—have indeed in the pages that follow been assumed by the narrator. He lived a natural man, as frank as minute in personal talk, eager always for experience, taking a rare pleasure in the company of lowly and, therefore, natural folk. Had he lived to be old, he would still have died young. The gods loved him. For him the prayer chiseled on stone in the ancient church at Cuernavaca: *La misericordia del Señor tenga su alma en vida perdurable.*

Next, to the lovely and delightful grace who made the ward of Godmother Death skip along the edge of the moon and for one evanescent while on this sublunary sphere strew petals of roses for the Flower of his Life to step upon.

Finally, to the *mozo* of the pack trail—particularly to one—who in guiding and administering to his *patrón* serves him as loyally as the idealized slave of the Old South ever served his master and who when the day is done and the camp fire is genial will, if his master be *simpático* and kindly and his ears be open, pour into them that lore of marvels and common things alike that is his inheritance.

CONTENTS

vii

TONGUES OF THE MONTE

CHAPTER
1

Machetes and Fairies

JUST as I rounded a bluff I sighted the waterhole in the spread-out cañon. At the same moment four vaqueros, yelling and spurring, approached from another direction, partly dragging, partly driving a lanky brindle bull. They halted between the water and a tree from which hung a few camp things, and instantly one of them lassoed the animal by the hind legs. While it was stretched out between him and the rider who had it already roped about the head and horns, a third man quickly dismounted and by a jerk on the tail brought the bull to earth.

At this juncture three other vaqueros dashed up, each as he reined from full speed to a halt giving his horse the same savage lash with the quirt he would employ at starting from a halt to a run. Yells more eager than vigorous expressed the belly anticipation that animated the whole group.

1

"Wait until I get my little cup of Juan Perulero!"

"Just long enough to say '*adiós, mamacita!*'"

"Plácido wants to catch pure *toro* breath in a bottle and carry it as perfume to the painted lady in the cane patch."

"Hurry! Shoot him with a quince seed!"

"Don San Antonio! Here the family is!"

"Chihuahua! We are about to get drunk on the blood of a bull!" A diminutive fellow whose teeth stuck out as if they were meant to eat pumpkins through a fence chirped this last expression.

Meantime all the vaqueros had dismounted, and now two were holding the bull down, the riderless horses keeping the ropes taut from saddle horns. One vaquero grabbed a blackened can, two others got porcelain-lined cups, and another, the eldest of the group, who had said nothing, stood whetting a long, heavy-bladed, sharp-pointed *belduque* on a rock. A few seconds later he raised the knife upward, called out playfully, "Off for Heaven!"—evidently to the soul of the bull—and then drew the blade across the animal's throat. It gave a hideous gurgle, and the blood spouted out in waves to be caught by the can, in which it was subsequently cooked, and in the cups, from which the holders eagerly drank. Meantime amid the general buffoonery one of the crew, imitative of the mistress of Cortés in *Los Matachines*, in which folk dance-play this man himself may have acted a part, dipped his blue bandana in blood, and kneeling with it spread out before the bull-stabber, quoted:

> "*Tengan, tengan sangre*
> *Del toro que mató mi padre.*"

2

MACHETES AND FAIRIES

(Take, take this blood
From the bull my father has slain.)

Some of the gore was allowed to soak into an old sack. This sack the riders were later to drag at the end of a rope through a certain part of the range so that any cow brute scenting it would give the "blood bellow"— certainly one of the wildest sounds on earth—and thus become liable to capture.

During the swift operations of the killing I had ridden to within a few yards of the group and halted. Blood-drinkers are rare among vaqueros, and I was enthralled by the sight. My *mozo*, who led the pack mule, knew one of the group, and now there was time for the invitation to make camp together. As I like good camp company as well as any vaquero and as the day was drawing towards its close, I was well pleased to abide.

The place was deep in the eastern cordillera of Mexico, not a great distance from where the states of Coahuila, Nuevo León and Zacatecas all corner. The range here, like millions of other arid acres in northern Mexico, was unstocked and had since revolution denuded it twenty-five years ago lain largely idle. Nevertheless almost every *ranchito* had its little flock of goats; the settlements and towns all kept some domesticated horses, burros, mules and cattle; and out in the wild country a few other such animals ran wilder than the deer. The men I had come upon were out hunting wild stock—the *cimarrones*, or outlaws.

This was not the kind of cow camp familiar in the states. There was no chuck wagon; there were no pack mules with bedding, cooking utensils, and provisions. Probably not one of the vaqueros had ever been in a

3

tent. Unhampered by things, each could tie his blanket on saddle, stuff his scant rations and cup in *morral*—the fiber bag carried at the saddle horn—and be off instantly. Their horses were trained to whirl inward the moment the rider lifted foot towards the stirrup and to leave in a rush, for there may be times when a vaquero wants to get away quick from a bandit or a fighting bull. If their heavy, ungraceful spurs were an encumbrance upon the ground, they helped to balance the rider immediately he swung into the saddle and to keep him planted there.

The vaqueros had left home well supplied with *tortillas*. Each had a metal cup. Some had a small portion of coffee—the kind mixed with parched chickpeas, but not one had any sugar. There was one coffee pot among the seven men and salt was not lacking. Their principal diet, on this hunt at least, was meat, although at home they lived mainly on corn and dried *frijoles*, or beans, which from their universal use in Mexico are commonly called *nacionales*. Despite the fact that only one man among the lot had a gun, a .30-30 Winchester for which he professed to have but two cartridges, I learned that they had been rather fortunate in getting meat. During preceding days they had roped two musk hogs and a doe. Now they were butchering an old outlaw bull that it would have been impossible to drive away from the cañons.

Ribs were spitted over the fire; the hide was pegged out to dry; on the morrow the meat would be cut into strips and hung on stretched ropes—jerked. Meantime a heap of coals smouldered in a hole dug near the fire. A handful of *orégano*, a kind of wild marjoram, which one of the men had brought in tied to his saddle, was

4

stuffed into the mouth of the bull head to add flavor. Later the head itself, the hide still on it, was wrapped in grass, bound in place by strings from the leaves of Spanish-dagger that had been lightly roasted in ashes to make the fiber pliable. Then, the coals having heated the pit and burned out, the head was buried and some chunks of fire were placed on the earth covering it.

"It will not be so hard to cook as the head of Padre Ayala," said one, alluding to a Franciscan reputed to have been killed by Indians in Spanish times but to have had such a holy head that after three days of boiling in an *olla* of water it still "did not want to cook itself."

Over such a bounty both present and prospective the vaqueros were hilarious. Amidst such a plenty of beef they barely touched their *tortillas*, for *tortillas* will always keep. After they had gorged in silence, except for the noise attendant upon gnawing off and swallowing meat, and had drunk abundantly of the sugared coffee from my pack, true to their nature and to my expectations they began singing. There are two creatures that will always sing at night after a good fill of meat: one is a coyote and the other is a Mexican vaquero. And there is something common to the songs of both. I wish I could convey the effect of a vaquero's song as it rises and dies far out in the mountains or *monte*,[1] whether from *jacal* or camp. I cannot. It is a wail; it is a yell, long-drawn and quivering, that seems to go up to the stars; it is a rhythm—not a melody—out of the primordial elements. It is, no matter what the theme of the

[1]A generic name for *forest, brush, thicket;* the word is commonly used by English-speaking ranch people in the Southwest. Less locally the word also means *mountain.*

5

song—whether of love and lust, a bandit's career, a dead child, a rider killed by a horse, a patriot returned from "North America," or a wild bull—a note of solitude, of something far, far away. It is wild; it is barbaric; it makes the blood run both hot and cold. Prisoners of war in Montezuma's camp or flower-festooned maidens of his own blood destined to be sacrificed to the Aztec gods might have wailed out such notes on their way to the sacrificial stone.

On this night, of "Lupita" (with some extra verses not found in print), of "The Four Fields," and of "My Dun Horse" the vaqueros sang. Two coyotes that sounded like twenty responded to them from the dark distance.

"Mama, I'm hungry," vociferated three young vaqueros. I called for "When I Went up to Kansas"— a ballad of cattle trails never again to be traveled that for three quarters of a century Mexicans from San Antonio to Zacatecas have wailed out. Only one of the vaqueros, an oldish man, knew it. As he sang it, after much persuasion, I saw the *corrida* of Mexican cowboys leave the border with a herd of steers Kansas bound; I tarried in their camps and rode slow with their drags until away up beyond the Arkansas River they put the cattle in a pen. There the steers stampeded and killed the youngest hand. Then I heard the others, returned home, tell the boy's mother why he did not come back also.

Immediately that this doleful relation was finished, someone took up the words:

"Lunes y martes y miércoles—tres,
Jueves y viernes y sábado—seis."

(Monday and Tuesday and Wednesday—three,
Thursday and Friday and Saturday—six.)

6

With the exception of two vaqueros—one the old fellow who had stabbed the bull and the other a man of about thirty-five who sat moody and choleric throughout the evening, no song in him—the whole crew joined in. They repeated the words again and again, with each repetition chanting louder and faster until my head was in a whirl.

I was sitting next to the old bull-stabber, and said, "That is a very strange song. What does it mean?"

As he was starting to make reply, a youngster who had been particularly loud in chanting the names of the days of the week laughed towards him, "Have care not to come out with a Sunday seven."

To "come out with a Sunday seven" is to say or do something foolish. I had often wondered how such a phrase came into use. Before the old vaquero had fully answered my question, I learned.

"You know what a *jorobado* is?" he asked.

Yes, I knew what a hunchback is. In fact, for luck, I wore a Mexican ring carved of horn and inlaid with the mother-of-pearl figure of a tiny hunchback. On the streets of Mexico City I had seen people touch the hump of a hunchback to make the lottery tickets he sold bring them luck; in Juárez I had seen a hunchback kept by a gambling house to give gamblers confidence in their luck—and luck itself, perhaps, to the house. I had some knowledge of the "humpbacked flute-player" that Indians of the Southwest unknown centuries ago depicted on the walls of caves, a puzzle to modern archæologists.

Now that the weathered vaquero felt the responsibility of conveying to me a piece of important information, he seemed to gather dignity and become conscious

7

of being, if not immediately an *hijo de algo* (son of somebody), certainly a descendant, even though by the left-hand route, of the Cid.

With great formality he said, "As *gente de razón*, you, *señor*, well understand that the bucket comes not up before the rope has been drawn in."

"Certainly," I assented.

"Well, then," he began, "one time a long time ago, as the old ones say, two hunchbacked men lived in a village in the mountains far, far from other population. One of them was a woodcutter, and he was bright and ready in his mind; he could make *versos* and sing them too. The other was a little stupid, and in his heart he had envy.

"And you have to know, *señor*, that there is nothing worse in this world than envy. For example, if two individuals go out to dig up a treasure and one of them has envy, the gold, even if the *envidioso* finds it, will be turned into charcoal or some other matter without value. Did you ever know a rich baker?"

Offhand I could not assert that I ever had actually enjoyed acquaintance with a rich baker.

"There is one explication," the old vaquero went on, looking around him as if to see that the point went home to every man. "While the Most Holy Virgin and San José were journeying with El Niño Dios, they came to the house of a baker. He was baking and the Niñito picked up a bit of dough that had dropped on the floor. La Virgen María took it and composed it into a little bit of loaf and asked the baker permission to cook it in his oven. He was willing. When, after a while, the oven was opened, he saw that the little piece of dough had baked into a loaf larger than his own. He quickly exchanged the two. Because of that envy a baker even if he work day and night will never become rich.

"*Bueno*, as the relation goes, this second hunchback had envy. But because they both had humps and because they were both ridiculed at times on account of their deformity, even though people did touch their humps and shake hands with them for luck, they were good *compañeros*. Yes, they were such good companions that they were at the point of licking each other like two friendly oxen.

"One day the woodcutter took his two burros up a mountain a long way off. He cut the wood, loaded it on his little beasts, and started back. He knew, however, that he could not reach home that night. So, late in the afternoon, he camped. The hobbled burros were grazing in a little flat off to one side of him and he was resting against a sharp hill that rose to his back when all of a sudden he heard voices. The country about him was so covered with brush that he could not see any distance, but no one lived in that part of the world. This he knew. He was very curious; also he was cautious. In order to get a view of the ground whence the voices seemed to be coming, he climbed the hill.

"When he reached a good place for the vista, his eyes fell upon a wondrous sight. Down there below him, out in the midst of the brush, was a clearing shaped like a *comal*. In the center of this basin a huge fire was burning, and there, dancing madly about the fire, a crowd of dwarfs and elves and fairies were singing at the top of their voices:

'*Lunes y martes y miércoles—tres.*'

(Monday and Tuesday and Wednesday—three.)

9

"These words the little people kept saying over and over. It seemed to be the only line of song they knew. Yet everybody knows that a song has to have more than one line and that the lines must rhyme. Well, after the hunchback had listened to the monotonous chant at least forty times, he stepped out into full view and just as the singing folk came again to '*tres,*' he added in his rich voice:

'*Jueves y viernes y sábado—seis.*'

(Thursday and Friday and Saturday—six.)

"A great shout of joy came up from the *comal*. The dwarfs and elves and fairies whirled around more madly and sang even louder and faster than before the rhyming lines:

'*Lunes y martes y miércoles—tres,*
Jueves y viernes y sábado—seis.'

• HUNCHBACK SONG •

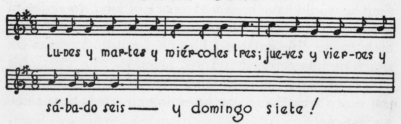

"And then they were so happy and so grateful to the hunchback for having completed their song that they rushed up the hill and began dancing around him, all the while singing. But when they saw how deformed he was, they suddenly stopped and said something magical, at the same time softly touching his hump. Behold! In

10

an instant his back was straight and he stood as erect as any soldier that ever saluted. Then quickly they ran with him down the hill and prepared a fine feast. While they ate, the little people continued to leap about and sing their song. It was dark by now and the moon was up. All at once they stopped, each with his finger on his mouth.

"'Listen!' one said.

"*Bum, bum, thump, thump.* Sounds like that, low and heavy, were coming from this way and that way.

"'It is the big devils,' whispered the fairies. 'We must scatter and run. But you,' they said to the woodcutter, 'climb into that cottonwood tree so thick of leaves and you will be safely hidden.'

"Immediately they were gone and the woodcutter skinned up the tree. He settled himself into a fork. Nor was he too soon, for three enormous devils coming from three different directions—the east and the west and the north—met right under the tree. As they began talking, the poor woodcutter up over them was more afraid than he would have been had a pack of lobo wolves been howling at his heels. He dared not move so much as a little finger. He flattened himself against the limb on which he was perched and just listened.

"'Well,' said the devil from the east to the one from the west, 'what have you been doing all this time since we last met?'

"'Oh, I have been very busy. I have been over there in the west country called Otilo, and I have made all the people stone blind so that they cannot see a thing, not even the sun. What have you been doing?'

"'I,' replied the other devil, 'have been working day and night in my kingdom, Soleste, in the east, and I

11

have made every person in it dumb—just as dumb as a stone.'

"Then both these devils turned to the third.

"'Do not think that I have been idle,' he replied. 'Up there in Borsete, my kingdom to the north, I have made every being so deaf that not a soul can hear it thunder.'

"All three devils clapped their hands and bellowed with laughter and congratulated one another on their accomplishments. The poor woodchopper held in his breath to keep his heart from beating so loud.

"'Now,' the devil from the east said to his fellow from the west, 'I know you would not want to restore the sight to those blind people in your kingdom. You would not think of doing such a good deed, but just suppose for fun you did. Could you bring back their sight?'

"'Very easily,' the devil from the west answered. 'As nobody can hear us, I'll tell you what I'd do. I would get up about four o'clock in the morning and, taking some gourds with me, I would go out and collect them full of fresh dew. Of course it is a lot of work to collect a gourd full of dew, but taking a drop off this leaf and a drop off that leaf and half a drop off a blade of grass now and then, a person can finally fill a gourd. Well, after I had collected the dew, I would go in among the blind people and, using my finger, rub a little on the eyes of each one. Then as soon as the dew evaporated on the grass, every blind person who had had his eyes moistened would see as well as a buzzard.'

"'It's a good thing nobody can hear us telling such secrets,' said the devil from the east. 'Of course I wouldn't think of curing my people of their dumbness, but it could be done.'

"'Of course you wouldn't do such a deed,' said the

devil from the west. 'But, just supposing for fun you did take a notion to cure the dumbness, what would you do?'

"'The cure is as simple as skinning up a tree,' said the devil from the east, gesturing up the cottonwood. 'Over there in my kingdom grows a bush called the *cenizo*. It has gray leaves, and after a rain it bursts into bloom with thousands and thousands of lavender flowers, so thick that they almost hide the gray.

"'Well, to cure this dumbness I would wait until the *cenizo* bloomed. Then I would take some sacks and go out into the hills and I would gather them full of leaves and blossoms mixed. Then I would brew them into a tea. This I would let settle until a wind blew away all the ashes from under the pot. Then I'd carry an *olla* of the *cenizo* tea among the people and with a spoon made out of horn ladle it into the mouth of each one. As soon as a person swallowed it, he would immediately say, "Thank you!" After that he could talk as well and as fast as a cañon-full of piñon jays screaming out to the deer that a hunter is coming.'

"Now the devil from the north was questioned.

"'It takes more knowledge to cure people of deafness than of blindness or dumbness,' he said. 'There is not only just one way to cure them; there is just one place where they can be cured. Up there in my kingdom, beside the capital city, is the Cerro de la Campana. Well is it named Mountain of the Bell, for on its slope next to the city is a round, bare boulder made out of the hardest flint on earth.

"'Now, if I led a deaf person out close to that rock and then took a hammer and struck the rock, the sound would be so bright and sharp that it would go straight through the deaf one's ear, even if he had a pillow tied

13

around it. Then he would be so acute of hearing that he could hear the beating of a gnat's wings away over on the other side of the cañon.'

"'Wonderful! Wonderful!' exclaimed the devil from the east and the devil from the west.

"'Yes, these are wonderful cures,' said the devil from the north, 'but nobody else knows them and we'll never use them. Now let us go south and see what mischief we can do down there. Then we'll separate and visit our kingdoms. A year from tonight we'll come back here and rejoice again over the evil we have caused.'

"Still laughing and congratulating each other, the three devils started southward.

"After he had waited until he knew they were a long way off, the poor woodcutter, who had been flattened up in the tree like a rusty-lizard, managed to limber his legs and arms and climb down. He had certainly heard some wonderful things.

"A bright idea came to him. Here for years he had been working like a slave, earning barely enough with his axe and burros to buy *frijoles* and corn for *tortillas*. Now he was the possessor of secrets that not all the doctors on earth knew. He decided that he would be a *curandero*. He would set out to cure people of blindness and dumbness and deafness.

"So when daylight came, he and his burros traveled straight west. When he came into the country called Otilo, of a truth he found all the people blind. He borrowed some gourds and early in the morning went out to gather dew drop by drop from the leaves of bushes and the blades of grass. Then he took it among the blind, moistening the eyes of each one. When the sun dried the dew on the grass, the people whose eyes had been dampened saw. There was great rejoicing, and the people gave this curer gold and silver and many beautiful things, to say nothing of their blessings. By the time he had brought sight to all the blind, one of his burros had a *carga* of pure riches.

"Then the *curandero* traveled into the east. It was raining when he got into the kingdom of Soleste. *Cenizo* plants by the thousands burst into bloom, and hillsides covered with them miles away looked like clouds of lavender. The people in this country were accustomed to weave sacks and mats and ropes out of the fiber of the *lechuguilla* and *palma loca*. So the *curandero* had no trouble finding sacks.

"He filled some of them with the leaves and blossoms of the *cenizo*. Then he boiled the tea in a big *olla*. After the wind had blown the ashes all away from this pot and the tea had settled, he began ladling it with a spoon made of horn into the mouths of the dumb. As soon as a person swallowed a mouthful of the tea, he said, 'Thank you!' After that he sang for very joy, all his dumbness gone. The cured ones loaded the *curandero's* second burro down with wealth.

"He bought a third burro and struck out towards the north. He found the capital city of the kingdom of Borsete, and on the Cerro de la Campana near it, as the devil had described, he found the bare boulder of the hardest flint on earth. He gathered together all the deaf people in the country and led them out to this rock and then struck on it with a hammer. Bright and sharp, the sounds penetrated the dullest ears. And when the people found that they could hear, they leaped and laughed, and they gave the *curandero* still more riches and still more blessings.

15

"By this time he was as rich as a Potosí, and with all the good he had done and all the blessings he had received, he was very happy. He had been away from home nearly a year. He decided to go back.

"Everybody in the village was amazed at his straight back and at his fortune. He gave gold to all the needy and he told the story of his adventures. The hunchbacked *compañero* was almost crazy with envy. He wanted to suck the bottle also.

"'Show me,' he begged, 'the place where the *duendes* sing and the devils tell their secrets. I want to get rid of my hump and be rich.'

"The *curandero's* heart, like his hand, was open. 'Prepare yourself,' he said. 'One year ago tomorrow night I heard the devils agree to meet a year thence. I can lead you to the very cottonwood tree under which they will talk.'

"So the two traveled. The *curandero* showed the hunchback the tree, told him to get up in it and be quiet, and left. About dark the waiting hunchback heard the devils tramping and muttering. They stopped under the tree. There was no laughter from them now.

"Said one, 'All those people I left blind a year ago can now see. Their eyes are so good they can see the shadow of a butterfly flying over brown grass. Some stranger came along and rubbed dew on their eyes.'

"'Thunder and horns!' roared a second devil. 'That same stranger has been in my kingdom to the east. He pulled up hectares of *cenizo* plants, brewed the tea, and ladled it into the mouth of every dumb man, woman, and child. Everybody there is singing and talking gayly. I had to shut my own ears and leave.'

"'Devils and more devils!' stormed the third evil one.

16

'To the north in my kingdom a foreigner found out about that flint boulder that rings like a bell. Actually a devil can't step on thistle-down in the country now without being overheard and chased away. We have been outraged.'

"Then all three devils set in to blaming one another and everybody else because somebody had learned their secrets. They were still quarreling, and the envious *compañero* up in the tree was wondering if they were ever going to say anything profitable, when he heard a medley of glad voices and saw come skipping into the moonlight a bevy of dwarfs and elves and fairies.

"They came right up to the tree and began dancing around the big devils. Perhaps the little ones were happy because so many people in the world had been cured of being blind and deaf and dumb. They had no fear of the devils now, but danced right over their tails, twitched the long hairs growing out of their ears, skipped through the prongs of their pitchforks and teased them in other ways. Then they took up the song they loved best to sing:

> '*Lunes y martes y miércoles—tres,*
> *Jueves y viernes y sábado—seis.*'

"Over and over they sang it, at each repetition faster and louder. The three devils could not get in a word, even to quarrel. After a while the ambitious hunchback became so disgusted at not hearing any secrets that he decided to add to the song, devils or no devils, and at least win a straight back. So at the end of the verse he screeched out:

> '*Y domingo siete.*'

(And Sunday seven.)

17

"At that the little people instantly vanished and the devils all looked up.

"'There's that scoundrel who overheard our secrets and used them,' they cried. 'Get him!'

"One of them skinned up the tree and with a jerk tumbled the eavesdropper down. Then they grabbed him and taunted him—

> '*Y domingo siete,*
> *Y aquí está su pisiete.*'

> (So it's Sunday seven,
> And here's your blemissen.)

"With that they put a second hump on his back—his *pisiete*. Then they turned his pockets wrongside out and kicked him and told him to go home and tend to his own business. True it is that honey was not made for the mouth of a burro."

At the end of the story there was silence for about a minute. Then the choleric-looking vaquero who up to this moment had not smiled or spoken a word said, "That story does not end correctly."

"Certainly," I took the liberty of saying, "the relator of this story has not come out with any Sunday seven, but how should it end?"

"Why, *pisiete* is not a word at all," the critic retorted. "It means nothing. After the *domingo siete*, the devils said:

> '*Échale otro piquete.*'"

> (Give him another wound.)

He looked very wise and well satisfied, and nobody contradicted him. The old story-teller merely repeated one of those jingles often quoted at the end of a story:

"The cup is broken.
It fell on the *metate*.
Whoever so wills
Can wrap his *sarape*."

"Furthermore," the critic added, "the tea of *cenizo* is a laxative that will cure jaundice, and it is good for the blood and for the system and also to cure the *susto*.[1] But who ever heard of a person's taking it for dumbness?"

"Yes," added another, "and because it is the first of all plants to bloom after a rain it also helps women to be fertile."

It must not be thought that the critic displayed any animus; indeed, his words had a singularly impersonal tone. "Anyhow," he concluded, "there are no such things as devils and fairies. These are matters for priests and old women. No good citizen of Mexico who has *Adalante!* (Forward!) for his guide will give them credit."

As I came to learn, this man had been among the "Golden Ones" composing Pancho Villa's picked guard. His name was Feliz, although he generally appeared rather *infeliz*. He wore a heavy full moustache, not very long, that would have distinguished any man anywhere, for, divided exactly at the middle of his lip, half of it was white and half jet black. On account of this oddity he was called Bigote Blanco. White Moustache was not always moody; he could be quite agreeable. At the same time he seemed always to have something locked up

---

[1] Literally, "fright." Mexican folk become ill with *susto* and waste away from the sickness in a manner unknown among the "North Americans."

19

inside of himself. Despite an ostentatious skepticism, he was exceedingly credulous. He rode the best horse in the outfit, a brown named Recuerdo—Remembrance—from the fact that he was out of a mare presented to the owner by *"mi general"* Pancho Villa himself.

As for the old fellow who told the story of the hunchbacks, I liked him from the moment I saw him standing over the brindle bull with a gleaming *belduque* in his hand. I was to come to know him better than I know most men and to owe him my life. In certain ways he justified his name—Inocencio. The younger vaqueros called him Don Inocencio. He never admitted to me that he could not read; even if he could not, he knew more about his world than most college professors know about theirs, and his knowledge was always refreshing. Early in life he had been a muleteer, but most of his years he had been a vaquero. For three of them he had been with the *rurales*—the mounted police of Mexico organized under Diaz—and this experience accounted not only for his wide knowledge of trails and ranches in the whole north country but also, in part, for his conservatism. In walking he appeared lame in both legs, but he was merely stiff. He wore thigh-high leggins, whereas most of the other vaqueros wore leather or rawhide *chivarras* that come to the waist and are supported by a belt. His voice was very soft and his eye as clear as a child's. His beard, though as long as a mestizo's beard will usually grow, was short.

After Inocencio had finished drawing up the "rope" of his narrative and while White Moustache was still throwing mud in the "bucket," the old vaquero in a very casual manner pulled from its long scabbard the knife with which he had stabbed the bull and began whetting it on a stone taken from his *morral* and evidently carried for the purpose.

Now and then when the knife was at a certain angle the firelight made it gleam brilliantly. I had already noted that its handle was made out of horn carved into the head of an eagle.

"That looks like a particularly good knife you have," I remarked.

"Yes, *señor*," one of the other vaqueros spoke out, "and it has a name and it has a history."

"What is its name?" I addressed the question to the man who had given me an opportunity to ask it.

"The Faithful Lover," he answered with a laugh. "Read what it says for itself."

The speaker chunked the fire into a blaze and very modestly Inocencio allowed me to turn the blade so that the inscriptions upon it could be deciphered. They were stamped in crudely but plainly: on one side, "*Yo te amo*" (I love you); on the other,

> "*A quien pica esta víbora*
> *No hay remedio en la botica.*"

(For whomsoever this snake bites
There is no remedy in the drugstore.)

The part of Mexico in which I now found myself is not predominantly a machete region, the machete being most characteristic of jungle land, where every man— and often women and children—whether a canoe paddler, a mail carrier on foot, a cotton-picker, or a rooster-fighter, carries it, just as nearly every Tarahumare Indian in the mountain forests of Chihuahua carries an axe, or as footmen as well as horsemen in parts of Sinaloa

21

and Sonora carry a rawhide reata coiled and ready for use. Nevertheless, the machete is almost as national as *frijoles*, whether used to mow down sugar cane on the wide plantations of the hot lands, to clear jungle growth for a tribesman's patch of corn, as a shillalah on prisoners in state penitentiaries, as the instrument with which Zapata—so Diego Rivera has pictured him in the frescos of the palace of Cortés at Cuernavaca—cut down landlords in order to give their lands back to the Indians, or as the dueling weapon that an occasional peon, left arm and hand wrapped in shielding *sarape*, flashes while Death clicks his heels in harmony with the strokes of steel. One wielder, so story tells, could flash his machete overhead so dexterously and swiftly that even in a driving rain it would keep him as dry as a roof.

Now it happened that I carried in a scabbard on my saddle a very fine machete I had years before procured in Oaxaca, where men in whose family the secrets of Toledo steel have been kept for two hundred years forge the best blades in the three Americas. Knowing how pleased nearly all human beings, and especially vaqueros, are with some novel object, particularly if it connects with their life, I went to my saddle and brought the beautiful machete.

Every individual in the group handled it admiringly—except the aloof Feliz—and two or three spelled out aloud the brave mottoes that embossed the steel: "*To conquer me you need what the bamboo lacks*"; "*Don't flock together, little doves, for here comes your hawk.*"

"A certain *señor* presented Pancho Villa with a machete maintaining mottoes more *bravos* than these," said Feliz.

"How?"

"'*I am the friend of guts*' and '*Get ready, lice, for the comb.*'"

"Before robbers of the Villa party took it away," Inocencio said, "there was a machete at the Hacienda of the Five Wounds bearing this, '*Now is when the mint is about to season the soup.*'"

"Oh," exclaimed another vaquero, "there are *dichos* on blades as many as the stars that light up San Pedro's Road," and he swept his arm to indicate the Milky Way. "'*Come on, chinche, to the bite.*' '*The bird that sings much has little tallow.*'"

"'*Give me the kiss of love,*'" put in another vaquero without explanation. Then, stimulated by attention, he called out, "'*I am the cock that sings with joy when he gets up.*' '*Don't wrinkle yourself, old hide; I want you for a drum.*' Also, '*Frijoles shrivel at the first boiling.*'"

"Now this machete of mine," I said, "is a virgin without a name and it has no history. I am waiting for that of the Faithful Lover."

"The matter is not personal with Don Inocencio," spoke the vaquero who had introduced the older man's knife.

"No, it is not personal," Inocencio answered. "I will speak. During the times of revolution, years ago now, Destiny took me above the mouth of the Río Soto la Marina, there in the Huasteca. I was not with bandits. For a while we kept camp in a pueblo where the men fished and where there was a priest. He was a good man but he always went by rules in books. He was an *Italiano*.

"One day while some women were washing down at the edge of the water a *chamaco* waded out to catch a

23

horse of the devil[1] with red wings. It went farther out and the boy followed. He was just playing. All this the mother told. She heard a scream and saw a shark cutting him in two. She rushed to the rescue, but all she got was the legs and part of the trunk. Poor little one! Poor little mother! Poor little father!"

"*Pobrecitos!*" came voices of other vaqueros out of a silence as profound as the night.

"The father," Inocencio continued, "was in his house just a little way off. It happened that I was talking to him at the moment when the cries of the women came to us. He grabbed his machete. It was always at his hand. When we got to the water and saw what was left of the boy, he ran for the priest.

"The priest came at once. He was not fat like many priests. He had no smile. He was straight, straight, like a pine tree, and there was no bend in his body. He looked at the pieces of the child. 'It is not possible,' he said, 'for the church to perform rites over this. The head is gone, the heart is gone. The home of the soul is not here, and it is for the soul that the church acts.'

"'Oh, *padre*,' the father of the boy said, 'I will pay all I have, my burro, my house, my skiff, and hooks.'

"'No, it is not possible.'

"Then this father turned to the mother. 'Show me exactly where the shark was,' he commanded. She pointed and threw a rock to indicate. He did not say a word. He first pulled off his shirt. He wore no shoes. The *calzones* were all he had on. Then with his knife he cut off a leg from the corpse and threw it into the water at the spot where the rock had fallen. He knew that the shark, hungry for more, was hunting, waiting.

[1]Dragonfly.

"As he cast the bait, he began walking toward it, his eyes searching, his machete arm free. He was not disappointed. The shallow water compelled the shark to show part of his body as he grabbed the leg. The man with the machete was against him. I could not say how long the two fought. I was without power to help. Every person there looking was stone still. It was nakedness with a knife against teeth and lashing tail. The water showed streaks of blood, but in the end the shark was dead. The man hauled him to the bank and slashed his belly open. There the head and heart of the boy showed themselves. They were white and partly gone but they were plain.

"The straight priest had not said a word during all this time, not one little word. Now he said, 'The church will bury the child.'

"'Thanks be to God,' the father said.

"But that was not all," Inocencio concluded. "Those people of the Huasteca are not like us. I do not understand. It seems that a long time ago they prayed to what they call the Shark God. That night the eater of *cristianos* was stretched out on rocks and wood was placed all over him. Then while the fire burned, the *gente* danced around and around the carcass, one old man beating a drum and all of them singing strange words. It was a thing terrible. Those people are not like us."

"And so this is the knife that killed the shark?" I asked.

"*Sí, señor.* For a favor the slayer gave it to me."

This favor, I judged, was a matter "personal" to the narrator.

When I lay down on my pallet, the vaqueros about

the low fire were still talking, their habitually low voices diffusing into night's stillness, the lighted tips of their shuck cigarettes working curious designs in the darkness. While early next morning, having, in Parkman's phrase, "performed my ablutions," I was walking towards the fire, Inocencio met me with a tin plate, which my *mozo* had procured out of the pack. Upon it was the choicest morsel of the bull's head—the eyes.

"Have you ever eaten such?" he asked.

"No," I said, for I did not want to deprive him of his triumph.

"Ah," he exclaimed, his own eyes kindling with the pleasure of one who luxuriates in pleasing, "they eat divinely well. Thus we *rancheros* are like the *zopilotes*, which consider the eye the greatest delicacy in a carcass and always eat it first. Sit down, sit down. Eat, eat."

Inocencio truly feasted in watching me.

"Delicious," I pronounced.

"Exquisitely delicious," he said.

He ran to the fire and brought back a *tortilla* toasted a gold color. "Here is a little golden one," he exclaimed. Then, with regret, he added, "Of course there are no more eyes, but you will have more of the head. And what part of it do you choose? In the head of a cow are all the meats of God's creation: the brains are eggs; in the jaw strips is chicken; in the marrows and the gristle-linings is fish; beef itself is in the tongue and other parts. And now, *señor*, will you have eggs or chicken or fish or beef?"

The *mozo* I had was employed only temporarily, and I cared little for him; he wore shoes and professed not to be able to drink coffee without sugar. On the spot I discharged him and hired Inocencio to act as my man. I was now in the vicinity of the hacienda where I intended to spend some time, most of the vaqueros, Inocencio included, pertaining to it. It suited me well that they planned to remain out several days. Thus in the open and in such company I could pass a long time *muy contento*.

Explanations are tedious. I discourteously abandon the company of people whose talk drags with them, skip the pages of books heavy with them, and instinctively avoid making them myself. If it be asked, however, how I came to be riding alone in this remote part of the land, where pleasure-seeking foreigners never come and where business opportunities are nearly as scarce as tourists, I reply frankly that I am not the first man to have crossed the Río Bravo del Norte, in either direction, without giving or wishing to give an explanation. And riding away across the Great River—that river towards which so many men for so many generations have yearned with hope or fear or lust for revenge or some other emotion making their hearts wild—need not imply moral guilt.

I was provided with sufficient funds to sustain me for a year or more; but when the prices of horses, *tortillas*, *frijoles*, tobacco, coffee, a *mozo*, and a bed either on the ground or at some equally ungrudging hacienda or peon ranch are considered, such a sufficiency for a solitary man amounts to a very modest sum.

On the Texas side of the Rio Grande I was born and reared among ranch Mexicans. I had spent much time in many places in Mexico itself. I was now among a people and in a land long familiar to me. Truly with the

arrieros of mule trains in the deep sierras I could sing—
or at least hum:

> *"Chihuahua's my country,*
> *And Sonora my land,*
> *Eating chile with pork,*
> *Tortilla in hand"*

The *gente* well say, "Whoever finds freedom finds his
country."

CHAPTER 2

The Magician on Horseback

THE place where we camped was called Charco de Queso, or Cheese Waterhole. When I asked of my newly acquired *mozo* how it came to be so named, he gave this explanation. Many years back a leader of bandits known as Diente Frío—Cold Tooth, on account of the fact that an eye-tooth fanged over his lower lip—secured himself in this region. A reward was on his head, and he came to suspect, not without reason, that a man by the name of Salomé who was entrusted with bringing supplies had traitorous designs. "That was when two eagles made their nests in the same tree."

One morning while the bandits were breakfasting, Salomé appeared in camp. Cold Tooth cordially invited him to eat. Breakfast consisted mainly of cheese, and the doomed man ate of it heartily. Then the bandit leader ordered, "Hang him and give him more cheese to eat."

So Salomé was hanged to a convenient limb, and a piece of cheese was rammed into his grinning mouth. It stayed there until some crows ate it away. A small mound of rocks supporting a cross of unhewn sticks indicated the tree where the cheese-eater had paid for his ambition.

On the night of either the third or fourth day after I arrived at Charco de Queso, just before I was about to lie down, Inocencio, who was at the time smoothing out my bed, said, "Master, if you wish to see something curious, come with me."

I went with him for perhaps a quarter of a mile, stepping with the same caution he took. As we came to a place where there was some broken stubby brush, we heard a voice, seemingly two voices.

Inocencio now whispered the explanation I had been awaiting. "White Moustache," he said, "caught a three-year-old horse a few days ago and tonight he is training him for combat against the enemy."

Keeping under cover, we drew a little nearer.

"Son of a blank," the voice sounded, "you have waylaid me. Now prepare for your destiny."

Then in changed tone a voice came back, "Nobody dies ahead of his time, but yours will come. Coward!"

Then the first voice, "On to him!"

With that, the man on foot and the horse by his side made a run. The object of the charge was a kind of scarecrow, which the man repeatedly slashed with a machete, all the time fiercely talking back and forth, now as himself, now as the enemy, straining to impart his fury to the horse. Finally the horse pawed the figure savagely.

Thus for the first—and only—time I witnessed the

training of a young horse for combat, a kind of training not very common in Mexico, I believe, but concerning which I had several times heard. A horse so trained is supposed to be of particular use in charging an ambush and in aiding his master if wounded to escape. My guide and I slipped back to camp before the lesson had ended.

The next morning while we were all preparing to ride out, Inocencio, as he held my horse's head, advised in a low voice, "Upon mounting it is always well to say, '*En el nombre de Dios.*'"

"But why," I asked, "should I say 'In the name of God' every morning I get up on a horse?"

"Because," he replied, "the sepulcher of the rider is always open."

It was something of a coincidence that this very day I saw one rider all but enter "the open hole." I doubt if he had spoken the prayer, for such piety as Inocencio's has become rather old-fashioned and odd.

This man, Luis, had the evening before struck tracks that he declared belonged to a wild cow known as Ramona. After the notorious Ramona we were all now setting forth. Late in the morning we startled her out of a thicket, running alone and as fast as a mustang. Luis cut across from his advanced position and on a steep gully-cut slope roped her. In wrapping his end of the reata around the horn of his saddle, he somehow dropped it, and the cow went racing on. "Don't turn her loose," the cry went up, and Luis spurred onward to retrieve the dragging rope. He was hardly ten feet behind the cow when he leaned over to grab it from the ground. At that instant, now hot and ready to fight, the cow halted, wheeled, and had her horn in the man's groin before anybody could do more than think.

While two men jerked the cow away, the others dismounted to help their wounded comrade. He was unconscious with the pain. The first thing they did was to swathe his head in a coat, primarily that he would not come to life looking into the bright sun and thus go crazy, and secondly so that he "would not catch air." Now, one may "catch air" in his leg, his arm, his neck, his eye, anywhere, even when no opening has been made for its entrance; hence the precaution of the most inured man of the *campo*, when a house is available, to shut the door—usually there is no window to shut—before going to sleep. Hence also a child born even in the hottest time of summer is heaped over with blankets so that it will not "catch air." But the effect of catching air through a wound is likely to prove so disastrous that the Indian forebears of the vaqueros fashioned grooves in the shafts of their arrows; then if the arrow-point did not reach a victim's vitals or if the preparation of rattlesnake venom smeared on the point did not infect the blood, the air entering down the grooves of the arrowshaft would prove fatal.

Conscious or unconscious, a smothered man will struggle for breath. The combined struggles of the gored vaquero and myself to get the wrapping from around his head were successful. Inocencio and another staunched his flow of blood with cobwebs. After he had been somewhat revived with water from a canteen and a poultice of roasted prickly pear had been placed on the wound, we put him on a stretcher made by fastening a blanket over two long poles and spent the remainder of the day conveying him to a solitary, meager ranch house well named La Soledad. Meantime I had sent back to camp for my pack. Although I could do little but apply an antiseptic I always carry, yet as a man of education and worldly experience I was naturally looked to for medical advice. I was a free being, absolutely untethered, and my staying by the patient for a few days involved no sacrifice. Indeed I was well rewarded, for thus I came to know the master of the Ranch of Solitude.

I had already heard talk about him among the vaqueros, and at the Hacienda of the Five Wounds, where I later stayed a long time, I was to hear much more. He was usually spoken of and to as Don Encarnación, those who were familiar enough with him to drop the "Don" shortening his name to Chón. He had a nickname, too, "Coro"—"because his voice had the strength of an entire chorus." As characters go, he was the chief novelty of a wide country wherein odd characters, in proportion to the population, were not rare. He was, in short, *un mágico;* he had read "in the Black Book"—a book that nobody had seen. Once he had made a pact with an "*espíritu* in the form of a mare mule."

White Moustache, who believed in neither devils nor fairies, but who had a profound interest in any matter even remotely pertaining to horses or horsemen, gave me the "history."

"When that old one," he said, "was young, an Indian prophet told him that in a cave under the Cuesta de la Cruz there lived a spirit in the form of a mare mule, frisky, full of kicks, and breathing flashes of fire out of her nostrils. The prophet said this *mula* had knowledge of the properties of all herbs good for the welfare of beasts. It was her destiny that to whosoever should mount her in darkness and ride her bareback she must communicate that knowledge.

33

"So the young vaquero went by night to the cave to watch and listen. About twelve o'clock he heard a formidable stampede that sounded as if a volcano were erupting, and then appeared the *mula*, breathing fire and kicking rocks right and left. He hid behind a big rock, and when she came by he sprang upon her back and put the spurs to her. She pitched up one cañon and down another and ran over bluffs, but he was a true *jinete* and could not be thrown. Then in exhaustion she came back into the cave and for a while stood trembling. There she indicated to her rider that he should dismount. After he was on foot she nuzzled his ear and communicated in a whisper all the secrets she knew. Thus the conqueror came to know better than anybody else the *remedios* of the *campo* that are good for horses and cattle and goats and all other animals."

True, the ancient was master of a "secret weed" that would drug a horse, but I suspected it to be the well-known "loco weed." He recommended tying a toad on the forehead of a windbroken horse, for the toad is cold-blooded, any windbroken horse has been overheated, and the natural antidote for heat is cold. This treatment is not unique. I know one gringo who, he claims, had such a severe case of erysipelas that an American doctor turned the case over to the gringo's *mozo*, with the result that after the *mozo* had rubbed toads over the inflamed flesh for four hours, the erysipelas went away. Old Encarnación's *remedio* for a crippled horse was to apply grease out of a coyote or the kidney fat of a goat with a hot bone, but I never became convinced that this was one of the secrets whispered to him by the "malignant spirit in the form of a mare mule"; it is too much like the common—and commonsense—*remedio* of applying

34

a heated maguey leaf, split open, to sprains. A prickly pear poultice will "draw" as powerfully as the maguey.

He was not a magician merely for magic's sake; he employed magic only as a vaquero. Too old to ride much now, the exploits attributed to him were out of a remote past. He must have been *muy valiente* in those days, but he himself never talked of the marvels he had performed, except to recount an experience with the rope or something like that. His silence on certain matters no doubt enhanced his reputation. Some said that he had a special kind of breath to blow into the nostrils of a horse. Others said that his power lay in his eye—an eye "more *poderoso* than that on an Irishman"—and all the vaquero world knows that the Irish have the most potent and powerful eyes for subduing fierce horses.

Yet he had a power not of the eye. While he was a young man, strong and valiant, as one common story went, he was unjustly treated by the *caporal* of range riders under whom he worked. He did not immediately reveal resentment, however; he bided his time. This boss had a wonderfully fine horse, tireless, fast-running, perfectly reined, expert in cutting and roping cattle; yet sometimes this horse would quit the *remuda*, and then he was such a *ladino* that he could hardly be caught. On one such occasion when the horse thus turned outlaw, the *caporal* sent three men to catch him. After they had spent two days running down that many horses apiece they reported failure.

Encarnación was present when they came in. Humbly he told the *caporal* that he would try to catch the *ladino*.

"How many men do you need to help you?" the *caporal* asked.

"Not one. I go *solo*."

35

So he went out alone. Within two hours he returned, the *ladino* leading docilely. The *caporal* at once saddled him.

As he was preparing to mount, one of his faithful vaqueros said to him in a low voice, "Have care. That horse will throw you and kill you."

"No," the *caporal* responded, "this horse is as gentle as a woman. His only fault is running off while he is loose. He will not throw anybody but a gringo, and that's because he does not like the foreign smell."

"That is true of the past," the adviser said. "Nor will the horse throw and kill you here, but when he has you off alone. This horse has been spoken to."

The *caporal* laughed, pulled up into the saddle, and rode away. The high-spirited *ladino* seemed, as always, gentle. During the day the boss cut off from his men to follow a wild steer into some brush. There the horse began pitching and screaming. The *caporal* had ridden many bad horses, but he could not stay on this one. After throwing him to the ground, the horse pawed him to death. Undoubtedly he had been whispered to.

It was said that the whisperer, now in his old age, took counsel with a terrapin as ancient as himself that he kept as a kind of pet. I saw this terrapin, one of a species common to the deserts of northern Mexico—too tough of shell for coyotes to molest much. The *gente* sometimes throw it into the fire alive and after the creature's legs have been burned off break a hole in its back, insert some salt and pepper, and allow it to roast. Chinese cooks stew it with chicken. The old man told me that he was one time saved from perishing of thirst by a little sac of water this species of tortoise carries hidden under its shell. More than once I saw him feeding his terrapin a piece of prickly pear, but I did not hear any words pass between the two. The constant marvel to me was that such a man of magic should speak of a kid's twisted foot, the itch bothering a dog, or some other equally commonplace matter.

Long, long ago when the river-watered plains to the north were ranged over by mustangs, Encarnación, people said, used to ride off alone and weeks later return with a *manada* obediently following him, though he had not touched with hand or rope either the stallion or a single one of the mares. They said that somehow the *manada* seemed to regard him as their stallion-leader, following him to grass, to water, on a trail, into a corral, wherever he led.

That there have been men in this world with an inexplicably subtle power over horses I am sure. Don Raymundo Bell, for example, who seemed to have been born without fear of any man or beast, would slowly approach any wild young horse in a corral, monotonously mumbling something that no one ever made out, now and then intermitting a sharp exclamation, until he had drawn right against the mesmerized animal. Then he would talk to it in a low voice, and within fifteen minutes from the time he began his ritual the subdued animal would be following him. He told me he had found one horse he could not subdue, because it would not let him look into its eye. I tried hard to wrest from old Encarnación some explanation, perhaps some secret, concerning his own power, but all I ever got out of him was a generality or a mystery: "Look! the buzzard sees, the deer hears, the snake feels, the horse smells. . . . When you wish your horse to leap an ob-

stacle, hurl your soul ahead of him and he will follow."
Yet he made concrete observations too: "A mule under
saddle can smell the trail of range stock better than a
horse can. . . . The hoof prints of a tired deer show closer
together on the ground than those of a fresh deer. . . .
For your knowledge you read books and go to colleges.
I read tracks. The *campo* has been my college."

He was an encyclopedia of *vaquerista* adages, such as
that the cream-colored horse with white mane and tail
called *palomino* "belongs to the race that never dies";
that of stocking feet "one is good, two are better, three
are bad, and four are worse"; that a "toasted (chestnut)
sorrel will die before tiring"; that when a man is pursued by a hot enemy "the zebra dun affords the best
wings with which he can fly"; that a horse with a cow-
lick in his mane at the point of the shoulders will not
stumble or be jerked down, etc. He conceded, however,
that "over colors as over taste, there is no argument."
He instructed me that if ever I had an opportunity to
pick a mount out of a penful of horses, I should enter,
give the bunch a scare, and then rope for my own the
animal that kept his head up and his ears pointed towards
me the longest. That horse is "made of the finest metal
—of the gold in the bell."

Late one fall, one of the current tales about the
vaquero-magician went, the *corrida* with which he as a
young man rode lost a herd of cattle through a stampede. While regathering them, the vaqueros ran out of
tobacco, corn for *tortillas*, coffee, salt, out of everything
but meat—and something in the meat turned their
stomachs against it. Who knows what? The fact remained that while every man was hungry, no man had
any hunger for meat.

On a particular night while the lungs of heaven were bursting themselves blowing out a norther, the outfit was compelled to stop on a plain where there was neither windbreak nor fuel. The slender greasewood switches and the pithy stalks of *lechuguilla* would burn readily enough, but in a minute they were consumed.

While the men were shivering and wishing for food, the vaquero Encarnación said: "At the hacienda today they slaughtered two fat hogs, cooked *chicharrones* (cracklings), made *tamales* with much chile in them, prepared many stacks of *tortillas*, and now our feast is waiting. With permission I go to bring it."

Then he stepped to one side, away from the flare of the fire. Nobody thought otherwise than that he was jesting. A vaquero named Presciliano followed him, however, and watched him. He saw the *mágico* cast off his *chivarras* and hat and then his pants and shirt, stroke himself a few times with the wing of an owl that he was carrying concealed, and immediately vanish. Presciliano gathered up the clothes, came to the gusty fire, and told what he had seen.

A few minutes later all heard a voice say, "Presciliano, throw me my clothes. How can you expect me to appear without them?"

Presciliano took the clothes and threw them out into the darkness towards the voice. Very quickly then the *mágico* appeared. He had a morral of *tortillas* piping hot, another bag of *tamales* stuffed with chile and *chicharrones*, an *olla* of *frijoles*, and another of hot coffee already sugared.

Some of the men tactfully excused themselves from eating by saying that they had already filled up on beef. Others devoured the food with much gusto. It was certainly bewitched, but it made no one ill. "There are many strange things in nature."

Another of the strange things of nature was that this vaquero of magic could enter invisible the room in which an enemy of his was plotting, and thus hear secrets. Once while an enemy was shooting at him he turned into a little dog and went through a hole in an adobe wall.

When he slept out at night during warm weather, instead of uncoiling around his pallet a black hair rope —which is supposed to frighten rattlesnakes away because it looks like their enemy, the blacksnake—and which therefore frightens them away, he merely drew a circle with his spur or a stick. No rattlesnake ever crossed the line thus made and crawled against him.

He would go out where the wild horses ranged, draw a circle on the ground as big as a corral, leaving a gap in it for the gate, and then, sometimes with other vaqueros to help him, run the mustangs into that corral. Once inside, not an animal could pass the line any more than if it were a rock wall ten feet high. *Absolutamente no!* After the *caballada* was penned, Encarnación would close the gate by drawing a line. Then he would lasso the mares to roach their manes, brand the colts, or do anything else with the stock.

He might while riding along come upon the bleached skeleton of a bull. "Wait a minute," he might say to other vaqueros. Then he would get down, lift the skeleton up, put *ánimo* into it, and stand off waving a red bandana in the manner of a *matador* flashing his scarlet cloth in a bull-ring. The bull would come bellowing, and there the play would go on until the *mágico* willed it to stop and the bull to turn back into the natural skeleton. He could get down upon his all-fours out on the prairie and bark so as to call coyotes up within his grasp.

In the old days, he liked to play tricks. For instance, one evening, after the *corrida* had been working in the corral all day and everybody was sweaty and dirty, he said, "*Compañeros*, how would you like a bath—a deep, cool swim?" There was not even a dirt tank within five miles and yet while the vaqueros were still laughing at the suggestion, they saw right beside them a *laguna* with banks lined by trees. They could even hear the leaves of the cottonwoods rustling in the air. It was "only an illusion and no water was there, but such was the power of the *mágico*."

His chief trick was with the quirt—a trick that Pancho Villa, according to common report, used to play also. Going along a trail, he would as if by accident drop his quirt. He would wheel his horse, make as if to recover the article, and then, noting some boy riding near at hand, very politely say, "My friend, please do me the favor to pick up my quirt." The boy would reach down to get it and just as his hand was about to grasp it, the quirt would suddenly turn into a rattlesnake buzzing his tail and rearing his head ready to strike. Swinging backward, the boy might exclaim, "Quirt of the devil!"

"How is that?" Encarnación would say. "It will be necessary, after all, for me to get down."

Then he would dismount, swiftly but cautiously pick up the "bell-jingler" and with one twist of the arm and wrist pop off its head—and there would be nothing in his hand but his old quirt.

As to his exploits with the lasso, they were more his-

torical and less magical. More than once he had dueled
on horseback with only the reata, he and his opponent
rushing at each other with swinging loops, and he always dragged the other vaquero off. Again, to win a bet,
he rode blindfolded on a well-trained horse behind a
steer let loose on the prairie and, running and roping
by sound alone, noosed him by both hind feet and threw
him. Another time he bet a rich *hacendado* fifty pesos
that with one end of the rope, not to be pulled on by
hand, tied to his own neck, he could forefoot each of
fifty mares in a pen and break their necks. More than
of pesos his bet was of his own neck against a mare's.
After he had broken the necks of the first five mares
run by him, the *hacendado* gave him the fifty pesos to
quit.

He could, while mounted and running at full speed,
rope his own horse by the forefeet and throw him. In the
act of forefooting a cow or a bull, he could so flirt his
rope over the animal's back that the jerk flinging it to
the ground would snap its neck in two. But this sleight
is not rare. Don Encarnación had been known to charge
suddenly upon wild ducks massed at the edge of a lake
and with finely plaited rawhide reata noose one from
the air before it could get out of reach. This feat would
be called rare.

The third night after I reached the Ranch of Solitude
Don Encarnación, Inocencio, and I were all seated outside the room in which the gored vaquero uneasily lay.
By my orders the door was kept open that he might
have plenty of the distrusted air. The full moon was
"dancing on her *patio*"; that is, was encircled by a ring,
and one could have read any well-printed book by the
light. A ten-year-old boy, grandson to the old *ranchero*,

42

was tormenting a skinny dog with his rope. After a while the boy went to scratching his head energetically.

Without speaking loud enough for the old man to hear, Inocencio remarked, "He who lies down with dogs may expect to get up with fleas."

"What, what?" The boy danced his question.

"Yes, tell me what it is," Inocencio propounded a riddle:

> *"Ground-work over ground-work,*
> *Over the ground-work a box,*
> *Above the box a cross,*
> *Above the cross a corn-mill,*
> *Above the corn-mill some lookers-on,*
> *Above the lookers-on an open plain,*
> *Above the open plain a thicket*
> *With some robbers in it."*

"Lice," the boy yelled. He had evidently heard the riddle before, and now for him had been opened an inexhaustible topic. For a minute he stood still, arms stretched out, face turned to the sky, sing-songing:

> *"A little basket filled with flowers*
> *Opens by night*
> *And closes by day.*
> *Unriddle it for me."*

"Why, the stars, of course," Inocencio answered. "And what makes the stars?" the boy asked.

"They are the eyes of young virgins who have died in love. But go, boy, go. You are a son now; you will be a father."

Silently, without another word, the boy picked up

his rope and began energetically to neck the dog to a child that had toddled out upon the *patio*.

But to me this night the riddle of riddles was Don Encarnación. For hours he had been silent. It seemed that if he would but speak I might learn some new thing. It is my nature to draw out of men anything strange or novel they have within themselves, whether the matter be fact or not. In truth I have no reverence for mere facts. So with the boy's rope for a snare I began leading the old vaquero-magician towards the subject of lassoing.

"*Amigo*," he finally said, "I am a very old man. I have been all my life in the sierras, on the *llanos*, amid the forests. I have seen much that the *gente correcta*[1] know nothing of and would not believe if told. Nevertheless, as to the use of the lasso you have asked me in frankness what I will answer in the same manner. When I was fifteen years old I was with the *Liberales* that fought the French at Puebla. For that victory we still celebrate the Fifth of May each year. Just before the battle the general of the cavalry made a speech. 'My men,' he said, 'some of you have machetes; a few of you have guns. That is well, but the true Mexican government we represent has no arms or ammunition to give you. You are going against trained troops well armed. There is but one way. Each of you has one weapon he can use. Each of you has a reata. Make it sing. Drag the royalists to death. Long live Benito Juárez! Long live Mexico! Long live the horseback-born! Charge!'"

"And did you rope one?" I asked.

"Yes, but it was not a Frenchman; it was a *gachupín*.

[1]Correct people, people of upper-class conventions.

44

And after I had dragged him a hundred *pasos* he got up and I had to knock him down with the butt of my quirt."

"I know something about the *modo mexicano* of combating with reatas," I answered, "for it is well remembered that the Texas scouts when out alone were sometimes roped off their horses and dragged to death."

Unwittingly I had made the best possible speech to spur the roper on—a speech that flattered racial pride.

"I merely wished to go back to beginnings," he continued. "I have roped something stranger than a *gachupín*."

I waited in silence. Don Encarnación looked at me and then he seemed to be studying the peaks of a mountain clearly defined under the moon twenty miles away. A coyote howled only a short distance off, then began yipping, then suddenly hushed. The dog rushed away from the boy barking, and a pet goat took after him.

When I laughed at the goat, the ancient glanced at me quizzically as if in doubt whether to trust me; again he seemed to seek advice from the mountain. Finally in a low voice but at the same time with a touch of apology that would not have been present had the gringo stranger been absent he said, "I roped a *nagual*."

I checked the exclamation in my mouth. I should not have been surprised had I been in the jungles of the Mexican peninsula, where Indians are yet to be found furtively practicing the ancient beliefs of *nagualismo*, at the birth of a child dedicating it to some animal, between which and himself as years go on the rapport becomes so close, so intimate, that he can—so adherents of the cult believe—turn himself into that animal. Yet even here I need not have been surprised, for what child of Mexico has not been frightened by the threat that the *nagual* will get it?—that old Indian, wrinkled, dirty, hideous, his eyes red, who knows how to transform himself into a shaggy-haired dog, a springing jaguar, a crawling snake, a creeping wolf, or some other feared beast of the wild.

"Pardon me, Don Encarnación," I said. "I thought I heard Luis mumble. After such a long sleep a little swallow of *tequila* will do him good."

When I returned, I brought the jug with the remark that we should ourselves make some "proof" of it. The old man of magic stood up, removed his great sombrero, tilted his head back, and drank deep. In the moonlight the white mixed with the dark of his long thick hair gleamed like wire silver under a candle. He unwound the red *faja* that sashed his waist, wiped his lips on it, and then regirted himself. Inocencio was not saying a word. Away off now, the coyote howled its laugh both weird and merry, and a faint bell, perhaps on a goat, tinkled.

Don Encarnación sat down again, leaving his hat on the ground. He pulled from his pocket a piece of buckskin wound around a short red cord of tinder, a bit of flint, and the steel *eslabón*. Having unwrapped these articles, he struck a spark of fire, which lodged in the tinder, blew on it, lit his cigarette, pinched out the fire, and then very deliberately rewrapped the articles and put them in his pocket.

"Yes," he resumed, "I once roped a *nagual*. I did not rope it because I was brave. I do not wish to deceive you. It was all so long ago that it seems to have been in another world—before the centuries had a beginning. I was young then, another man."

The old man's tones, not loud but deep rumbling, made me understand how he came to be called Coro. The "Chorus" went on.

"At the pueblo where I lived I arose one morning very early to give my sweetheart *las mañanitas*—the dawn serenade. All was quiet. I was as hot as if I were over a big fire in a cave; I was as cold as if I lay naked in front of the norther. I can no longer feel that way, only remember. I placed the guitar on my right knee and raised my hand to begin the music. Then something came to my ears. While my hand was still raised like this, I listened. Then the sound was clearly of hoof-beats. I heard them pound over the cobblestones in front of the *mayorazgo*.[1] They came on up the lane towards me. Then in the breaking light I saw the rider. He was a vaquero like myself. At the same time he recognized me. With a cry, *Aihaa!*, wild and high and far like that, he jerked his horse to a halt.

"I could not tell which was more used up, the man or the horse. The horse's nostrils were dripping blood and he trembled all over. I thought he should be bled at once above the hoofs, but I did not draw the knife. The man was terror itself.

"As he swung off his horse he came straight toward me, his hands reached out like those of a helpless child. '*Ay, Dios de mi vida!*' he was moaning. He half embraced me, trying to say something, but his mouth was so dry he could hardly speak.

"'*Ay, Ay!* Holy Mother of God! I have seen the *nagual*,' he gasped. 'Last night he drove away the horses. Tonight he will come for the goats. I tried to stop him, but he neighed like a stallion and fire came

[1]The house entailed through generations to the first-born.

47

out of his nostrils and he rushed at me. *Por Dios y todos los santos!'*

"The wild man had made so much noise and was still making so much that people were coming out of their houses and gathering round. Two or three men without faith were jesting, but mostly the people were silent. I myself looked at the vaquero thinking he could believe anything. He was just a boy, ignorant, a *campesino*.

"'With these eyes, I tell you, man, I saw the *nagual*,' he cried to me.

"Just then I noticed Teresa at the open window, to which I had come to serenade her. She beckoned, and I drew a little nearer. 'Tell me,' she said, 'is there really such a creature as the *nagual?* Does he wear moccasins soled with wool so that he can creep noiselessly? Does he make his eyes glow in the darkness like a green fire? Does he grow claws on his hands like a panther so that he can tear open the throat of some poor *cristiano* asleep in the night?'

"I could not tell how serious Teresa was or if she were playing with me. 'Some say yes; some say no,' I answered.

"'Perhaps yes,' she said. 'Look at this *pobrecito* of a vaquero. He has seen something. That is certain. Yet if a man were brave, not even a *nagual* could give him the *susto*. If such a thing as the *nagual* exists, I wish to behold it—here.'

"As Teresa spoke thus, I noticed that the people were indicating my guitar and smiling. Just then the owner of the ranch on which the vaquero worked called out above the crowd, 'Daniel, so while seeing my horses stolen, you ran away from the thief! How valiant you are!'

"The boy was now as much wilted by shame as by

48

fear. 'Get out of here,' his *patrón* cried, his voice in anger. 'Go at once and tend to your business. After the thieves!'

"The vaquero actually began to cry. 'I can't, I can't,' he said. 'The *nagual*, the *nagual!*'

"Then the *ranchero* went into a passion. 'Coward!' he yelled. 'If you won't go, are there no vaqueros in this pueblo who will go and protect an honest man's property?'

"I thought it strange that the *ranchero* himself was not mounting a horse. Teresa was gazing at me and her look was a question.

"'I will go,' I said.

"Then I was full of doubts. This *nagual*, I kept telling myself, may have existed a long time ago when only the Indios lived in the world. Now, I tried to make myself believe, he is just in stories. I thought to ask my grandfather, for he was a very old man, but I knew he would only look at me in the empty way. For years he had been out of his right mind. There was but one way for him to get well. We were all waiting for it.

"I got two other young vaqueros to go with me. By the time we reached the ranch the shadows of the mountains were long upon it. It was empty. While traveling we had drunk some *tequila* out of a gourd and sung and yelled. Now in the shadows we became as silent as the locusts when the heat of day falls into the coolness of dew.

"The herd of goats was coming into the corral, a dog guarding them. In front of the adobe house we built a fire. We warmed our *gordas*, ate them, and drank coffee. We did not speak about *naguales*. I told my companions that we would catch the thief alive, not kill him. We all kept our reatas by our sides ready. Each of us also had a machete in a scabbard. About midnight the others dropped off to sleep while I kept on watching.

"The fire was out, all but a few coals. The moon was overhead, and, standing there, for I could keep awake better by standing up, I could see the herd of goats in the pen down the slope from the house. A few were standing; most of them were lying down. Then, *válgame Dios!* I saw something that would have made a dead man spur his horse!"

When old Encarnación exclaimed "*Válgame Dios!*" his voice seemed to shake the ground. He rolled another shuck cigarette and struck fire to it. His ten-year-old grandson had been a silent listener. "Where is the *tortuga?*" the old man said to him. "In his bed," the boy answered and bolted off behind the house. In a minute he was back with the old turtle, which, held high in the air, put out legs and head in a helpless way. I wondered if the magician were going to have a consultation. "No, don't disturb the poor fellow," he said. "Leave him alone in his nest." And the boy ran back with the *tortuga*. Instead of consulting it, the ancient seemed again to consult the moonlit mountain peak twenty miles away.

"Yes," he broke out vehemently, "I saw it. With these eyes I saw."

His eyes at this moment also saw the jug, and again he tilted it.

Then with fierce energy the narrator turned upon me, although I had given no sign, not one gesture, of doubt. "Shake your head until your teeth one by one fall to the ground like hailstones from the sky. Wave your denying finger back and forth in front of your face so fast that it would keep the sand of a storm out of your eyes as well as the best Saltillo blanket. Shrug your shoulders until they cave in like the spine of a sway-backed mare suckled by two colts and loaded down with three *tercios* of potter's clay. Say *no* and *no es posible* until your voice is as completely vanished as that of a cow that has bawled for three days and two nights for her lost calf. Yet I know whereof I speak and I assert that what I tell is fact."

It appeared that the old man had not always found his auditors either respectful or credulous. It was very strange. Here was a man who had started out telling me a story because he liked both me and himself. Now he seemed to be telling it because he wanted to overpower a disbeliever.

"But Uncle Chón," Inocencio aroused himself, "have you eaten of game cock? What horsefly has stung you? Why, you are as hot as water for chocolate. Here we all are respectful, open of ear and closed of mouth. Yet suddenly you go to kicking at the *señor* as if he were a bed of ants and you were a mule standing in the bed. It would be just that you ask pardon and go on to tell of the *nagual*."

"There is no disrespect," the old man dryly commented. "I tell what I saw. Suddenly a great goat, taller than any billy goat in the world, was walking about in the corral. He removed the bells from four sleeping goats, took down the bars of the gate, and then began to drive the flock out.

"As the lead goats went through the gate, I found my voice. 'Get your ropes!' I yelled. 'There he is!'

"The two vaqueros sprang awake. The dog went to barking. Our horses snorted. I led the way, running toward the corral. At the same time I saw the big goat drop to all-fours and start running off. All the ground about was open, nothing growing on it but rocks. In the manner of goats the *nagual* was running uphill. As I gained on it, I saw that it had no tail. The other vaqueros were close behind me. I cast the loop, and it went true.

"The creature bounced into the air, hit the ground flat; then, like a wildcat that is knocked out of a tree, jumped up and ran down hill. I still held the end of the rope but was jerked down and dragged forty *pasos* before one of the others roped it and added his weight to mine. It had the strength to drag both of us, but not so rapidly. Then I saw the machete of the third vaquero in the air.

"'Don't kill!' I yelled.

"He gave a half-lick and half-cut behind the animal's horns that knocked it down.

"Remember, I wanted to take the *nagual* in alive to show to Teresa. When I got over it, still holding the rope firm, it was giving little bleats and gurgles and the blood was running black out of the cut. It had a very strange beard for a goat; it looked exactly like my grandfather's beard.

"Then while I was yet gazing at this beard, a voice from under it said, 'Chón, you have killed your own grandfather.'

"Those were the only words. The gurgling sound grew deeper. I started running towards the house to get some water. My *compañeros* had already fled. When I got back with the water, the *nagual* was dead. Yet its voice, its words, were still in my ears. Niño de Dios, it was frightful!

"By now the light was promising itself in the east. We all saddled our horses and started back for the pueblo. You may think me an antichristian for not burying the goat that called himself my grandfather. I was powerless to do anything but flee. Anyhow I knew well that no Christian grave would receive that body. I could tell you why.

"On our return ride the wish to please Teresa no longer burned within me. That wish had become something hard even to recall. When we got to my house, we heard women crying. They said, 'The candles are burning at the head and feet of your grandfather.' They said he had been found at daylight, lying on the bare floor, blood around him from a deep cut back of the head. It was thought that he had raised himself off his pallet in the night and fallen against something sharp."

The old man paused for a full minute. Then he ended with, "Now I have told you how I once roped something stranger than a *gachupín*."

Inocencio said, "But yes."

As for myself, it seemed to me that a gate to a question had been left open.

"You said, Don Encarnación, that you could tell why a Christian grave would not receive the body you rode off and left?"

"Yes, I can tell you. Not a great while before this a girl much against her mother's will went to live with a certain man. It is true, he was too poor to pay a priest, but he was a shameless one and never intended to have her by the right hand. The mother had reason. She tried to punish her daughter. The two fought with knives and the girl was killed. Her body was laid out, but the holy candles would not burn. Every time they were lit, a hand, a hand that came out of the air, would snuff them—like that. Then her body was put in a box and carried to a newly dug grave. The priest was there saying his words.

"But as the box was lowered with ropes, it twisted to one side and would not go down. The men shoved it down. As soon as they withdrew their force, it sprang back to the surface. Again they pushed it down; again it jumped up. Figure to yourself the box jumping thus out of the hole by its own force. For a long time the priest and the men tried to make it rest. They could not. Then they understood that God's earth would not take the body of a woman who had tried to take her own mother's life. The box was opened; the body was cast out on the ground and left for the coyotes and buzzards."

"That was the only resort," Inocencio agreed. Then after a silence he added, "I will take my *veinte pasos*"— the "twenty double steps" recommended between the supper table and bed. "I will change the horses."

They were staked about a half mile off. Curious to ask Inocencio something, I went along.

"And what do you think of this *nagual* Don Encarnación roped?" I asked when we were beyond the hedge of growing *ocotillo* stalks that thorned in a patch of pumpkins.

"The *nagual* I have never seen," he answered, stopping short. "I think it no more than a belief come down from the ancient times of the Indians. Don Encarnación is a good old man, and, as you know, 'the sayings of the little old men are little gospels.' Nevertheless, to understand what another is thinking it is necessary to put the head in his house. Perhaps this *viejito* is like the drunkard who heard the empty jug talking to him. Truth and roses alike have thorns. I mean no disrespect to him. What he says about God's earth, however, deserves attention. Listen, Don Federico, I want to tell you something."

As it was impossible for Inocencio to tell something important while walking, we stopped and sat on two convenient rocks.

"The earth is a judge," he began. "One time in Mazapil a youth came home very drunk. His mother whipped him. Then in a most barbarous manner he drew a knife and killed her. He was seized, but some said that because he was drunk he was not responsible. The only way was to let God judge.

"A hole was dug in the earth and the murderer was buried in it up to his navel. Three priests confessed him and prayed for him. He was sober now, and he wept out prayers to God for forgiveness. Weeping and crying, he was like La Llorona herself. If God pardoned him sufficiently to permit him to go on living upon the earth, he would gradually come out of the hole. If God were not willing for the earth to bear him up, it would swallow him.

"On the morning of the first day, as I have said, he stood buried to the navel. By the time the sun went down he had sunk until the earth reached his nipples. There were watchers day and night, and candles were burning, and the priests did not leave. By the morning of the second day the murderer had sunk so low that the earth came up to his neck. He no longer prayed aloud but only with his eyes. His tongue hung out black and swollen. The people were afraid to succor him in any way. The earth was the judge.

"The second night came and passed. At daylight no sign of the mother-murderer was visible. The earth had swallowed him entirely. No watcher had seen him finally go under. He had just disappeared. The earth is just."

When I left the wounded vaquero, rapidly recovering, and the man of magic, I rode directly for the Hacienda de las Cinco Llagas. I was already on ground that once pertained to it. I knew I should find a warm welcome there, for its owner was my friend. A man of twice my years, Marcelo Cienfuegos (Hundredfires) by name, I had come to know him well while he was a political refugee in San Antonio. There I had been able to do him a favor that cost me little, although it meant much to him. He had returned to his country years ago, a ruined man financially. After having received many invitations from him, now I was riding to his home.

As I was soon to learn, the agrarians had left him only a few plots of cultivated land and had even seized some that could never be counted on to bear a crop. Some claimed that the national government now had the estate in charge, others that the state government had confiscated it for taxes, and others that Don Marcelo was still in possession of the titles. As a matter of fact, neither he nor any official was clear on the subject. He lived on at the vast and decadent headquarters of the hacienda surrounded by numerous householders whose relationship to himself was as indefinite as his own to the land from which they drew a slender livelihood. By staying there I incommoded nobody, and I took care not to be an expense.

CHAPTER
3

The Five Wounds

LA HACIENDA DE LAS CINCO LLAGAS—the Hacienda of the Five Wounds—got its name, I suppose, through the piety of some Spaniard reminiscent of the nail prints and the sword pierce at the Cross. So far as records go, it began its history as a part of the millions of acres pertaining to the Marqués de Aguayo, whose perturbed spirit still haunts the domain. Doubtless some ancient document tells how in the presence of a representative of the King of Spain the Marqués or his agent upon being granted the land "pulled up grass, took water from the river and waterholes and drank it," all as a symbol of true possession. Dynasties of *hacendados* lived upon it and passed. Here industry throve, pride and power made each other grow big, and life flowed full, no matter how leisurely. But all this was in the long ago.

The stables, now empty, had been a monastery. Adjacent to them rose, nearly as high as the church tower,

the peak of a conical stone *troje*, or granary, no longer
used but in excellent condition, the narrow flight of
rock steps twisting about it on the outside worn down
by generations of peon feet. A pair of doors at the base
of "the cone," as the storehouse was called, opened
wide enough to permit one of the old-time heavy carts
to enter; and after the lower part of the *troje* had been
filled through these doors, *peones* used to carry sacks of
grain on their backs up the stairs and empty them
through a mounting series of narrow windows that
could be closed. Not far distant from "the cone" were
the circular rock wall and rock floor of a threshing pit,
or *era*, in which no mule had tramped out wheat for
generations of mule lives.

Three corners of the great walled quadrangle were
ruined heaps, but the fourth with its parapet and loop-
holes showed how all had been towered fortlets. The
wall itself was in many places leveled to the ground.
Just north of it mouldered in decadence three gigantic
adobe furnaces that had been cold for a hundred years,
and out from them lay imponderable piles of black slag
from which silver, and probably gold, had been extracted.

An open aqueduct of rock still brought water into the
vicinity from a spring a league away, first down a cañon
and then across some table-land. But water no longer
discharged into the ruined fountain within the main
patio or into the ample reservoir of masonry once used
as a bath; nor did it flow any longer through the in-
geniously contrived spring house.

Houses of adobe and rock scattered about sheltered
twenty families or so, some of them defiant agrarians
backed by the law, others living rent free by consent of

the landlord or paying with the household services of a girl, now and then a man's day of work, chickens, eggs, or a few liters of corn. There were times when most of the kitchens contained *"no más nopal sin sal"*—nothing more than prickly pear without salt. Almost any Mexican who wanted to come and live in one of the houses, for there were numerous abandoned ones, might have been admitted. What kept the horde away was that there was no employment and that no more arable land was available.

In the old monastery was a thick pine log fully sixty feet long that at some time in the last century had been pulled by oxen from mountains seventy miles away and hollowed into a trough to be used as a receptacle for melted goat tallow. The tallow had given the yellow wood a peculiar lustre. In the old days Las Cinco Llagas was stocked with goats by the tens of thousands, and the sale of hides, dried meat, and tallow provided a rich income.

One side of the wall enclosing the monastic stables served also as a side for another rock pen much larger, in the center of which a round corral with chute-like branches was overlooked by a kind of dais once roofed. This round pen had been used for bullfights and also for riding wild horses in, the dais affording the *hacendado* and his party a noble and comfortable view of either sport or work. Seated here, the lord of a million hectares could survey the whole system of corrals.

Another relic of vanished enterprise was a combined wine cellar and distillery, its massive walls and roof arching above ground. When the revolutions of a quarter-century ago broke out, this storehouse of *"licor divino"* became the chief object of interest to every band of liberty-inspired riders in the wide country. Finally, growing weary of its magnetizing effect, the owners cut down the vineyard.

As should be, there was a dungeon, or rather a series of three dungeon cells. The underground passage on which they opened was entered through the *zaguán*, and after running down hill a hundred yards or more it connected with a sturdy rock structure known as El Fortín. The tradition was that during the time of the Marqués de Aguayo, who during one period personally occupied Las Cinco Llagas, although it was but one of several properties comprising his vast estate, his *mayordomo* imported from Durango a number of the famous black scorpions that to this day take annually their toll of lives in that city. This *mayordomo* must have been something of a naturalist, for he was credited with having also imported from the West Coast the curious but harmless white lizard known as *cuida casa*—"house guardian"—the lizard that Peter Ellis Bean had for his only friend in the prison at Acapulco. Those were the times when, in order to take advantage of the bounty offered for the scorpions by Durango authorities, certain mean people bred and raised them. Some seasons they were so numerous that they were "bought by weight, crushed into masses like the ground corn dough."

The scorpions brought to The Five Wounds were secreted in pieces of decayed wood in one of the dungeon cells, and here any prisoner whom it was not diplomatic to kill but whose life was an inconvenience to his captors was placed. The *alacranes* could be depended upon. I strongly suspect that some of the *alacrán* traditions were imported from Durango along with the venomous insects.

According to one story, after various prisoners had here met a mysterious death, a certain young man black of hair and in love with life was given his choice of being shot or spending one night in the cell. He chose the cell, but when he came out next morning his hair was snow white. He said that in the pitch darkness he heard some animal scuttling out of a piece of wood, and then, through terror-sensitized ears, he heard it crawling toward him on the earthen floor. He had but one weapon of defense; that was his heavy felt *sombrero*. Guided only by sound, he placed the great hat over the unknown and unseen enemy and there, afraid to make another single move lest the thing escape, held it pressed down all night long, scarcely shifting a muscle. The candle of a guard come to look in, or perhaps to remove the accustomed dead body, revealed an enormous *alacrán*, "twenty centimeters long," strong with the life of its victims. The prisoner killed it with his foot and was set free. Afterwards lesser *alacranes* became a menace to the legitimate inhabitants of the hacienda. They were drawn forth from their hiding places in the walls and pieces of wood by the strains of violin music and all killed. For more than a hundred years the place has had no black *alacranes;* to experience them one must go to Durango. Their sting is said to be a sure cure for hydrophobia.

Yet despite changes and decay, the tone of life at Las Cinco Llagas remained essentially what it was when the Marqués de Aguayo rode; the traditions, the outlook on life, the ways of living here at the house of Hundredfires all belonged yet to the Age of Horse Culture, all remained true to the original hacienda, whereon power belonged to the horse, animal of both service and glory, and to the mule, the ox, and the burro. No newspapers came here, except an occasional one from Torreón, and so far as the problems of society were concerned the Industrial Age had barely been inaugurated. The peons distrusted an imported plow because "steel makes the ground cold," and corn and beans require warm earth. The mule too has "a cold hoof," and therefore in land to be sown in *frijoles* the plow had better be pulled by an ox. The man who guided the one-handled wooden plow, moving as slow as the Finger of Destiny writes, watched to see if the ox dragged his foot at the turn of the furrow—for, if so, it was a "sign of rain."

These people still believed that when new land was to be sowed, the grain should be dropped by an adolescent—one fertile with potency—although an old man might accompany him over the ground to direct him. Fallen into neglect, however, was the *fiesta* at the end of corn harvesting, when the tributary farmers carried in array the image of San Isidro before the *hacendado* and thus laid him under obligation to provide food and drink while everybody danced.

It was extraordinary how the figure of the Marqués de Aguayo of so many revolutions ago continued to ride on. Here, indeed, history was the "prolongated shadow" of an individual. It could not have been so except in a land yet ruled over by generals wearing spurs and yearning each to be master of a hacienda—a land in which the favorite song of the school children today glorifies the mounted *charro*, "proud symbol of our race"—a land in which with hardly a half-dozen exceptions unnumbered monuments are to men of blood and violence and in which the ballads sung nightly on a thousand plazas heroize the bandit always mounted.

This Marqués de Aguayo owned lands that stretched from the interior of Texas to Zacatecas, and he made a ride that is still the wonder of all this country of the riding tradition. Folk living on the haciendas to which he once held title sometimes yet see him in the night desperately spurring. As I myself rode and slept among such witnesses, the Marqués became far more of a reality to me than he appeared when I read the excellently documented book of facts written to refute the legend. But this legend belongs; I tell it as generations of vaqueros, drivers of wood-laden burros, and old women of the *metate* have blended it to make it their own *Cid* of spur and blood.

To begin, as the old ballad about the Marqués begins —for there is a ballad—"the ancient parchments tell not, nor do the chronicles point out with exactitude, the year or the day of this strange event." But it was three hundred years ago or so. Of the various subdivisions of land called *estancias* that the Marqués owned, his favorite—even above Las Cinco Llagas—was La Villa de los Patos. Here in mature but vigorous years he brought his young and beautiful wife Angela. Here also came as visitor and ward a comely nephew, Don Felix. The Marqués was often away for long periods, sometimes riding great distances both by day and night, overseeing his farflung enterprises, making war on savage marauders, and not infrequently halting to carouse and gamble.

One day, upon returning to Los Patos from a prolonged absence, he discovered something that made him as jealous as Othello. It was his nature to act swiftly, and now he was fury-bent. He had many horses that on the mountain trails were as fleet as they were sure-footed. He had many peons that obeyed without question. In those days it was the custom to travel with a *caballada* of horses for changes on the route. The Marqués ordered five peons, besides his *mozo* of the stirrup, to prepare to ride with him and twelve picked horses for his *caballada*. As soon as men and horses were ready, which was promptly after his order was issued, he set out for Mazapil, a combined mining camp and hacienda that was also one of his possessions.

Mazapil as the crow flies lies some twenty leagues—around fifty miles—south of Los Patos across a mountain-wrinkled basin. As the trails twist, the distance must be sixty miles. The country between the two points is without water or trees. About four leagues out from Los Patos the Marqués ordered one of his servants to halt with two horses and to remain there until he should return. Four leagues farther on he left another peon with two horses, and at like intervals over the entire distance arranged *postas*. He rode into Mazapil accompanied only by the personal *mozo*.

At Mazapil he had friends. It was not long after dark before, with plenty of grape cognac of Parras—where the cellars of the Marqués de Aguayo yet age the juice of grapes—they had begun a game of monte. Soon the Marqués took occasion to withdraw. "With permission," he said, and stepped out. His comrades went on drinking and gambling, deeply absorbed.

As he had ordered, he found his horse saddled and ready, *mozo* by the stirrup. He was setting out on a journey to which he wished no witnesses. Accordingly he seized the peon by the throat and quickly choked him to death, in silence and without marks. It took but

a few minutes to put the body out of the way. The place
for it had been prepared, for this "Crœsus of Mexico,"
it must be remembered, owned and ordered everything.
Then he rode.

He rode for honor, for death, for vengeance. There is
no way to tell how fast he rode; he rode without regard
for horseflesh. In an incredibly brief time he was at the
place where he had posted his last relay of horses. As
he dismounted, his horse spread his legs out stiff,
swayed, and then fell over dead. In a minute's time the
saddle was changed, and, leaving the peon to hold the
other fresh horse against his return, the Marqués was
again on the road, alone. Thus killing every horse he
rode but managing with fine precision to reach a *posta*
before the mount succumbed, he sped on to La Villa
de Los Patos—and to the room of Angela.

As he expected, Don Felix was with her. Anger did not
prevent finesse. He stabbed the woman before either
she or her lover knew that he was there. Then, over-
powering the nephew, he forced him to stab himself.
He left the knife in his hand so that the double murder
would have the appearance of having been done by the
betrayer of the bed. In the *patio* the Marqués found a
watchful house servant. The dead do not bear witness.
The Marqués was leaving no witnesses.

While getting a fresh mount from his stables, he met
another servant; this man also he killed. Then back
towards Mazapil he rode. He returned, if possible, more
swiftly than he had come. Only now, as he changed
mounts at the *postas*, he killed one by one the witnesses
of his night-time ride.

Just how many hours it took him to make the round
trip the story does not say. It was dark when with a

polite *con permiso* he excused himself from his comrades and set out. It was still dark and the game of monte was still going on when he re-entered the room at Mazapil and took his place.

When, the next day, news came of the deaths at Los Patos, the Marqués appeared to be stricken with grief. He ordered a royal funeral and made provision for countless masses. But despite the care with which he had removed all witnesses, despite the arrangement he had made of the dead lovers, and despite his own high position—or perhaps because of it, for the higher in station a man stands the higher up do enemies rise— he was suspected and brought before court. The only evidence was circumstantial, and the admitted fact that he was at Mazapil at both the beginning and the ending of the night on which the Marquesa and Don Felix met their death proved an alibi. That in the intervening hours he could have ridden to Los Patos and returned was considered humanly impossible. Some say that a little servant girl who had witnessed the killing of the Marquesa Angela appeared but was barred by law from testifying.

Investigations went on for many years. The viceroy of the King of Spain in Mexico City took a hand. At length a high judge—the *oidor*—from Guadalajara came to Los Patos, where, except for hirelings, the Marqués lived alone in the dark, gloomy house still pointed out as *la Casa de Cadena*.[1] His plan was to draw out a confession. Yet if such a confession were brought

[1]The House of the Chain, so called because, according to tradition, it was a sanctuary for anyone who passed the chain stretched between the rock pillars at the entrance of the surrounding wall. The medieval principle of sanctuary, fostered by the church, was never much exercised in Mexico, I believe, although *casas de cadena* are not extremely rare.

into court, the Marqués would deny having made it. The *oidor* foresaw this and foresaw the necessity of having testimony to corroborate his own word. Having, as he thought, gained the confidence of the Marqués, he one dark evening hid a man under the table, which was heavily draped with a green cloth, in the salon where guests were usually received.

After a good dinner at which both *oidor* and *marqués* fortified themselves well with wine, the two entered the salon. The candles but shadowly lighted it.

"Come, now, Señor Marqués," the *oidor* said in an easy way. "As you know, the court can do nothing with you. There is no testimony. Not as an official but as your friend and as a human being with intense curiosity, I burn to know how in one night you kept the game of monte going in Mazapil and at the same time that of daggers in Los Patos."

"I will tell you," the Marqués replied with a frankness that surprised his guest. "When a man who loves glory has achieved some remarkable thing, he itches for it to be known."

"Yes, yes," the *oidor* eagerly assented, "and your name, my Marqués, praised by the King of Spain in the Escorial beyond the ocean and trembled at by every savage Chichimec in Nueva Vizcaya, must be ever gathering to itself fresh renown."

"For that reason only, I talk now," the Marqués went on. He seemed absolutely careless. "Those who say that the dead have better memories than the living lack blood and are stuffed with fear."

But before beginning his story the Marqués pulled his chair up against the mantled table, on the side across from the *oidor*, who sat near the brasier of coals.

He told all in detail—of the relays stationed, of the ride, of the swift dispatch of lovers and witnesses alike. Then he concluded: "It was a dishonor that only blood could wash out."

At the end of the story the High Judge from Guadalajara arose and called out, "Witness, you have heard. Come forth. We have the confession."

But the witness under the mantled table did not speak or stir. The Marqués remained seated, at his ease.

"Witness of the court," the *oidor* called in a more commanding voice, "come forth. We have accomplished our mission."

Still there was no stir or response. The Marqués had not moved from his relaxed position.

A third time the *oidor* spoke. He was impatient. "Why do you not respond?" he called.

Then the Marqués spoke. "*Porqué los muertos no hablan.* Because the dead do not talk."

At these words he quietly pulled up the overhanging folds of the heavy green cloth. Huddled on the floor under the table lay the lifeless body of the secret witness. The Marqués had choked him with his sharp knees. The exercise of furious and constant riding, it is said, had given to Aguayo's legs and knees muscles that, even to a generation of men living on horseback, were astonishingly strong.

"You have authority," the Marqués added, looking at the *oidor*, "to hold inquests. Here is paper with pen and ink. You will write that this man, whose name I know not but who is known to you, died in my house on this night of apoplexy."

The *oidor* wrote and left. The processes of law never got further. Some say that the Marqués lived out his life as the cold-blooded *hacendado* he was. Others say that in his old age he became penitent and retired into a sharp-pointed mountain called Pico de Teira—to be seen from certain elevations overlooking The Five Wounds—there to expiate his sins as a hermit. They say that his sole property here was a small flock of goats, from the milk of which he made cheese, and that he planted in the sinks of the mountains a peculiar variety of very small black beans. I know that these beans— *frijoles encantados* ("enchanted beans") the folk call them—still grow at places on Pico de Teira; and it is a fact that they grow on no other mountains about. Natives with infinite patience gather them to eat. They have a certain savor, but they never struck me as having much to do with the ride that keeps the name of the Marqués de Aguayo alive. Nor could I ever discover the vague connection that a certain song wailed out by the singers at The Five Wounds was supposed also to have with the Marqués.

This song was of a man whose sweetheart had been taken off on horse by another. He went to the top of the famous peak to see what he might see of the elopers.

> "*I went up the Pico de Teira,*
> *I went up the Pico de Teira,*
> *To see if I could catch sight of her in the distance,*
> *To see if I could catch sight of her in the distance.*
> *Only the dust,*
> *Only the dust,*
> *Of the man who was taking her away.*"

Another story, if not of less antiquity, at least with more recent application, connected the hacienda with

69

a certain Señorita Magdalena. She was of a patrician family named Sánchez Caballero that a century ago owned enormous estates in northern Mexico, among them, so it was told, Las Cinco Llagas; but the men of the family sided with the Emperor Maximilian and upon his downfall were all killed or exiled and their properties confiscated. Las Cinco Llagas, however, belonged to an old woman of the family who took no part in the wars, so that in consequence her title was left inviolate. While Maximilian was still alive, she died, leaving the hacienda to her niece Magdalena.

This Magdalena lived in Paris, and she lived a very daring and luxurious life, without parents to direct her or guardians to restrain her. To maintain her extravagances, she mortgaged Las Cinco Llagas to a Mexican capitalist for 50,000 pesos. Before long she had spent and gambled that sum away. Then, with no more money forthcoming, she returned to Mexico and retired to her estate. It was very sparsely stocked, one armed party after another having fed itself off the cattle and goats. Nevertheless an *administrador* had more or less kept the property together. He was an ignorant Mexican of the *pelado* class. Without warning and without explanation Magdalena married him.

She married him; then forbade him ever to darken any door entering her quarters. This order he respected and, though husband, remained but a steward without caste.

Meanwhile the note for the 50,000 pesos approached maturity. The creditor and others for a time thought that an uncle of Magdalena's might come to her aid, but something happened that made them lose all expectation for relief from that source. This uncle was a bishop. It was his custom to make annually a tour through the principal cities and towns of his bishopric for the purpose of inspecting ecclesiastical properties, administering spiritual affairs and collecting funds due the church. On this particular tour he left Monclova one morning in a great coach loaded with himself and approximately 50,000 pesos in silver. Besides coachman and footman he had various outriders. Between Monclova and Castaño, at a defile, his coach was suddenly set upon by a numerous party of what he later reported to be Apaches. Every man with him was killed, all the mules and horses were driven away, and the coach was burned up. By a miracle, as he reported, he alone escaped.

At this time it was the law in Mexico, as it is still the law, that any sale of land by process of foreclosure must be held on the property involved and that the person who bids it in must within twenty-four hours produce cash payment at the place of sale. Forced sale of Las Cinco Llagas to satisfy the holder of the 50,000 peso note had been legally advertised. On the day appointed authorized officials arrived, accompanied by the holder of the mortgage. He apparently would be the only bidder.

In formal manner the property was offered for sale. The mortgage holder bid something a little less than the amount of his note. Then to the surprise of everybody present Magdalena bid 50,000 pesos.

The conductor of the sale hesitated. " Very well, Madam," he announced, "your bid is highest and by law the property will remain in your hands—provided you produce the money within twenty-four hours."

"In much less than twenty-four hours you shall have it," she replied.

Thereupon she ordered her husband to take fifty men —all of the peons of the hacienda were present, for the sale had been made the occasion for a kind of *fiesta*— lead them into her rooms and bring out the fifty *talegas* of silver he would find stored there. A *talega* contains 1,000 pesos, in those days weighing sixty pounds. The *administrador*-husband led his men to the rooms he had never before entered and soon they were emerging with the fifty sacks of silver. This was delivered to the officials, who in turn delivered it to the creditor, and thus Magdalena remained in possession of the hacienda.

The story goes on that after the 50,000 pesos had been receipted for, the *administrador* became a husband in deed as well as in name. According to conjecture he earned this reward by conducting the "Apache" raid and delivering the *talegas* of silver at the hacienda. I will add as a kind of commentary that Don Luciano Sánchez Caballero, chief of the tribe, is said to have sent an agent over from Paris, where he was exiled after Maximilian was shot, to fetch 50,000 pesos he had left secreted at Los Patos. Fifty thousand pesos seems to have been a common multiple with the Sánchez Caballero family. As another story goes, Don Luciano was one day riding in his coach drawn by six white horses, a rider galloping ahead and calling out to everybody he saw, "Clear the road. Sánchez Caballero comes." But a peon refused to clear the road. He knelt in it, hat off, head bowed. The carriage stopped, and Don Luciano called out haughtily, "When you ask for a charity stand like a Christian to one side and not like a robber in front."

"But, Sire," the old man responded, "I do not ask for a charity."

"Then what do you ask for?"

"I kneel but to tell you that what you left at La Bonanza is still there."

"What are you talking about?"

"Why, the 50,000 pesos in the garden."

"Oh," Don Luciano cried. "I had forgotten. Many thanks," and he tossed the old man three pennies.

I have heard the tale of the heiress Magdalena and the *administrador* she married told as having its setting at the great and famous hacienda La Babia far to the north in Coahuila. I set it down as pure legend but nevertheless as something belonging to the life of Las Cinco Llagas.

The most incongruous appurtenance to The Five Wounds was a spread-out mass of boilers, engines, vats, presses, flywheels, and I know not what other parts of machinery that had been installed by an American company to extract rubber from the *guayule* plant during the World War and the years immediately following when rubber was so high. With the fall of prices, however, the little gray scattered plants that have to be pulled up from the desert, packed in on burros, and then put through various processes before the rubber is marketable could not compete against rubber trees. The company gave up its lease on the lands and, after having guarded the machinery for a decade, abandoned it.

Near by on the rich irrigable land once planted in grapes, rows of *guayule* plants that had been set out in their place flourished.

"Why don't you dig them up and plant once more the grape?" I one day asked Don Marcelo Cienfuegos.

"Nobody here knows how to make wine," was his ready answer. "There used to be an expert wine-

73

maker from France, but he was cut down like the grapes."

"Then why don't you dig up the useless plants and grow corn or wheat?"

"Who knows? Perhaps some day they will be very valuable and somebody will buy them." A pause. "Besides, the women of my house do not lack corn to grind on the *metate.*"

Don Marcelo shrugged down a little more firmly on a cottonwood log that had been blazed with an axe and placed as a bench against the wall under the *portales* in front of the house. It was adjacent to the great doors that opened into the *zaguán*, or entrance hall, through which carriages once entered. To the east, facing the *portales* that shaded the log bench, was the church, and between them and the church was a fountain of fresh water supplied by the aqueduct and utilized by all households of the hacienda.

After a long time, during which I listened to the locusts in the cottonwoods and watched three girls carry *ollas* of water away on their shoulders and heads, Don Marcelo commented, "My friend, you are young yet. After a while you will comprehend that against the Winding Sheet and *Suerte* [Fortune, Destiny, Luck] there is no escape."

Then Don Marcelo waited a long time to say anything more, bending his left hand slowly at the wrist back and forth in front of his chin as if to motion away an invisible fly or an invisible fate. It was a characteristic gesture with him that took little effort. Then he added, "If your trouble has a remedy, why worry? If it has no remedy, why worry?"

Two or three old-time friends of the house of Hundredfires whom I met and talked with judged Don Marcelo, not without sympathy, pretty much according to his own philosophy. *"Cuando el Dios no quiere, los santos no pueden"*—When God does not will, the saints are powerless—one of them quoted to me, without meaning to suggest that Don Marcelo was a saint. After all, he had done pretty well, been pretty fortunate in holding on at all. Many *hacendados* had fared worse. Aside from the futility of going against Fate, it was just as well that he not make much stir, for "when bad fortune falls asleep, let no one wake her." Certainly Don Marcelo was not prevented from repose by any kind of divine discontent or cast down by regrets for lost splendor. As Inocencio once sagely remarked, the *patrón* had, without apparent discomfort, "drawn up his legs to fit the length of the blanket."

If troops of vaqueros no longer rode forth in the morning at his command, those towards the north mounted on black horses, those towards the south on *pelicanos*—browns with white hairs in their tails, those towards the east on *grullas*—slate-colored like the sandhill cranes after which they are named, and those towards the west on coyote duns, he yet retained one symbol of vanished principality. That was the maker of his personal cigarettes. She was old, old, more than a hundred years old, "older than fire itself," it was said, and here her cigarettes marked the passing of time as softly as any sundial "numbering only the hours that are serene" ever marked them in a monastic garden of flowers and sunshine.

Before the little old woman's cigarettes were ready for her *patrón* to inhale, the black leaf-tobacco and the corn shucks in which it was rolled had been curing for

two years. A year more or less meant nothing to her—
or to him. She seemed to take more care with the shucks
than with the tobacco. They were home-raised, not
imported from Portugal as certain *hacendados* of the
swelling times of Don Porfirio Diaz used to import them.
The ancient *cigarrera* would pick the shucks for soft
grain, pliability, whiteness; she would moisten them
with water and dry them in the shade; she would
scrape them, and then with brandy moisten and re-
moisten them, turning them every so often, until at
last they were cured to suit her. The process was a
ritual.

She delivered the finished cigarettes in little round
bundles tied with shuck string, each *cigarro* tightly
rolled, the shuck twisted into a point at one end and
doubled inside at the other. It was a formula with Don
Marcelo to bite off the doubled end, unroll the shuck
very, very slowly, and reroll it. He was generous to his
friends, and no paper ever manufactured adds to the
flavor of tobacco as does a well-selected and well-cured
shuck.

Yet Don Marcelo was in no way a patrician. His
swart features suggested little of Castilian blood. He
made no pretense to any "nine-hundred-years-old-
name." One time after he had been to Mexico City, a
nephew recounted to me, he declared that he had
rather hear a wild bull bellow down a cañon than listen
to three choirs in a cathedral. The same nephew re-
lated another anecdote about his uncle, of whom he was
very fond. When Don Marcelo was a young man, he
went one night to a dance at which the *chiquiado* was
being played. In this waltz a young lady seated in a
chair must be approached with verse, often improvised.

76

The youthful Marcelo, very much embarrassed, composed this *verso:*

> "*You mount and sweat the croup*
> *And I will tighten the girt;*
> *To nicker to a filly like you,*
> *My voice it needs a quirt.*"

I heard so often, not from him but from others, a story in which Don Marcelo's grandfather figured as a swineherd that I grew to believe it. This ancestor's name was Antonio. He had about sixty hogs, half of which were his, the other half belonging to his *patrón*, owner of the Hacienda de las Cinco Llagas.

"Take care of those hogs well," the *patrón* often said to Antonio. "Without their meat and lard I do not know how we should live."

"You talk like a poor man," Antonio would say. "How much will you take for this hacienda of yours?"

"I will take three burro-loads of gold."

Sometimes Antonio singed prickly pear for the hogs. In the season of ripe prickly pear "apples"—*tunas*—he herded them towards the fruit. For them he knocked down "dates" from the royal palms and with machete felled the succulent stalks of the maguey. "Hogs are like people," he would say. "The *quiote* (fruit stalk) of the maguey will not only nourish and fatten them; it will make them breed with great desire and bear fruitfully. Truly when the old *cura* saw people eating the honey of the rose from the *quiotes* during a prolific season and said there would be many baptisms the next spring, he knew facts." Taking his swine wherever the maguey was in stalk, Antonio explored far places.

77

One hot noon the hogs took shelter in a cave. In some places the floor was of rock, in others earthen. The earth was cool and the hogs rooted in it. Suddenly Antonio heard one of them give a terrified squeal; he rushed to examine the cause. He saw a hole, and through it he heard the squealing animal. It was too dark down there for him to see; he got a dried maguey stalk, lighted it, and looked. A secondary cavern, not very far below, seemed to run back under the first. Antonio dropped down to it. He rescued the hog, but he saw something that interested him a great deal more than swine. He saw gold bars, stacks of them. Now for Antonio the vast crumbling adobe furnaces at the hacienda that had not been fired for generations and the mountains of black slag beside them took on a very definite meaning.

He was astute. He carried nothing away, said nothing. With rocks and earth on a support of tough stalks he covered up the hole so that nobody else would discover what he had found.

In a few days he saw his *patrón* again.

"How are the hogs?" the *patrón* asked.

"They are eating all the *quiotes* they want these days," said Antonio.

"Good—as good as gold," said the *patrón*.

"Yes, there was never such a summer for *quiotes* of the maguey," said Antonio. "The hogs will breed and breed and breed. How many will you take for the hacienda?"

"No, when you buy the hacienda, you will have to bring me gold, not hogs," laughed the *patrón*.

"And how much gold did you say?"

"Oh, three burros well loaded."

"Will you sign a contract?"

The swineherd's idea seemed a great joke to the *patrón*, but while laughing he agreed to sign a contract whenever he and the peon should be together before a justice. He had no idea that this would ever be. But Antonio knew the *patrón's* habits, and the next Saturday he rode to Mazapil. The *patrón* was there, and boldly the swineherd reminded him of his agreement. Half in good nature and half in resentment at such presumption, the *hacendado* signed the agreement before the justice. The president of the police force, who was also the town's chief buyer of ore, and two other men acted as witnesses.

"We are all in your favor," these witnesses said to the *patrón*, "and we sign, but we see no reason why you should so humor a herder of swine."

"It is my word," said the *patrón*.

Antonio owned but one burro. He borrowed two others. With only his son to help him, he went to the cave and loaded the gold on the three burros—loaded them heavily. Then Antonio delivered it at the hacienda, with witnesses to see. And that is how he became *Don* Antonio, owner of The Five Wounds, and progenitor of Don Marcelo's father.

"Yes, animals often favor *cristianos*," concluded one of the sandaled historians. I shall always remember this man for his having—according to his own testimony—been an eye witness to the "charming" of a filly by a panther that slowly waved its tail in the grass and thus attracted its prey within leaping distance. "Especially do hogs and chickens favor Christians. I remember when my mother, who was a widow, rented a house for twenty-five centavos a month. She complained that the adobe of the floor was all worn away and that the dirt

was loose. She had nine or ten chickens. One day soon
after we moved into the house, those chickens scratched
in the floor so as to expose the mouth of a *cántara*. It
was a big jar. My mother counted 400 pesos out of it.
With the money she bought the house and no longer
had to pay rent."

As a symbol of what may have been his ideal of the
justice that Fortune had dealt him—for to the fortunate
all good fortune is just—Antonio adopted a brand
known as the *Balanza*. I saw it, burned thus, ⚖, the
"Scales" still perfectly balanced, on the few cattle and
horses about The Five Wounds.

▲▼▲▼▲

CHAPTER 4

Sunset in the East

Don MARCELO was hardly a reticent man; he was merely not talkative. Immense in stature and infinite in a deliberativeness that much flesh seemed to add to, he daily sat and smoked and looked into space, or merely sat and looked without smoking. As I contemplated him, I often wondered what was going on inside of him. At many times perhaps nothing. Yet he was not stupid. He was possessed of a sense of humor and even of a kind of fancy, but it was a rare day when these prompted him to tell an anecdote or play audible variations on the ironies native to his race. He was not hampered by any kind of religious beliefs; he shared in few of the superstitions that surrounded him; yet without protest or question, apparently, he took for granted whatever was according to *costumbre*—and to say that "it is the custom" is in Mexico considered sufficient explanation of anything. Politics bothered him

81

as little as did the church, despite the fact that politics had given his land to the agrarians. In short, when it got ready to rain it would rain, and if it did rain the corn would yield whether it were cultivated or not.

There were no luxuries at Las Cinco Llagas, and therefore Don Marcelo could hardly be called luxurious in habits, but he had a way of putting brown *piloncillo* sugar in his *mezcal*. Once when he made some remark about the inconvenience of weight, I suggested that if he would grow grapes and eat them instead of so many *tortillas* and so much *piloncillo* his pounds would shrink. His only comment was that "if a man is destined to be fat, belts will not reduce his thickness."

One summer forenoon while during a long and comfortable silence I was idly watching the "air snakes" whirl up dust as they twisted across the plain, I noticed eight or ten women and two or three men climbing a trail that led to a kind of hut-chapel on top of a low mountain fronting the hacienda. Don Marcelo noted them also and asked me if I knew what their purpose was. I had visited the hut, perhaps eight feet square, seen in it a crude wooden cross, rocks that candles had burnt out on, and some wreaths woven of the time-resisting yucca leaves, but I did not know the purpose of this particular *romería*, or pilgrimage.

"They are praying for rain," Don Marcelo explained. "It is the custom." There followed a silence for the length of a cigarette. I could see the pilgrims kneeling before the little *capilla* on the mountain.

"It seems that these people are not hungry." Don Marcelo at length again broke the silence.

"How is that?"

"The prayer is not short enough for a hungry stomach."

"I am going to tell you something about praying for rain," Don Marcelo went on in his deliberate way. "This was some years ago. The custom then was to get a priest to bless the seeds of the corn and the *frijol* on Candlemas Day. Then followed the planting. The year I am talking about the seed rain did not fall until close to the Day of San Isidro, the fifteenth of May. It was not much of a rain, but it sprouted the corn. For ten days the corn grew; then it stood still. Then it began to twist and wither. Unless rain came it would surely die. The *gente* were taking the images and pictures of San Isidro outside and imploring him to make it rain. Some whipped San Isidro. Day after day passed and not one cloud drifted into sight.

"Well, as everybody knows, the time for the rainy season to begin is the Day of San Juan, the twenty-fourth of June. This day was now at hand, and still it was dry. Then one morning the *peones*, all of them, came in a group and one of them said to me, '*Patrón*, we want to borrow La Virgen María from the church.'

"'Why do you want the Holy Virgin?' I asked.

"'We want to have a procession and pray for rain.'

"'Very well.'

"They took her, the wooden image, and carried her on a platform and went up to the *capilla* and over the fields, stopping at crosses to pray. Then they brought her back to her place.

"The next day the rain started and it did not stop for two days and two nights. The clouds poured themselves out. It hailed. The wind blew. It was a barbarity. When the sky was clean again, there was no corn.

83

What had not died from drouth had been beaten down and washed away. Then once more the *peones* came.

"'What is it now?' I asked.

"'Why, *patrón*,' the spokesman said, 'we want to borrow *El Señor* from the church.'

"'And why do you want *El Señor* at this time?' I asked.

"'We want to have a procession.'

"'*Válgame Dios!*' I said, 'you don't mean to tell me you are going to take *El Señor* out to pray for another rain right now?'

"'No, *patrón*. We want to take him out and show him what kind of Mother he has. Just look at the fields and see what she has done!'"

Don Marcelo had a collection of jokes on priests, neither respectable nor respectful, that he did not relate in the presence of his wife, Doña Josefa. It was not, however, that their broadness prevented him. She was exceedingly broad herself in at least two senses of the word, and she was more pious than she was broad. She often made me think of a certain hen that John James Audubon admired on shipboard—because she "exhibited a pleasing simplicity of character"; yet I sometimes felt that she resented my own lack of faith. Anyway she let drop many words and instances to convince me. For example, one Saturday after I had noticed her and some other women, in preparation for a special service, perfuming the hair, powdering the cheeks, and attaching new laces to the dress of Nuestra Señora de las Margaritas, the *patrona* of the hacienda church, she said to me, "This Lady has brought to pass many wonderful things."

"I have interest and respect," I replied.

The history of La Señora de las Margaritas was not unique; rather it was representative of the miraculous origins ascribed to patron saints in churches all over the nation—imitations, however ingenious the details, of the now hackneyed history of the Virgin of Guadalupe. Although the date of the arrival of the Lady of Daisies at Las Cinco Llagas was forgotten, the manner of it was known to everybody. One morning, as the story went, while a priest was at the altar, the doors of the church being closed, he heard a loud knocking. He went to the door, but upon opening it saw nothing but a jenny with a large package, wrapped up, on her back. He closed the door. Again came the knocking. Presently he discovered that the jenny was kicking the door. He opened it wide to go out and drive her away. She bolted inside. He tried to force her out. She would not go. He went for help. The jenny simply would not leave and men could not drag or carry her out. Nobody knew to whom the animal belonged or whence she had come. Finally it was decided to take the load off her and then try to drag her out. The load, it appeared, was some sort of wood. Upon being unwrapped, it discovered itself as the image of Nuestra Señora de las Margaritas. When the jenny saw that her sacred burden was in the place for which it was intended, she voluntarily walked away, and there the image remained.

"She was here when the mines were working," Doña Josefa went on with her argument. "There was then among the hundreds of people on the hacienda a woman by the name of Lola, the wife of one of the miners. She was not a true wife, however, for she had eyes and more —yes, very much more—for another man. This other man was a watchman, and every day at noon while

Lola's husband was away in the mine, she would carry her lover a basket of warm *tortillas*, cheese, and other things he liked to eat.

"But the husband after a while heard talk and he had suspicions. One day a little before noon he appeared without warning just as Lola was leaving with the basket. It was covered with a white cloth embroidered with *margaritas*.

"'Where are you going?'" the husband said to her.

"'I was going to the church to kneel before Nuestra Señora de las Margaritas to pray for your safety in the dark mine,' Lola responded. 'I was not looking for you, but now we will go back into our house and I will prepare you a delicious hot lunch.'

"'Yes,' the husband answered, 'and what have you in the basket?'

"'I have some *margaritas* to place on Our Lady's altar.'

"'That is well,' he said. 'I should like to see them.' With that he grabbed the basket and snatched off the white covering.

"But what he saw was not a warm lunch of *tortillas* and rice with frijoles, and quince cheese and other things. The basket was full of daisies, so fresh that the dew was still upon them. You see, Nuestra Señora de las Margaritas always protects her worshipers. What could the jealous husband do? The Lady had changed the food into flowers. The husband took off his hat and went back to work."

Concluding this story, Doña Josefa laughed heartily, and I for some reason thought of Lupita, who was perhaps at that minute sprinkling the floor of my room. I also thought of Luz and Martín. Luz, the young and sturdy mother of a child whose father remained for me invisible, spent most of her time in the kitchen grinding corn; Martín, who wore his straw hat more *alacranado* ("scorpioned"; that is, tipped back in the rear) than anybody else, carried wood, watered horses, and did other chores. Both of these individuals called Don Marcelo *papá* and Doña Josefa *mamá* or *mamacita*, though neither was ever considered as belonging to the family. However, at opportune times each of the two, with a certain pride at once solemn and jocular, assured me privately that "Don Marcelo *es mi papá*. Yes, indeed." The way of the *hijo natural* was not hard.

We were on the theme of piety. The most ardently pious of all people on the hacienda was undoubtedly the old cigarette woman. She was quixotically religious, always saluting in the antique manner, instead of saying simply "*buenos días*" invariably using the antique and ceremonious "May God give you a good day," etc. On account of her extreme age she was popularly regarded as being a *miramuerte*, having power to see *muerte*, death, coming from afar.

This belief was strengthened by a birthmark on her cheek and throat in the form of a hand, "the hand of God." It was visible only when she was excited, at which times the aroused blood in her body made the fingers of the "hand" stand out against her dark, withered skin. In explanation of the mark it was told that her father, having been murdered with a knife before she was born, appeared one night to her mother, his hands red with his own blood as at his death, and commanded her to fulfill an obligation he had left undone on earth. She questioned the authority, the authenticity of the ghostly visitor. "Leave me a sign," she said.

"With this hand," he answered and vanished. The next day her child was born, on its cheek the unmistakable sign—the print of the red hand.

The old woman harped often on the times when the hacienda kept a *padre* of its own to say masses in the chapel. The most revered of these bygone *padres*, Father Ceferino, could—according to her—work miracles. Whether she had actually seen him in her childhood or whether she knew him only by tradition it was impossible to tell, but there was nothing vague in her telling about his miracles. The most remarkable he performed was at the tower of the church, right there in front of us. It seems that Padre Ceferino had been so fertile with miracles that authorities over him finally ordered him to cease working them for a while. Their fame had gone so far that the bishop announced a visit to Las Cinco Llagas.

He arrived before all preparations for his advent had been completed. A mason was resetting some stones on the coping of the tower displaced by lightning. There he was hurrying to finish when the bishop went inside the church, followed by Father Ceferino, who, however, soon bustled out to see how the work was progressing. Just as he got well outside and looked up, the mason lost footing and began falling. He saw the miracle-working father below and cried out in the most supplicating tones for deliverance.

"I am interdicted from working any more miracles," Padre Ceferino hurriedly explained. "However, stay where you are while I go within and seek permission from the bishop to save you!"

In mid-air the stone mason was held by invisible powers; the kind-hearted *padre* went in, explained to his superior the situation, and received permission to perform "one more miracle." Emerging, he moved his hands and said something and the mason descended to the ground, head up, at an easy and orderly rate. This was the last of Padre Ceferino's miracles.

Next to him the old *cigarrera's* favorite religious character seemed to be El Mal Hijo—not the biblical Prodigal Son, but a penitent who must from all accounts have roamed over the Southwestern states as well as Mexico. She used to dilate on him to edify the children, and she could repeat by heart his whole speech enjoining charity and respect for elders.

She would describe how the Mal Hijo rode a burro, calling out *"todo el mundo es mi tierra*—all the world is my country"—and showing a withered clenched hand. This hand was his text. "I raised it," he would cry, "to stab my own father. He was poor and houseless, and I was rich and living in splendor. When he came begging, I in my pride raised the knife against him, but it twisted and entered my own wrist. Look at the crimson scar and see how the wages of sin are paid. Behold! And now I, without where to lay my head, knock at your door."

He was always invited to enter, and upon entering he always sat and read.

"What did he read?" I asked the *cigarrera.*

"He read the language of the Bible—*la Latina.*"

Then after he had read he always talked: "*Todo el mundo es mi tierra.* I have sinned the unpardonable sin against God. Ungrateful one, I turned my hand against my own father. Look how it and the arm are withering, withering, withering as year by year I seek what is not to be found. Condemned to wander over the face of the earth, I shall never, never find rest in this world, no, nor in the world to come. Woe is me! Profit by my words! Take warning against disobedience and lack of gratitude!"

As the *cigarrera* quoted the harangue—she could quote enough to fill several pages—she would rock her old body back and forth and with clenched and palsied hand imitate the posture of her exemplar, the "hand" on her throat and cheek emerging like letters of invisible ink when the paper on which they are written is held before a flame. I don't know which had a more terrifying—or more moral—effect upon her young auditors, the account of El Mal Hijo or her imitations, back in the deep shadows of the tobacco room, of "Old Hook Woman" and "Burro Ears." The "hook," ghastly in pantomime, was to catch children who did not behave, and the enormous ears, simulated with hands covered by the black cotton *rebozo* she always went shrouded in, were to hear all lies and evil words that children spoke even in a whisper.

She had, too, a whole repertoire of *cuentos* in which, although the elements of horror and fantasy might overshadow the moral, the didactic application was flatly made. Such was her story of "The Thorn of the Flower," a story well fitted to her reputation of being a "beholds-death."

There were three brothers, of whom the youngest was the mother's favorite, not because he was least but because in addition to being always obedient and good of heart he had been the most trouble to raise. Soon after birth he was apparently going to starve to death, though the mother was a good milker. The child was nothing but a skeleton and certainly within a few days would have become an angel when it was discovered that an *alicántara*[1] was coming by night into the bed, sucking the woman's breasts, and putting its tail into the infant's mouth. The snake was killed and then the boy gained. As he grew up, the two elder brothers showed themselves each day more jealous of him, and they came to persecute him with cruelties and inhumanities.

This mother was a widow, and one day she told her three sons to dig a well out in the brush so that the little goats and the little burros and the other *animalitos* could have plenty of water. According to their manner, the two big brothers forced the other to do all the work, while they spoke hard words to him and idled. Now as he was digging down he found two gold nuggets. The brothers saw the gold and they had more envy of him than they had ever had.

"We will take it to our mother," he said.

"No," they said, "you will not prejudice her against us any more." Then they went against him and killed him and took the nuggets for themselves. They buried him behind some brush and went home. There they told that he was hunting for a rabbit.

When an hour passed and her favorite did not come, the mother grew very anxious, and she sent the two brothers to look for him. After a while they returned without any news. Then she herself went seeking and weeping, but she could find no trace of her lost son.

A long time after this, a poor man went out one day

[1]The coachwhip, called also prairie racer. Among Mexicans the *alicántara* is this and not a poisonous snake as the name implies in some parts of the world. The snake is also called *víbora de vaca* (cow snake), because —so the *gente* assert—it sucks cows, often to the extent that they give no milk at the pen.

to cut *zacatón* grass to thatch his roof. Now the proper time to cut this tough, coarse grass is not when the moon is "tender" (crescent), for if cut then the grass will rot within five years; nor is it when the moon is "thick," but when the moon is dying. That is the time, too, when deer graze late in the day, not having light to graze by during the night. Thus it chanced that along late in the forenoon this poor thatch-gatherer saw a buck browsing on some *palo verde* brush. He had no gun but very quietly he watched and then he noted a beautiful, beautiful white flower growing obscurely against the bush. After he had watched the buck a long time until it grazed away, he stepped to examine the flower.

It was solitary on a long stem. He had never seen any flower like it or any other so beautiful. It was a marvel. He would pull it and take it to his wife. As he broke the stem, the flower sang these words:

> "*Pity me, pity me, my dear friend,*
> *Pity me now in this sad hour,*
> *For in the field they murdered me—*
> *I am the thorn of this flower.*"

Yes, a flower singing! This must have some significance, the man thought. So he carried it to the king and told him how he had found it and what it had sung.

When the king took the flower in his hand, it sang the same words it had sung to the grass-gatherer. He was filled with wonder and suspicion, and he at once called one of his servants and commanded him to go through the town presenting it at each house. The flower was silent until the servant reached the home of the murdered boy. The boy's sister came to the door and took the flower in her hand, and at once it sang:

> *"Pity me, pity me, sister dear,*
> *Pity me now in this sad hour,*
> *For in the field they murdered me—*
> *I am the thorn of this flower."*

Then in astonishment the sister passed the flower to her mother, and again it sang:

> *"Pity me, pity me, mother dear,*
> *Pity me now in this sad hour,*
> *For in the field they murdered me—*
> *I am the thorn of this flower."*

A riddle and a dagger in the heart! But the mother was thinking something, and she called in the eldest of the three brothers and gave him the flower, and when it was in his hand it sang:

> *"Pity me, pity me, brother dear,*
> *Pity me now in this sad hour,*
> *For in the field you murdered me—*
> *I am the thorn of this flower."*

The second brother heard and tried to escape, but he had to take the flower also and in his hand it sang the very same verse it had sung to the eldest. Then the mother and the sister went with the servant to the palace, and the king called the grass-gatherer who had brought the flower, and the grass-gatherer guided them to the place in the brush where he had plucked it. The mother asked that they dig a hole at the roots of the

plant. In this hole they found the body of the murdered
son.

Meantime the soldiers of the king had made the two
guilty brothers prisoners. They were hanged to a tree
overlooking the hole. "Thus nobody goes from this
world without paying what he owes."

There seemed to be no particular time or place for the
cigarrera to dispense her counsels. It was when she felt
in the mood and the children were handy. Sometimes
when they wanted a story she would not give it; again
she would pour one out as easily as breathing. One evening about sunset I happened to encounter her as she was
carrying an old five-gallon kerosene can half full of
water; her strength was not sufficient to allow her to
carry it full. Eight or ten children were at hand in a
ring playing not very noisily "La Cabrita" (Little
Nanny Goat).

At this instant I happened to glance towards the
mountains to the east and, although dusk was approaching, the sun having disappeared, I saw one of them aglow
with a soft yet brilliant blanket of light, rose and ame-
thyst and golden, misty like a veil and at the same time
pellucid, surpassing in beauty and strangeness and effect upon the imagination any light my eyes have ever
beheld. The flame of fire that Moses saw out of the
midst of a bush was not more *extra*-phenomenal than
this one incandescent mountain among its somber
fellows. The light kept shifting and changing with un-
believable rapidity. Now it was a spectral red, like the
lips of the woman-mate to Death in "The Rime of the
Ancient Mariner"; now a smouldering luster of copper
like the un-natured and ominous hue of a full moon in
midnight eclipse; now, again, all misty loveliness, and

at the last a dying blush as soft as the half-caught aroma of honeysuckle hidden in the dusk. I have read of the Mountains of the Moon on which *la luna tuerta*— the "one-eyed moon"—shone blood red, and I have walked both dreaming and waking under a light that never was on land or sea, but only this once have I experienced, whether amid the realities of dreams or the unrealities of wakefulness, such a sunset glow.

For some minutes I stood still, and then by instinct I called to the slow-moving old woman, "Look! Look! What does it signify?"

She had, I suppose, although I had not been aware of her actions, halted to observe. Now she set her can of water on the ground, and said casually, "The sun is putting itself down."

"Yes, and in the east," I said.

"Why not?" she answered. "Just so one early morning a frog said to a buck deer, 'Let's make a bet as to which can see the sun's earliest ray.'

"'With all pleasure,' the buck agreed, for he was very proud of his eyesight. 'But what do you want to bet?'

"'Twenty-five heel-flies,' said the frog. 'They will taste delicious.'

"The buck laughed and said, 'Very well.'

"Then he turned himself to look eastward. But the frog turned himself to look at the highest peak of the sierras, which was to the west. Soon he saw the peak growing bright. He called out, 'There it comes.' The buck had not yet seen a ray of sunshine, but when he turned and looked where the frog was pointing, he had to admit that his bet was lost.

"Yet he could never pay his debt, for a crow over-

95

heard the buck and the frog talking and he told the heel-flies how they had been made a forfeit. They began stinging the buck and they have stung deer ever since and they never get near water where a frog can lick them up."

I suppose the old woman had seen such phenomenal sunsets before. Nevertheless, she stood gazing, and the children stopped their play and gazed too. The intense rose of the light turned to the softest violet, then to dark purple, and in six or eight minutes the mountain of celestial fire faded into the duskiness of other mountains around and beyond it.

Then a little girl came close to the *cigarrera* and said, "*Tata*, tell us about La Llorona that came out of the Red Mountains, and don't show us Old Hook Woman."

The old woman raised both arms high above her head and, swaying them and her body right and left very slowly, began to moan and cry in a weird, thin voice, "Oh-o-o-o-o-o-, my child, my child, my child, oh-o-o-o-o."

The children, the little girls especially, drew closer together, in a delicious ecstasy of fear. "But tell what made La Llorona say 'Oh-o-o-o,' " one pleaded.

Without another word, still standing, her features growing dimmer in "the hour when no man knows his brother"—the twilight that lasts so long in mountain country—the *cigarrera* began the story of "The Crying Woman."

"In the times that are passed while the Españoles still were owners of this country there lived far to the south in a town in the Red Mountains a beautiful lady. She was most fair, with rose on her cheeks and lips, and her hair was golden like the sunlight on the mountain you saw just now. Then she married and had a little girl. But in a duel a man killed her husband.

"This man was the lover of the beautiful lady. He was a hard man and whatever he did, he did as if he were leaping a wild horse across a gully. He did not like the girl baby; he hated the little innocent and spoke hard against it. Nevertheless the beautiful lady loved him. Who knows why? Perhaps God knows. She took the baby down to the river and threw it in and it drowned.

"After this became known, the soldiers seized her and the judges tried her and she was condemned to be burned alive. On the day of the burning all the people came to the plaza to see. They were all saying, 'Poor little one,' and she was weeping but still beautiful. There was much delay and it was dark before the fire was lighted. Then they all saw something white and bright, exactly in the form of the beautiful lady, fly out of the fire and go towards the river where the baby was drowned. As the form passed, all could hear the cry, 'Oh-o-o-o-o-, my baby, my baby, my baby, oh-o-o-o-o-o-o.' What pity! What horror! Terrible!

"But she could not find her baby at the river, and she flew following it down to the sea, and she followed it up to the deep *barranca* in the Red Mountains. And then she flew to other rivers, up and down the Río Grande of the North and along the seashore. And she flew into the City of Mexico and went up one street and down another, always crying and crying and crying. Then she went to Guadalajara and to San Luis Potosí and to Chihuahua and to Saltillo and to Durango and to all the other cities, and she passed by all the ranches and all the haciendas. She is still looking and searching and crying, and she can never find her baby. Poor thing! Poor thing!"

In the dimness I could feel the fright of the huddled children, and I saw or imagined I saw for an instant the flush of "the hand of God" on the old woman's cheek. With tenser voice she continued.

"Where men are hanged La Llorona comes, and one near such a place can feel her breath as she passes. At any place where bandits bury a dead man to guard treasure she appears also. She smells out the dead a hundred leagues away and down in the ground as deep as a well, because she is always searching for her dead baby. There are times in the late evening when her voice comes out of a long white cloud. This cloud is always passing, never still.

"Sometimes she walks instead of flying. Then it can be seen that she wears a white *rebozo*, perhaps holding her arms thus as if she were carrying a little one. One night a bold man who met her in the street, not knowing who she was, said, 'Pull back your *rebozo* so that I can look upon your beautiful face.' At once she uncovered her face and he saw nothing but bones of a skull, each one of them as bright as a coal of fire in darkness and every tooth brilliant like the point of a ray of lightning. Figure that to yourself! This man felt her breath on him colder than ice. He fainted to the ground. At last he recovered enough to crawl home and tell what he had seen." Here the old woman was down on her knees groping towards the children. "But that night," she added, "he ceased to be.

"Yet very seldom does La Llorona speak. She cries and weeps and weeps and cries. One time when I was a little girl a vaquero on the Hacienda Bonanza who was sitting on his horse asleep while he guarded the herd, awakened to see her paused in front of him. It seems that neither the horse nor the cattle sensed her. 'What time is it?' she asked. 'By the stars it is twelve hours of the night,' the vaquero said. 'At twelve hours of this night I have to be in Saltillo,' she said. 'Oh where shall I find my child?' And then the vaquero heard her wailing and wailing through the air in the direction of Saltillo. She can be seen in Saltillo and in Mexico City or some other place at the same hour of the same night. Thus she passes."

"But have you heard the cry?" one of the boys asked.

"Why not? If I had not heard it, how could I repeat it to you? Once another *señora* and I were carrying water after dark just as I am now, and the crying came from right over our heads."

Here the *cigarrera* repeated in her thin voice the notes of the cry, "*Oh-o-o-o-o, mi bebé, mi niña, oh-o-o-o-o-o-o.*" The children broke pell-mell for the lighted kitchen of the big house, and I think the old woman herself hurried beyond her wont to get away from the place.

What I saw of these children of the hacienda was mostly during the long waits between nightfall and our always late supper. During this time they were to be found, with various dogs and oftener than not a pig or two, either in or near the enormous kitchen with its stone ovens, two little girls acting as slaves to a man-child. While the offspring of the *patrón's* immediate family gnawed *tortillas* or sipped coffee, the children of lower rank, showing neither hunger nor envy, went quietly without anything. As the hand-stone rubbed back and forth on the *metate* and deft fingers and palms

99

slapped the ground-corn *masa* into *tortillas* as thin as
wafers and as round as the moon, sometimes the children shouted rhymes that went with the *rub, rub, rub*
and the *pat, pat, pat:*

> *"When they feel cold*
> *And when they want to eat,*
> *The little chicks say,*
> *'Cheep, cheep, cheep.'"*

> *"Here comes the moon*
> *Eating a* tuna
> *And dipping her spoon*
> *In the* laguna."

> *" The cross-eyed cat*
> *Had a beard on her chin*
> *That tickled her fat—*
> *Shall I tell it again?"*

And then at "tell it again" the whole bevy would
begin repeating the nonsense jingle, their treble voices
rising higher and racing faster with each repetition until
their tongues and my head were twirling like a set of
fandango dancers. Some of the children wore, as amu-
lets against the Evil Eye, red beads strung around their
wrists, and the flashing of these amid the waving and
clapping of hands seemed to add swiftness to the whir,
the whirl, the race of tongues.

They had a kind of chant:

> *"Pájaro cú, cú, cú,*
> *Pájaro cú, cú, cú,*
> *Poor little bird, cú, cú,*
> *And poor owlet cooing too."*

And this chant made me remember and repeat to them a little story with which my own childhood was instructed by one of their blood. I perceive that nearly everything connected with Las Cinco Llagas runs into a story, and I suppose that the inclusion of this additional one will not spoil the broth. So old Comancha, as we called our washer-woman because she was so dark in her copper swarthiness, told it to us children.

In the beginning of the world, maybe one thousand, maybe two thousand years ago, the eagle called all the birds together. He was king over them and they all obeyed him. At the assembly there appeared one totally naked, without one feather to hide its nakedness. Now the king eagle was of the *gente decente*. He was very proud and he and some of the other birds, the official ones, were much offended. He ordered the shameless bird to be put out.

But the dove took pity on the poor naked creature and said that she would give him a feather and that each other bird might give him a feather and thus he could be clothed and saved from being outcast.

"That will be all right," said the eagle, "but someone must act as his sponsor and be responsible for him."

"You are wise, Señor King," the peacock spoke up. "The naked beggar must have a sponsor, for with all the many-colored feathers he is about to receive he will grow offensively vain. I very much doubt the wisdom of this proposal anyway." The truth is that the peacock was jealous of a rival.

During the discussion the owl had said nothing, for the assembly was in daylight, and the owl was sleepy. Now he spoke up and said, "I will act as sponsor." Many of the birds feared the owl and all knew him to be so wise that he could tell when anybody was going to die. As is said yet, "When the owl sings the Indian dies." So the matter was settled and right away the birds began giving the naked one their feathers.

The redbird and the scarlet tanager gave him red feathers, and the robin another shade of red. The blue-bird and the jay gave him blue feathers, the parrot and the hummingbird green. The canary gave him yellow, the oriole orange. The blackbird, the crow, and the buzzard gave him black. The mockingbird, the gull, and the pelican gave white. The tall *grulla* gave him a long mouse-colored feather, and the wren gave him brown. The quail contributed speckled feathers, the guinea silver, and the turkey bronze. Oh, the naked one had feathers of more colors than the rainbow, and he had so many that they were thicker on him than the down on a goose. Now he was clothed in a glory that no other bird on earth ever enjoyed. And he was so vainglorious that he would have absolutely nothing to do with the other birds. He would not even speak to the peacock. That night he left the country.

The next morning the king eagle called again all the birds to give them counsel. The one who had been naked and clothed was not there. Then the eagle was very angry.

"I told you what would happen," the peacock said.

Other birds showed spite also.

"You agreed to act as sponsor," the eagle said to the owl. "Now you are charged to bring in the truant. Go at once."

But the owl went to weeping and said he was too blind to hunt during the day and must wait until night to search.

"You said nothing about this when you agreed to act as sponsor," the king eagle cried out. "I order the hawks to make you prisoner at once."

At that the owl flew into a black cave where nobody could see to follow him.

But the kind-hearted dove felt responsible, for she has a very tender conscience. "I will go hunt for the lost bird," she said. Then she started out to hunt, and the little Aztec doves, and the big white-winged doves, and the plump pigeons and all other members of the dove family went with her, flying here and there through the woods calling, "*Cú, cú, cú.*" The paisano, or road-runner, undertook to search also, looking close to the ground. He could not say *cú*, but, as now, he went *cru, cru, cru*. Also he took the owl a lizard to eat. That night the owl searched faithfully, calling *whu, whu, whu* into every dark corner of the woods.

But the *pájaro-cú*, as the lost bird came to be called, could not be found anywhere. Nobody knows where he went to, but he went somewhere, and the owl at night still goes about looking for him and asking *whu, whu, whu*, and by day the paisano with his head and his tail stretched out level with his back runs up and down trails, stopping often to look sharply in this direction and that direction, often rolling out of his mouth as fast as his eyes can wink, *cru, cru, cru*, and all the dove people too, especially in the evening, say softly as they think it is their duty to do, *cú, cú, cú, cú*. But the doves don't expect any answer. It is very strange that a bird with so many bright feathers like the *pájaro-cú*, cannot be seen, but thus it is. It is thought by many that he went to a foreign land.

CHAPTER 5

By Sun Time

Don marcelo's generation of the house of Hundred-fires had included other men, all gone now. One of them, Anselmo by name, was often visible to me through his handiwork, although the "law of flight" had during the Revolution sent him beyond making further terrestrial impressions. This Anselmo, it seems, had cared very little for any kind of derivative from grape juice, but he did have a positive inclination towards juice of the maguey in the forms of *mezcal* and *tequila*. It was his custom after taking a siesta in the middle of the day to arise and begin fortifying himself. At a certain stage he would issue forth for his seat under the arched *portales*, a servant accompanying him with a goatskin—no doubt dyed green or magenta—for his master to sit upon, a bottle of the white liquid, a bone-handled American forty-five sixshooter, and a belt of ammunition. Having got himself properly entrenched, Anselmo

104

would undertake to ring the church bell without pulling
the rope. He was a faithful churchman, and it was a
principle with him that the sound of a church bell more
than anything else inclined the hearts of listeners
towards holy things. Occasionally one of his bullets
would slap the ponderous metal into a dull reflex of
sound, but most of them went wild or against the rock
pillars of the tower.

Seldom now did the bell call listeners to peaceful
meditation, but, sitting there in the shade of the *portales*
under the pit-marked church tower, it was easy for me
to be peaceful and to contemplate and to wish for the
soul of the bell-ringer of bullets' repose and the tones
he liked.

Inocencio's *jacal* was nearly as good a place in which
to linger and remember and forget as were the *portales*
of The Five Wounds. Although Inocencio was a kind of
appurtenance to the *hacienda* and now as my *mozo*
spent much time at it, his *ranchito* was apart in a pocket
of a valley by a diminutive spring a long hour's ride
distant. It was known as El Pirul, from a lone pepper
tree—the tree imported from Peru by the *conquistadores*
and now naturalized over much of Mexico. Here I
liked to go because the welcome was always genuine.
It was invariably accompanied by some sort of apology,
such as, "Your poor house lacks everything but hearts
with a desire to serve you."

Shaded from the intense sun by the *ramada*, the arbor
of poles and grass thatch leaning against the hut,
Inocencio and I would sit *para platicar*—"in order to
talk." During warm weather his barefooted wife kept
her *metate* out under the shed and often she would pause
from her everlasting grinding to join in. Or if there was

no talk, I might merely listen to the rubbing and get the same sort of lulling sensation that an idler gets from the sound of water running over stones. I suppose that reformers are right in regarding the *metate* as the emblem and implement of female servitude. It is the "nether millstone," older than Nineveh, which the law of Scripture made a household exemption from debt. Before daylight you can hear the poor servant girl grinding corn on it; after dark you can hear her still. Yet the rubbing sound seems in place. Hands, arms, legs—bodies from toe to scalp—swaying over it in rhythmic motion, this is the stone that for unnumbered millenniums has enforced grace upon the drudges of Mexican kitchens, whether the prematurely aged peon wife sheltered in some mountain crevice or the rich bachelor's saucy *criada* in a city house.

Whenever I was a guest at El Pirul, the *tortillas* must be as white as driven snow. To make them thus, the black base of each grain of corn had to be picked out, one by one, with the teeth. While Nicolasa—for that was the name of Inocencio's wife—ground, I would watch the hulls work to the side of the *metate*, like scum along the edge of swift water. Then the soft white *masa* —call it not not "dough,"—without salt, leavening or grease, would be patted into thin *tortillas* with a dexterity that has never grown commonplace to me, and cast upon a plate (the *comal*) over an open fire to bake.

With the rubbing on the *metate* in the ear of memory, I can hear Inocencio saying now, "Listen, Don Federico, I want to tell you something. A man is what he eats. The Mexican, what does he eat? Why, *frijoles*, of course —the 'national ones,' as we call these beans. We eat them 'on foot' [boiled] and we eat them 'horseback' [fried], and the little bean soup puts strength into a man as well as *frijoles* themselves. You know how we say of one who is weak, 'He lacks *frijoles*.'

"But *principalmente* the food is corn. Now look at it preparing itself on that piano with three legs and one hand," and here, well pleased with himself, the philosopher made an extended gesture towards the three-legged grinding-stone upon which his wife was moving the hand-stone backward and forward.

"Look at my corn-grinder there. When God made the world He made man, and then, seeing how man needed food, He gave him *tortillas*.

"The *tortilla*," he went on, "has in it everything that the corn supplies. It does not change from its source as does the white bread made from wheat. So the Mexican, except when his head is closed [closed to reason, ideas], is whole.

"Now the corn that he eats, where does it come from?"

That no response to this rhetorical question was expected I knew well enough. Yet I answered, "It has developed from a native grass, and if I ever go to Guadalupe y Calvo in Chihuahua, I shall know in what *barranca* to look for this grass, provided the Tarahumare Indian told me truth. The Mexican corn is both the thriftiest and the most savory corn in the world because it belongs where it grows."

"*Absolutamente*," Inocencio agreed. "I will tell you of its origin, as the history came to me from my father and to him from his father, from a time so far back that only one like the priest who knows Latin could count it. Thus the *historia* goes.

"When Jesucristo was a baby, his mother stopped

107

one day under a tree of black bark and green leaves to let him suck. I do not know what tree it was. Perhaps it was a mesquite. Well, after the Niño took the breast and got the milk to flowing free, he pulled his mouth away and let some drops fall on the ground.

"'Why,' said the Mother, 'do you let the milk of Nuestra Señora'—Inocencio gestured skyward—'drop to the earth?'

"'In order,' answered El Niño, 'that your brothers may eat and take nourishment also.'

"And the *maíz* grew there, grew purely through the favor of God. Thus, ever since, when the corn is in milk men eat of the same substance that El Niño was nourished with."

"The only trouble with the *maíz*," I commented, "is that in this dry country, even though it be native like the grass, it often fails for lack of water."

"Perhaps," Inocencio admitted, "for in this dry land our patron, San Isidro, has one bad year and then another worse, but remember that if there were chicken every day the cookery would grow bitter, and do not think that God gives *atole* with the finger.[1] There are the *tunas* of the prickly pear, to eat cooked as candy, to eat raw, and to drink as *colonche;* there is the fruit of the *coyoniste* cactus; there are the beans of the mesquite, good in their sweetness for man and beast and to be made into bread as *mesquitemal*. There are the dates of the *palma real;* there is sotol, alimentary when roasted as well as good for liquor; like it, the maguey serves for both food and drink. Oh, el *buen Dios* plants even the driest desert with many blessings."

[1] *Atole*, corn gruel. To "give *atole* with the finger" is a proverbial expression meaning to deceive with false promises.

"Yet, looking at it, I could wish it were green," I said, as I pulled my hat down over my eyes to diminish the glare rising from the bleak hills far and near.

"But, *señor*," Inocencio retorted, respect in his tones more than in his words, "we in Mexico think that the green color is more for cows than for men."

"Also," Nicolasa put in here, pausing from her grinding, "the corn in the *tortillas* keeps the teeth white and sound."

"Some say it is the lime in the corn," I remarked.

"Perhaps. I do not know about such things," she went on. "But our son Juan, who lived in los Estados Unidos for three years, has talked much about what he saw there. He says that the *Americanos* eat soft bread and many sweets and that the dentists there are as many as bakers. He says they all drink coffee very hot, like you. That will crack your teeth. It is bad. He says that the *gente* up there all eat with knives and forks and spoons and do not use the *tortilla* to dip up *frijoles*."

"That is true," I said, "but even though I want my coffee boiling, I like Montezuma's spoons."

"Montezuma's spoons," she laughed. "But what are they?"

"Why, don't you know that?" Inocencio answered. "They are *tortillas*."

"Yes," I elaborated, while they both laughed, "when Hernando Cortés was approaching Tenochtitlán, capital of the empire of Montezuma, this emperor sent an ambassador to meet him.

"'I represent,' said Cortés, 'the mightiest empire in the world. It fronts the ocean as a house overlooks an anthill, and the ships of its emperor command the commerce of all other nations.'

"'The empire of my emperor,' returned the ambassador, 'fronts two oceans.'

"'My emperor,' Cortés spoke, 'lives in a palace the very hangings of which are gold.'

"'And mine,' responded the ambassador, 'sleeps upon a golden bed in his palace and eats from a golden table.'

"'Hear!' said Cortés. 'That is nothing. The emperor of Spain, my emperor, goes so far in riches that the very vessels upon his table are gold and silver richly carved and even the spoons with which he dips up his food are golden.'

"'That is nothing,' replied Montezuma's ambassador. 'My emperor never uses the same spoon twice. For every morsel of food he scoops up he has a fresh one.'"

"Thus it is," Inocencio concluded, his eye upon his wife. "Thus the spoons of Montezuma had their commencement."

The household of Inocencio did have three pewter spoons, but that day I dipped up my soup with replenished *cucharitas de Montezuma*, and we were merry.

"Do have some more of the little soup so beautiful and fat," Nicolasa kept saying.

At El Pirul doves were always numerous about the spring in the late afternoon.

"Listen, Don Federico," said Inocencio one evening.

"I am listening."

"I want to tell you something."

"My ears are always open for what you have to tell."

"What do the doves say?"

"Who knows? Perhaps you can translate for me."

"Yes, I can tell you. Listen to them again. One says,

'*Qué quieres, pastor, qué quieres?*' (What do you want, shepherd, what do you want?)

"The other responds, '*Comer comas, comer comas.*' (To eat *coma* berries, to eat *coma* berries.)

"And the *torcazito*"—the Inca dove—interjected Nicolasa, "says with great humility, '*Peccavi, señor,*' but his mate without any thought of sin answers, '*Comer tunas.*' (To eat *tunas.*)"

"Of a truth," I consented, "I can hear very plainly now what the doves are saying, but to understand them one must understand the *idioma*. They speak in Spanish, not in English."

"Exactly! The creatures are *nativos*, like the Mexicans. Here you have the crows. Always watching the hunter and waiting for his kill, they cry, '*San-gre, san-gre.*' (Blood, blood.) And the piñon jays, when they see a man coming, scream out as a warning to the deer, '*Piñ-on-es, piñ-on-es.*' (Piñon nuts, piñon nuts.) The turkey gobbler says, '*Gordo, gordo*' (Fat, fat), quick, like that. The little friar [killdeer] likes to run in the water's edge and never roosts off the ground and when he gives the alarm at something approaching, he says, '*Qué frío! qué frío!*' (How cold! how cold!) The duck says, '*Paz, paz.*' (Peace, peace.) All the *animalitos* say something."

"Yes," Nicolasa, who had been laughing, added, "and do not forget the *coyotito.*"

"What does the coyote have to announce?" I asked. She laughed more. Then she told.

"*Bueno*, at night when the coyotes come out upon the prairies to seek their life, always you will hear the old lone male howling for his mate. Then you will hear her answer. Afterwards you will hear many, many

111

short, quick, gay yelps in one place, and that means that the coyote people have gathered around their leader and are playing a game. They form in a circle and run round and round, each trying to catch the other's tail, all of them all the while yip-yip-yipping. Perhaps there will not be more than four of them, but they will sound as if they were as many as a people gathered together for Easter mass.

"And now the leader howls a long, long cry, and back and forth he and his mate make a dialogue thus:

"The leader: 'Let's go to the blue corn.'

"The mate: 'What for?'

"The leader: 'To make *atole*.'

"The mate: 'With what will you stir it?'

"The leader: 'With the tail, with the tail.'

"The mate: 'It's not of bone.'

"The leader: 'Yes, it is of bone.'

"By the time the leader and his mate have decided that the tail has enough bone in it to stir *atole* from the blue corn, the other coyotes all join in the chorus, 'It's not of bone,—yes, it is of bone; it's not of bone,—yes, it is of bone.' They keep that up as long as they want to or until they are tired of running round in the circle trying to catch each other by the tail."

No doubt Nicolasa had chanted the chorus of the coyote's tail bone to her little ones many a time, but I am sure that she never had a more appreciative audience than the day she chanted it to me. Of the "untroubled fancy" of another day I remember this.

"Don Federico, you and the *patrón* of Las Cinco Llagas were talking of the old vineyard there. Listen, I want to tell you something."

"I want to learn, Inocencio."

"The vineyard of Las Cinco Llagas was cut down in its third stage."

"In its third stage?"

"Yes, in the third stage. Wait a little while and you will comprehend. 'Little by little,' as the cart-driver said to his oxen, 'we go very far.' I am going to tell you the *historia*.

"One time there was a drouth worse than any other known to the memory of man. It became so dry that the mesquites did not bear. The spring no longer afforded enough water to keep alive even the flowers in pots. Every drop that seeped was drunk by the people and the few animals not yet dead. But the people had one vine that they would not let die. It had been given them with a promise. So they killed peacocks and *guacamaya* parrots and watered it with their blood. It flourished.

"Finally there were no more peacocks or big green parrots to take blood from. Then they killed bulls and tigers and lions and irrigated the vine with their blood. It grew and flourished and spread over a wide plot of ground. But in time there were no more bulls or tigers or lions to kill and take moisture from. Then the people turned to the hogs and killed them, irrigating the vine with their blood. It flourished and bloomed and bore fruit. It bore grapes, and the juice of these grapes the people now drank themselves.

"It was very good. No matter whether they were hot or cold, hungry or full, it tasted divinely delicious. And, as was natural, in the first drinking these irrigators of the vine strutted like peacocks and chattered like *guacamayas*.

"Then when they drank more deeply, they grew

fierce and eager to fight, like the bull, the lion, the tiger.

"In the third stage of the drinking they became like the very hogs that had given their blood to the vine. Thus by the elbowed trail that winds round and round the mountain instead of by the trail that cuts straight across the plain I have brought you to why the vineyard at Las Cinco Llagas came to be cut down."

If I stayed at Inocencio's overnight, as I did several times, I could after I had lain down on my pallet hear him and his wife pray, pray for the sons absent, for souls dear to them gone from the earth, and always for *el extranjero* present.

The last time I was at El Pirul, I remember, Inocencio upon my making ready to leave said lightly, "Why now? While life lasts there is time to spare."

"Yet you know," I answered, "how the saints weep over lost time."

"But the saints favor charity, and when you consent to abide here they are joyful."

How long I stayed on at Las Cinco Llagas, "losing and neglecting the creeping hours of time," honestly I do not know. Many times in pueblos and cities of Mexico, as I have been kept awake at night by clocks insistent not only on marking hours but every quarter-hour, I have wondered why a people who regard time so indifferently would wish to have it announced so constantly. I think it was in the plaza of Nombre de Dios, in the state of Durango, that, having arrived late, I struck a match in order to examine the face of a sun dial I saw obscurely beside the walk. Thereupon a watchman rushed up with the solemn information that this "apparatus" did not give time at night.

In a "house of guests" at another place, where not

another stranger had stopped for perhaps three months, I was one freezing night availing myself of the meager kitchen fire while two old women and a younger one busied themselves with the supper dishes and pestled in a stone mortar the variety of seeds to be used in the morrow's *mole*—a dish, as Mexican newspapers say of a boxing match, "truly emotional." Presently another ancient figure wrapped in black *rebozo* came in.

"What hour is it?" she asked.

"The hours are eight," answered one of the dames, peering at a loud-ticking American-made alarm clock on a shelf.

"Is this *tiempo de Calles?*"—the daylight-saving time decreed by President Calles—asked the stranger.

"No, it is *tiempo porfiriano*"—time as it was under Porfirio Diaz—responded with some asperity the old woman who stood as guardian to time. "We do not use *tiempo oficial*. Leave that to the 'coyotes' and 'hawks' of the government."

"Ours is *tiempo astronómico*," elucidated the younger woman.

"It is *el tiempo de Dios*—the time of God," spoke with finality the ancient crone who had first consulted the battered clock.

"So, so," I translated as freely as I quoted, "and an hour ago it was seven o'clock and when another hour has passed it will be nine o'clock. Then in the morning all the men will lie in bed until the 'cloak of the poor' drops down from the sky to warm them."

"Yes, yes," they all agreed.

"Only," the most ancient moralized, "who has promised any of us tomorrow?"

And *el tiempo de Dios* ticked on.

One morning I was in the *zaguán* at The Five Wounds looking at the mountains framed by the great doorway when a blanketed peon came into the picture. Standing in his drapery at the edge of the *portales*, he slowly rolled a shuck cigarette and more slowly smoked it, never shifting a leg or a shoulder. He and the ancient masonry that sheltered him and the mountains forever beyond, all seemed to be in a harmony that was timeless. And when the shadows of evening lengthened and the swallows dipped nearer and nearer the ground and, as invariably as the cricket's chirp diminished in tempo with the lowering of temperature, the occasional human voice within sound softened to harmonize with twilight, the concord seemed primal, elemental, something destined never to change.

Sometimes I meandered afoot about the hacienda, perhaps to squat and watch two men weave fiber into ropes or spin mare's mane into twine for making cinches, perhaps to consort with a boy guarding the corn against crows. He was deft with the sling and had but to show himself within shot of the crows to put them to flight.

"You do not get to kill many of them," I said to him one day.

"No, that is because the crow is the most astute of all creatures in the world."

"How is that?" I asked.

"Well, did you never hear? Then I will tell you. One time a crow and a blackbird who were talking together saw a man coming.

"'Right now,' said the crow, 'we will have to stop our conversation and fly away.'

"'Why?'

116

"'Because yonder comes a man.'

"'He has no gun.'

"'No.'

"'He has no stick.'

"'No.'

"'He has no rock.'

"'In sight, no.'

"'Then,' went on the blackbird, 'why should we leave yet? I am afraid of an armed man, but I am not afraid of an unarmed one.'

"'Well, I am,' the crow said. 'I have a disconfidence in all men. That fellow might have a rock hidden in his pocket. *Adiós.*'

"The crow flew away. The closed-head stayed. The man came near, slyly put a hand in his pocket, drew out a rock, and threw it straight so as to kill the blackbird. The crow was in sight looking and learning, but he was out of reach."

This boy guardian of the corn usually had time to talk. "The crow is more sagacious than even the coyote," he went on—but the moral of that story is tedious.

Sometimes, sitting in the afternoon, Don Marcelo would remark, "The sun is all right in the morning. The sun of morning is good, but the sun after midday is evil. It will make the head sick." I suppose that Don Marcelo really believed what he said about the sunshine; else he would not have said it so often. But how in the light of his own rather active experience during younger days and of the experience of others he could think the afternoon sun evil, I do not know. "It is the custom" to so believe.

Occasionally as Don Marcelo noted my gazing at the weathered church tower and the silent old bell, he would muse, "Just think how many bullets Anselmo shot away! Thousands and thousands!"

Somehow Anselmo grew for me into a very real and cheerful sort of person. He seemed to have lived in and to bring me back to "the innocence of the old age." Yet the chief remembrance of Anselmo's existence at The Five Wounds was not the bullet pits but his motherless daughter Dolores, who was treated as one of their own by Don Marcelo and his fat wife. *Dolores* means *sorrows*. It is a very, very common name in Mexico, yet not so common as human destiny. I first became aware of her—though before this I had daily met her, glanced at her, spoken to her, and heard her voice—one morning long after my arrival at the hacienda.

Very early, at the hour when dawn first promises itself, I heard while not yet awake the voices of children and girls singing. At first they seemed far, far away as in a dream; then they were so near that I could distinguish the words. The song was the "Mañanitas de San Juan," the loveliness of which may not be translated.

> *"Qué bonitas mañanitas*
> *Como que quiere llover;*
> *Parecen las mañanitas*
> *En que te empecé a querer."*

(How beautiful the little dawnings are, as if it were going to rain; they seem like the *mañanitas* in which I began to love you.)

> *"Despierta, mi bien, despierta,*
> *Mira que ya amaneció;*
> *Ya los pajarillos cantan,*
> *La luna ya se metió."*

(Awake, my love, awake. Look how dawn's light has come; the birds are already singing and the moon has gone to rest.)

Then the verses changed to a more lightsome gayety:

> *"What pretty songs of the dawn*
> *King David used to sing*
> *To the pretty girls he knew*
> *Before he went psalming."*

> *"Mr. Twilight, Mr. Twilight,*
> *Please do me this favor:*
> *Put out your lantern's glow*
> *Or love might begin to waver."*

As I learned upon arising, it was Dolores's saint's day, and, according to custom, it had been inaugurated with the dawn serenade. She was seventeen years old, and now somehow she suddenly appeared to me as fresh and lovely as the morning of the first day. It is not often that in a Mexican home a strange man more than glimpses the unmarried daughters, except at meals. I was ceasing to be a stranger in the house. Anyhow, on the evening of this day Dolores was present when somebody told a story of a young lover who rescued a girl from the Comanches and carried her to safety on his horse. That made me remember a story I once heard in Chihuahua, and as I told it I could feel Dolores listening. Through it I meant—partly meant at least—to tell her how fateful it is for a maiden to fall in love; at the same time I know now that I was conscious of the "mighty magic" almost any tale of love and fierceness would have upon this maiden, a solitary rosebud that, whether she knew it or not, all the winds and sunshine in a garden yet pristine to her were calling, pulling, drawing to open into a flower with petals as red as the blood of the heart and stamens lush with golden pollen.

This is the story.

During the time when Maximilian, backed by France, was emperor of Mexico, a *gachupín* by the name of Esteban de Pardiñas lived on the plains against the Sierra Madre of western Chihuahua. He had a beautiful daughter named Jovita, a boundless hacienda, and an enormous debt. In order to relieve himself of the debt he contracted his daughter to a low-bred but wealthy *hacendado* of the region named Juan Látigo. This Juan Látigo professed to be enamored of Jovita, and, although he was repulsive to her, she prepared to obey her father's orders.

Now at the time the engagement was made it happened that a troop of cavalry under a French captain came to the Pardiñas hacienda and there remained for several weeks. The captain fell in love with Jovita, and either despite her engagement or because of it, she fell in love with him. They were discreet; nevertheless Juan Látigo soon discerned what was happening.

Out on the plains of the hacienda and in the valleys between the sierras there grazed in those days many mustangs. Among them was a pacing white stallion reputed among the *rancheros* to be the swiftest animal in the world. He had so often eluded traps, lassos, and chasings that many believed he bore a charmed life. He went by the name of El Blanco, for while there were other white horses, this was *the* White One. In the caves of the sierras overlooking the plains on which El Blanco led his *manada* of mares, then lived, as they yet live, the swiftest and most enduring runners known to the

Americas, the Tarahumare Indians. They have never taken to the horse; they can travel more rapidly afoot.

Juan Látigo was part Indian himself. His passions—lust, jealousy, desire for revenge—spurred him into an idea. He went to a certain band of the Tarahumares and offered them a mule load of salt and another mule load of *peyote*, which they eat in order that they may have visions, if they would deliver El Blanco alive in his corrals. Eight days later they brought in the pacing white stallion. They had run him down as they run deer down.

Of course Juan Látigo had continued to appear gracious towards his betrothed and her family. He now saddled a strong and swift but gentle horse and rode over to the Pardiñas hacienda. He hitched his mount near the garden gate. A half hour later he was walking in this garden with Jovita and her mother. As they neared the gate, he quickly snatched his promised bride through it, swung her into the saddle with himself, and was gone.

In his own corrals El Blanco was waiting, captured but untamed, his back yet untouched by saddle or man.

"*Señorita*," Juan Látigo said as he drew rein by the magnificent white stallion, addressing her for the first time during the ride, "I am going to present to you the only animal on earth worthy to bear you on his back. I ask pardon for the ride I have caused you to make on my own unworthy beast. No man has ever, no man will ever, profane the back of El Blanco. He is for you alone."

Calling two vaqueros to hold El Blanco, Juan Látigo now with his own hands proceeded to tie Jovita upon the horse. Then without bridle or rope they turned the mustang loose to regain his native range. As the maddened creature sprang out through the gate, Juan Látigo said, "Ah, *señorita,* now truly you in grace ride a white horse."

Among the ranch people of Mexico to say that one "rides a white horse" is to say that he rides towards death. Yet the white mustang did not pitch or fling himself to the ground. He paced, paced out of sight of the man who had lashed an innocent upon his back, paced straight for his wildest haunts.

As for Jovita, who can describe her feelings on this Mazeppa-like ride? She was chafed and lacerated by her position on the madly flying stallion. Bushes and the limbs of trees raked and scratched her. She prayed for death, she hoped for rescue. A great thirst came to consume her. One day, two days El Blanco paced, pausing only now and then to drink from a stream or to snatch a mouthful of grass. Jovita lost all sensibility.

Meantime Juan Látigo had ridden straight to the camp of the French cavalry officer.

"Sir," he announced, "I have for a long while perceived that you are enamored with the Señorita Jovita de Pardiñas. Also I have perceived that she receives your feelings with pleasure. Yet it is well known that we have been betrothed. Listen! We are no longer betrothed. I have resigned my claim. I have released her. Released her on the back of the only animal in the world worthy to carry her—El Blanco. You may have her if you can catch him."

The captain of the French did not wait to make formal challenge in order to kill Juan Látigo. He had heard of the pacing white stallion. What horseman of the north had not heard of him? He knew also of the running powers of the Tarahumares. He went to them by the same road that Juan Látigo had gone. Naturally it did not take the Indian runners so long to capture the harassed steed as it had taken when he was fresh. And Jovita lived.

When I had done with the story everybody exclaimed, "*Qué barbaridad!*"

An hour later as I was passing through the *patio* on the way to my room, I met Dolores.

"Don Federico," she asked gayly, "what became of Jovita?"

Before this, I recollected, Dolores had on the few occasions when she addressed me used the more formal *señor*.

"She lived," I replied, "how happily, who can say? El Blanco was released to the freedom he loved so well. The freedom of that wild stallion is what stirs me."

I do not believe that Dolores before this had given the horse a thought. I saw her head lift and her nostrils quiver in the manner of a proud and beautiful mare sensing something strange, something that may be dangerous. In my own mind, held forcibly against the pull of senses and emotions, was the idea that had been pounding there all day: the knowledge that a wall higher and broader than the great wall of China prevented my ever taking this lovely being for wife. As for all else, she was the charge of my dear friend and host.

During the pause I made, Dolores said nothing, only looked in that proud, something-comprehending way. Speak directly I could not. "For your own good and happiness," one part of me wanted to say, "let us never take even one short ride together under the morning sun across the open phlox-dotted mesa." What I said was this: "Jovita's ride is the one disproving case in

123

history against the wise Spanish adage, 'He who rides the tiger cannot dismount.' "

"Yes, *señor*," she answered, "Jovita disproved because she was brave enough to dare."

Then, without a *buenas noches* and without allowing me time to remark that so far as the ride on the white mustang was concerned Jovita had no opportunity to exercise her own will, Dolores was gone. What amount of contempt, what amount of hurt pride, what note of challenge there was in her speech I spent many hours that night debating within myself.

I resolved to see her as little as possible. For several days I wondered how I had ever experienced tranquillity under the *portales*. Indeed, I wondered if I had ever experienced tranquillity anywhere.

There is, however, a physical basis for love as well as for life.

CHAPTER
6

Tiger Claws

THE majority of rooms in the great house at Las Cinco Llagas were not used at all, the family of Don Marcelo and his hangers-on, kinsmen and non-kinsmen alike, being satisfied with remarkably few. Several iron bedsteads, two or three mirrors, a like number each of iron washstands and pine tables, a few chairs, all of which were uncomfortable, a sewing machine, and a squeaky old phonograph comprised most of the furniture. Adornments consisted mainly of calendar pictures that advertised patent medicines under the benediction of the Virgin of Guadalupe. The house had at one time been richly furnished, but *revolucionarios* had cut carpets covering wooden floors into saddle blankets and right in the *patio* had barbecued beeves on fires made out of the flooring and carved furniture.

The room assigned to me was well back from the center of household population. In front of the door a bougainvillea vine that seemed to bloom perpetual purple flowers afforded a screen against passers through the *patio*. A heap of sand around its roots was daily moistened, and in this damp sand Lupita always kept buried, except for the neck, a jar of water that I might drink it cool.

Lupita cared for my room. She had ripened into a firm lushness beyond the soft milk-corn age at which Mexican girls of her class usually marry. I was customarily, not always, away when she came to sweep, sprinkle the earthen floor, tidy up the bed, and replenish water in the *olla*. A straw mat carpeted the standing place against the bed. A stubby kerosene lamp half filled with blue-black oil sat on the little table, but as it had no chimney I burned candles, supplied by myself. The recently whitewashed walls reflected the dimmest light, whether from a candle within or from the sun or stars without, into a subdued luminousness.

Once when Lupita came while I was in the room, I told her not to put oil on her hair—she anointed it with marrow when marrow was procurable and used olive oil also—but to keep it washed and clean. After that her hair was always naturally fresh, like the rest of her person. For a shampoo she used suds made from the roots of the abundant yucca plant called *amole* or *soyate*, and she rinsed her hair in "tea" of the *toronjil* plant. These secrets of the toilet I did not learn immediately. I found out also that she was purifying her complexion by applying a moistened compound made of the ground heart of melon seeds and powdered bone or deer horn that had been burned, the mixture savored with a bit of *romero*—a bush that every Mexican woman knows. Her dress of calico was always clean.

126

Lupita's mother was the chief *curandera*, or herb-woman, not only of the hacienda but for the whole country round. While her house was not stuffed with the extraordinary variety of dried herbs—together with dried frogs and snakes, shells brought from the sea, and powdered insects—to be found throughout the markets of Mexico,[1] yet it contained a wide assortment of leaves, roots, and barks gathered from the countryside: the leathery blood-of-the-dragon for sore mouth and diseased gums; "herb of the charcoal burner" for catarrh; the "gut of Judas" for rheumatism; "herb of the angel" to awaken the appetite, and "herb of the drunk man" to favor digestion "when it is sorrowful"; thirst-leaf for indigestion; aromatic royal salvia for the heart; bark of the molar tree for allaying toothache and also for repelling fleas; bark of the wild cherry for coughs and tuberculosis; seeds of the Guadalupana vine, each one marked with the image of the Virgin of Guadalupe, to be soaked in *mezcal* and applied to cuts and other wounds; *tumbavaqueros* (it-throws-vaqueros) for epilepsy; leaves of the *anacahuita* tree to be rubbed over ringworm; marigold to be brewed into tea for the stomach, and walnut bark into an elixir for the blood; "flower of the dead man" to be sipped in the form of tea in the morning as a defense against melancholy; roots of the herb of the bad woman (bull nettle) for the kidneys and seed of the same for oil beneficial to the complexion. These are but samples. If an ailment for which the *curandera* had no *remedio* presented itself, she knew

[1]The pharmacopœia familiar to Mexicans in the border states as well as in Mexico itself is simply incredible. Anyone interested in the subject is referred to *Las Plantas Medicinales de México*, by Professor Maximino Martínez, México, D. F., 1933. This work lists something like 1400 names of medicinal plants, many of them duplicates, however.

where the proper herb could be found. Often the plant must be used fresh. In truth she "could rightly spell of every herb that sips the dew,"—"God's little herbs," as the *curandera* called them, "for His children."

Her most highly recommended cure—superb for any *enfermedad interior*—was, however, not herbal. It was broth of rat. She usually had one or two dried rats, their long stiff whiskers appearing to have grown longer after they had been gutted and hung up. As a charm to prevent any of the ills for which her pharmacopœia contained remedies, she was ready to supply a necklace made out of "the three Marys" (three small red seeds), "the three queens" (three small red-and-white seeds), and "the three kings" (three large red-and-white seeds).

Once while she was teaching me her lore, Lupita not far away, she pointed to a bundle of yellowish stems hanging above a jar of pulverized dried rattlesnake flesh, this latter a sovereign cure for the malady that Spanish men are reputed to have introduced among Indian women.

"That herb," she said, "would serve you well."

"But I am not sick."

"No, no, you are very well. That is it. Now with this little herb the *señoritas* will follow you like a *manada* of mares behind their master."

It was not alone the diseased who came to the *curandera*, and some by stealth. Certain people even claimed that she had powers of a *bruja*—a witch. Towards most of her patients she maintained an air of secrecy, and this air had given her an habitually sinister look, in it something dark that was not, however, profound. I could never learn precisely how she cured the *susto*—something worse than "fright." She could cure it only in men, for it takes a man to cure a woman that has been *asustada*.

Now that we were at the threshold of the unknown, for the mysteries of the physical are no less than those of the metaphysical, I said, "Tía Patricia, I have heard that there is an herb tasteless when mixed with food but deadly poisonous."

She gave me a swift look. "Many people say so," she replied. "Ask of the educated ones. Ask, for example, Dolores."

Then, as if considering that she had said too much, she added, "It is the young who are always trying to find out secrets."

In gathering simples she took Lupita with her, and sometimes they spent the whole day out together. It was as if an artist had painted a hand as rich in the juices of life as that of Mona Lisa against an old cowhide dried and shriveled in the sun. Once while riding alone I came upon the two at the spring that watered Las Cinco Llagas. El Siestadero it was called, because the shade there by the cool water was in the summer time so conducive to siestas, I suppose.

Lupita had just dressed from bathing in the pool and while her long black hair hung free to dry, she was gathering roots of the *flor de peña* (flower of the rock) on the cliffs. I dismounted to help her; and as I saw her there I had a revelation of why she was the freest and most graceful play-fellow of the winds and waters among all the Mexican girls of her class I had ever seen. Most of them never get beyond the *metate* for grinding corn, the rock for washing clothes on, the *olla* for carrying water in. There were married women at The Five Wounds who, though born and brought up at the place,

129

had never been as far away from it as this spring. Lupita had a laughing smile; this day it was as bright as a new *sarape* in the sun.

That very night at the hacienda I heard a voice in a certain song that made me ask whose it was.

"Feliz is singing."

I had heard White Moustache once grinding out in a tuneless manner the truculent words of the revolutionary song "El Treinta-Treinta":

> *"Companions of the plow*
> *Enslaved and starved and dirty,*
>   *There is but one road now—*
>   *Grab your thirty-thirty."*

But I did not know he could sing. I knew now, however, that he was singing for Lupita. I had noted his eyes as he looked upon her. The words of the song were very clear; two verses went:

> *"If you wish that I forget thee*
> *Ask of God that I may die,*
>   *For in life I must remember,*
>   *A world apart or closely by.*

> *"For the moon I'd give a peso,*
> *For Lucero[1] a silver rope,*
>   *For the eyes of my loved one*
>   *Life itself and eternal hope."*

Now the *curandera* had a little garden in which she raised certain herbs, carrying water for them, and here also she kept various potted flowers. Among them was a

[1] The morning star.

perennially blooming geranium of an intense red hue at once brighter than scarlet and darker than crimson. On the morning after listening to White Moustache's song I returned to my room, to find it, as usual, fresh and clean —and in a crease patted into my white pillow lay a sprig of the leaf and flower of that red, red geranium. I had an inclination to wear it, for I like to wear red flowers; instead I put it in a glass of water to keep it fresh.

That day I rode with White Moustache, Inocencio, and another vaquero to capture a certain wild mare. White Moustache was on his brown horse Recuerdo. The two other riders split off from us. Along in the afternoon he halted. "Yonder she is," he said, pointing into some brush probably five hundred yards away. I looked but could make out nothing, though I knew that the way to hunt is to disregard the background and pick out what is supposed to be against it. "Keep looking but make no noise," White Moustache said. Presently I thought I saw a tail switch. "Now stay here and pretend that you notice nothing," White Moustache instructed. He rode off and twenty minutes later I heard the shouts of the three men as the wild mare and her little bunch bolted out. There was a long and hot chase; it did not surprise me when White Moustache roped the mare.

On the way in, leading the mare, we came to the spring. When we halted to drink and let our animals cool, I plunged in, my companions watching me with a kind of listless amusement. White Moustache had a way of appearing listless without being passive. While I was in the cool water I saw him kill a brown lizard— "because this animal runs down people's throats." During the day I had remonstrated with him against

131

killing a horned toad, but I did not convince him of the absurdity of believing that this innocuous creature sticks its "horns" in the hoofs of horses, causing them to drop off.

After I had dressed from the swim, I gathered some of the deep yellow *flor de peña* growing where I had helped Lupita gather roots of the same flower. White Moustache remarked in a manner as cold as the spring water that the *curandera* could tell me a *remedio* for which they were good. I put my nose into the petals and threw them away. I thought it just as well for the pacific way of life that I had not worn the geranium.

On the way in at a place where the ground permitted two horsemen to ride abreast I told Inocencio to prepare for a hunt, which I had hitherto only aimlessly considered, in the Barranca de Víboras three days' ride from the hacienda. All I knew of this *barranca* was what I had heard, that it was a profound gorge among mountains clothed with great trees, that in it harbored jaguars, that out from it deer and turkey were plentiful, and that Indios, whose tribal name seemed to be unknown, came into it. I had a curiosity to explore it, and told Inocencio to get plenty of *tortillas* and *gordas* cooked and to catch up my pack mule, a sorrel that went by the name of Durazno (Peach).

"Your best horse is not a very good one," I said. "Perhaps I had better buy one for you to ride."

"That will be wise," he replied, "but never buy a horse from an enemy. He may have been taught tricks."

As we ascended a hill overlooking The Five Wounds I picked out half a dozen dim lights made by meager fires in the houses surrounding the hacienda quarters. I wondered if one of them might be from the *curandera's* kitchen. After the hard ride, the swim, and then the late supper of peppered solids I should have been sleepy but was not. Nevertheless I went to my room.

The door was closed. As I opened it and struck a match to light the candle, which had its place on the table beside the *olla*, wash basin, and glass, I noticed that the geranium I had left was gone. I thought I heard a breath, and as I glanced about in the dim light I saw the form of a woman by the window, apparently gazing out into the night.

Lupita turned. The red, red geranium flower was in her hair.

"*Señor*," she said, her voice very low, "since preparations are being made for your going away, I have come to ask for any commands."

I saw that the door was closed and for a full minute looked without speaking. I could not help dwelling on the dark flower in the hair. While I was still gazing in silence, a knock sounded at the door.

There was an exchange of glances, both directed towards a corner of the room across which a curtain that descended to the floor cut off a kind of wardrobe. Without making any more noise than a mouse would have made, Lupita glided behind the curtain.

"Pass in," I said, as I opened the door wide, leaving it ajar.

The visitor was White Moustache. This was the first time he had entered my room, though Inocencio often came there. Without removing his hat, thus keeping his hands free, and without showing any more animation than was his wont, he took the chair I offered. He shifted it slightly so as to face the curtained corner, the only obscured spot in the room.

He spoke. "As a long journey calls for a good horse, I have come to tell you I have decided to let you have Recuerdo, since you have expressed so much interest in him. I . . ."

At this instant a voice came from the open door. "Horses either borrowed or rented have no hearts." The voice was that of Inocencio. He stood in full view, placid. By the law of association, which, doubtless, Inocencio expected to work, I remembered what not two hours before he had said about the horse of an enemy.

If White Moustache was surprised at the appearance of Inocencio, he betrayed no sign, but in reply to what my *mozo* had interjected he said, "I was not thinking of renting the horse or of lending him. As you know, a *ranchero* will sooner lend his wife than his best horse."

"Why," I said, meaning to be pleasant, "I did not know you had a wife."

His countenance as unexpressive as ever, White Moustache said, "I will sell the horse, if you will pay enough."

"Thank you," I replied. "I will think about the matter."

Then I turned to Inocencio. "I did not mean that we are to leave tomorrow or even the next day. We'll settle the date later."

The men considered themselves dismissed and left. I stepped out behind White Moustache, remarking as I carefully closed the door that I wanted a drink of fresh water from the fountain. After we had walked across the *patio* and out beyond the *portales*, I saw him depart in the direction of his house. While I was standing alone sipping water that I did not want, Inocencio appeared.

134

"Not everybody," he volunteered, "is willing to let the water he cannot drink himself run on down its course."

I did not propose to be detained further by either wisdom or the lack of it. "Inocencio," I said, "tomorrow I am going to drink this fountain dry."

"That will be good for the health," he replied, "just so you do not let the water get in your eyes."

As I walked back through the *zaguán*, the orphan boy whose business it was to bar the outer doors every night was ready to close them. They were always opened very early in the morning, and thereafter until dark exit and entrance were free from anything like a formal watch.

When I entered my room, the candle was no longer burning. I did not need it to light my way to the dim window, through which there came faintly the fragrance of a *huele de noche*—"smells by night"—jasmine that grew in the enclosure beyond. The aroma of flowers makes a man remember; the fragrance of the clean hair and the healthy fresh body of a ripe woman makes him forget.

"So, after all," she said, "you are not going—at once?"

"No, Lupita. Not yet. I have become naturalized here. I have become a veritable Hundredfires and each one of the hundred is burning for you like a conflagration eating up the forests of the mountain."

I told her how I had gathered for her the yellow blossoms of the *flor de peña* where we together had got only their roots but how I had thrown them away.

She told me how she had long avoided White Moustache. "I know not," she said, "perhaps Dios knows,

135

but it seems now that I was waiting for you. It is the *suerte*."

The next morning I told Inocencio all the preparation for travel he need make at present was to hunt up the pack mule and shoe him. I sat all afternoon under the *portales* hoping that Lupita would come to the fountain. She did not appear. Then after sound sleep and two cups of coffee made by pouring a little black, thick *extracto* into hot milk I seemed to see all things in the world through a crystal clearness. I recalled Don Marcelo's saying that "against *suerte* there is no escape."

If Lupita avoided me for one day at the fountain, she did not avoid me at all times and places. Days drifted by. I heard that White Moustache had ridden to pay a visit to Nuestro Señor de los Guerreros at Tizonazo, a place in Durango where every year thousands of people go to make devoir to "Our Lord of the Warriors." Men especially go, and it is well known that this was Pancho Villa's favorite shrine, where his bloody right bower Urbino worshiped also.

One morning after having saddled my horse and ridden a short distance, I returned to my room to get a package of tobacco. As I approached it I saw Dolores silently gathering purple clusters from the bougainvillea growing, as I have noted, in front of the door. I heard the voice of Lupita within singing. Dolores seemed startled. We had not met apart thus for two weeks. She saw my eyes shift from her face to the flowers she held.

"You like blossoms, *señor*," she said lightly—too lightly for naturalness. "I will give you one." She gave me a single blossom from the rich mass. Then she was gone.

I rode immediately to El Pirul and told Inocencio to prepare for the trip. I was anything but contented. Daily here I saw Dolores, and a thousand times daily the wall that separated me from her rose up broad and high. Stealing the very glances I gave her lovely features, hardly trusting myself to address the most commonplace remark to her, many times straining my ears to catch the music of her voice as it separated itself from other voices of people not visible, wondering what thoughts might lie back of the light in her eye, imagining what the mere touch of her hand would be like, now planning to stake all on one word, one move, now considering cold impossibilities, I was becoming to myself a mockery of indecision and fatuousness. As for Lupita, she was, as she knew, but an incident, yet an incident that at the time somehow complicated what I felt for Dolores. The only remedy for mental and emotional trouble I have ever found is to remove myself from its source. This may be because when I travel out I leave old things behind, do not drag my accustomed environments along with me.

We took with us a fierce Airedale dog that one of Inocencio's neighbors had somehow acquired but that knew nothing about hunting and an old hound that an American hunter had two years before given to Don Marcelo to help keep the colt-killing panthers down. Neither Don Marcelo nor any of his *gente* was good at hunting with dogs, and I had no idea how this hound, Lead by name, might trail. I hoped to kill a jaguar for his beautiful hide.

As might have been expected, the Barranca de las Víboras proved to be more than three days away. By the end of the third day we had, however, come into a beautifully timbered, though rough, country; the rains of late summer and early fall had set streams usually dry to running and there were camping places everywhere. We pitched against a creek known as Arroyo de los Arrastres, across from a wraith of smoke from a solitary cabin, as silent as the smoke itself, inhabited by a native into whose veins had never been injected one drop of the blood of the conquerors. At sundown I heard a turkey gobble. "We will stay here a day or two," I said to Inocencio. I was where I wanted to be. The fever in the blood and those perplexities that prevent a man from being whole were all gone.

There were no noises in that country either by day or night except earth sounds. After darkness had fallen there came to us from the low mountain across the arroyo something like the bellow made by a bull calf.

Early next morning the native from the solitary cabin appeared.

"Did you hear that tiger up on the mountain last night?" he asked.

"Yes," I replied, "he has horns about three inches long and he thinks he is a grown bull."

"A *tigre* for sure," the native gravely responded. "I heard him again before daylight. I can prove it with your dogs."

The Mexican name for the jaguar is *tigre*.

Instead of hunting turkeys I took the dogs tiger hunting. On a narrow "coyote spine," or ridge, that broke away into gulches on either side and led to the tableland of the mountain, the hound Lead let out a deep-throated bay and coursed off like a bullet. "He knows something," exclaimed the native, and I felt jubilant in the knowledge that I had a genuine hunting dog. The fierce Airedale started too, then suddenly tucked his tail and bolted for camp.

We followed the course of the hound and soon in a patch of soft moist earth saw what the dogs had scented.

"*Ca-ramba!*" Inocencio ejaculated.

"Of a truth the wind does also blow in San Juan," exclaimed the native.

All eyes were fixed on such tracks as no mountain lion or jaguar—the only large animals of the cat tribe native to North America—that I ever heard of could make. They showed as plainly as if they had been moulded in plaster of Paris. The print of each of the four feet was as big as a saucer—and each had the outside toe missing.

Meantime, although Lead had passed out of sight, he was not out of hearing. What a voice he had! Then, suddenly, he was silent.

"He was probably going so fast that he jumped the track," I explained. "Let us wait a minute and we'll hear him again."

We waited one minute, many minutes. No cañon wall could have cut off the sound of the dog's voice. We scouted out severally. Lead was not to be seen or heard. While I was up on a high point I saw in a kind of swag a considerable distance down what appeared to be a small mound of twigs and leaves; it was against a madroña bush. I was not curious enough to descend and examine it. After we had scouted and listened until the sun was halfway to its zenith, we returned to camp. Lead never did reappear.

His sudden and utter disappearance remained a mystery. The extraordinary tracks remained a mystery. Indeed we were in a land of primeval and aboriginal mysteries. Above our camp the *arrastres* after which the creek was named had century-old trees growing up through their rock-floored bottoms, and no one knew whence the ore that Spaniards once ground in them had come. In all the country between the Arroyo de los Arrastres and the Barranca de las Víboras there was no ranch, mine, or hacienda, only two or three cabins. The land was not fit for farming; it grew no grass worth a cow's grazing and only a few bushes worth a goat's browsing; the timber on it was too remote for utilization. It belonged to deer, lobo wolves, panthers, jaguars, and other things of the wild. I found that the native who knew the difference between the bellow of a bull calf and *something* else—but what was it?—knew many other things. I liked him and for a pittance he was delighted to accompany us. His name was Estanislao.

Three days after we saw the outlandish tracks we rode for four hours and camped on a stream cutting down into the Barranca de las Víboras. Here we were lucky to find a little bench of land level enough for comfortable pallets. Above it the mountain-side rose at a steep angle; below it the water went talking over rocks and breaks. Twisting along between the bench and the stream was a deeply worn trail. Vegetation and jutting boulders prevented our seeing either up or down the trail very far. Other campers had been here, and the place was called Camp of the Forty Moons. I know not why. It was over the world and under it both, and was in a solitude as primeval as creation.

After we had settled in camp, Estanislao told me about a tiger hunter who lived "towards yonder very far away." Now there is not a wild animal in the world I had not rather live close to than kill, and every hour I spent in this Barranca de las Víboras territory I was more pleased with living and less inclined to wish myself where there were women or electrical appliances. Nevertheless, I wanted to kill a jaguar. With the disappearance of the hound all chance of trailing one down was gone. Estanislao kept watching ravens and buzzards for the purpose of locating a kill by their flight, but not even a fresh kill would exactly locate the killer. I sent Estanislao to bring the tiger hunter.

He left afoot, was gone two days, and returned after dark with his man, also afoot. This *tigrero* wore a blanket, and after he had eaten and was squatted by the fire I saw that all he had on underneath his blanket was a pair of *calzones*. I saw too that one side of his nose and face were all gone, so that the teeth on that side looked out.

For a long time I sat secretly looking at him and wondering what had happened to him. He was silent. Then when he opened his blanket to get a cigarette, I noted great scars on his chest and a naked rib sticking out, the wound healed over but the bone uncovered. Curiosity prevailed over breeding.

"Excuse me," I said, "but were you burned?"

"*No, señor.*"

That was the only answer and we were silent a while longer.

Then once again I tried. "What did happen to you?"

"*Un tigre.*"

That was all. Again there was silence, but I had to know.

"*Señor,*" he responded after a question that he could not evade, "you have sent for me because I am a hunter of the tiger. I call them to me with a caller made by stretching skin over the opening of half a gourd, and then sawing a stick back and forth in a hole made in the skin."

Here he showed me his drum-like *bramaderas*, one to imitate the cry of the male jaguar and one that of the female. He made the wild calls—and I was at the moment half relieved that no response came to them.

"When I go out," he went on with his explanation, "I hide myself where my back will be protected and where I can see in front and around me. Then I call. If a tiger hears, he will respond. I call again. He responds nearer. At last he may come into view and then I shoot him.

"I used to have two dogs. They would always point their ears and whine low and show terror when the tiger approached. I watched them so as to be ready to shoot, for often I could not see far on account of the growth.

"One time I went out with my dogs and my *carabina*. I planted myself in a clump of little trees under a bluff facing an open space. I made the call. At once, far down the *ramadero* a *tigre* answered. After a while I called again; he answered and this time he was not so far away. I knew exactly how he would approach, and I moved a little outward from the trees, my shoulders still to the bluff, bushes in front to obscure me. Now he was getting near but showing more caution. For a long while I must wait yet, I thought, and be very cunning with the calls.

"But my dogs suddenly grew very much excited. They whined hard. They had been taught not to bark. Their hair stood up. They were not looking towards the tiger approaching. They were looking behind me. I looked too, and there on the bluff right above me was a tiger, immense, ready to spring. I pointed my gun with-

142

out time to aim. The tiger was already springing and the bullet missed him. He knocked me to the ground and one claw caught my face. He seemed to be trying to eat it as the dogs fought him. He clawed my breast. Then I do not know what happened.

"When I came back to life, I felt a great burning and my lips were like meat baking on coals. I felt something touching one hand. I moved it. I heard a whine. My dog, one of them, was licking my hand. His moist tongue came to my face. I could see out of only one eye. With that I saw my other dog dragging himself to me from a bush. All his entrails were torn out. He whined as if he were sorry for me. As he died at my hand, I had a tear for him.

"After many hours I saw a man on a horse passing on the hillside across from me. I managed to shoot my gun and attract his attention. He carried me to his house and I lived. I still hunt tigers."

The fall nights in that country, for we were camped far above the bottom of the *barranca*, are sharp. When we lay down to sleep that night, a fire of juniper and oak wood was burning into coals that would still be warm at dawn. I lay on the side of the fire next to the trail. The other men lay on the other side of it. The Airedale, as usual, bedded as near the fire as he could get.

I was not yet asleep and was craving the experiences of a jaguar hunter when I felt an extraordinary noise. I say *felt*, for I felt more acutely than I heard. The sound was first a kind of swish through the air. Then it went *we-ahh*, very much like the expiring sound made by a toad when a heavy boot or hoof mashes the air out of it. The noise was not at all loud.

"Did you hear that?" I asked, not knowing if any of the men were awake.

"*Sí, señor,*" Inocencio responded.

"What was it?"

"*Quién sabe?* Perhaps a bird."

By now I had raised my head on my elbow so as to look about. I could see nothing out from the small circle of light made by the fire and, turning towards the fire itself, I saw a blurred object making off from it. I thought it might be some camper's burro that had wandered up the trail, and I called to the Airedale to "sic." The dog did not respond. I looked at the spot where he had been all night keeping himself warm. He was not there.

All this took much less time than it takes for me to tell of it. Then from the slope above our location there came to my ears the faint click of displaced stones. That slope was too steep for any but a wild burro to climb voluntarily. Besides, the sounds were not those made by hard hoofs.

"We'll look for tracks in the morning," I said. "Let nobody disturb the ashes."

When light broke, the soft ashes out from the fire revealed the prints of four feline feet. Each was as big as a saucer; from each the outside toe was missing. Only one animal in all the sierras of Mexico could have made that track. The jaguar hunter said that no *tigre* ever grew feet to such proportions; I was sure that no mere mountain lion ever made such tracks.

We worked up the steep mountain slope on which I had heard the thing displacing rocks the night before. Hardly two hundred yards from camp we found the Airedale's body covered over with leaves and twigs. The fate of the old hound Lead and the significance of the mound I had neglected to examine while I was looking for him were now clear. Both mountain lions and jaguars cover their prey in this manner. If this animal had the same habits, he would in all likelihood return the following night to finish his meal.

Inocencio had brought along two small steel traps, of the size used to catch coyotes. I had no faith in their power to hold the unknown beast even though he should step in one of them. Nevertheless, we set them with great care in a natural runway near the dead dog. At daybreak next morning we were climbing to the traps. Before we got within sight of them, we heard the rattle of chains and the growl of primordial savagery. Then we saw. The animal was caught in both traps.

In general it looked like a mountain lion, but it was far larger than any variety known to American hunters or naturalists. Its breast was enormous, its flanks lithe. It had devoured, excepting for the head and neck, the entire carcass of the Airedale—probably thirty pounds of flesh; but it did not appear to be gorged and was certainly not torpid. It was turning gray with age. It was a female. Even considering its size, its four-toed feet appeared abnormally large.

I was anxious to preserve the skin. After I had shot the animal, we three men had to exert our strength in carrying it down to camp, where the bench of level ground would make the process of skinning comfortable.

The carcass had been deposited beside the trail and I was drinking a cup of coffee when, as noiseless as a drift of smoke, four sandaled Indians trailed into sight. Close behind one another, in single file, they came on until the leader was right at the dead animal.

"*Válgame Dios!* (May God defend me!) It is an *onza!*"

Without even saluting, thus he exclaimed, and not pausing one step, passed on. In turn each of his followers echoed, "An *onza!*"

"And what is an *onza?*" I cried, but the exclaimers were already going around a shoulder of rock that jutted against the narrow path immediately above camp. They were as shy as wild turkeys and evidently averse to any kind of parley.

As they passed out of sight, I turned to the tiger hunter. Surely, I thought, he knows what an *onza* is. *Onza* means *ounce*, but the ounce proper is no more an inhabitant of the western hemisphere than is the Bengal tiger. It was occurring to me that this tiger-scarred man, through fear, through shyness, or for some other reason was withholding something that he knew or believed when an old, old Indian, too slow to keep pace with the others of his party, hobbled up.

He had two dried bloom-stalks of the sotol plant for walking sticks. The blanket over his shoulders was shredded and patched. His sandals were worn out. The skin of his face was as dry and weathered as the hide of a cow that has died on the range and been left to carrion and the elements. A tuft of his long straight hair stuck out of a hole in his squaw-thatched straw hat.

"*Caramba!*" he croaked as he halted, leaning over on his sticks and peering at our trophy. "It is the *onza*. *Válgame Dios!*" He went to poking about the paws of the *onza* with one of his walking sticks.

"*Onza*, yes. That is what the others say," I shouted, for I presumed that the old man was deaf—though he wasn't. "But *por el amor de Dios* tell me what an *onza* is."

"It is," the old man replied, shaking one of his sotol

146

stalks in emphatic gesture, "the very worst animal in the world. Sometimes—sometimes, I say—it is a cross between a bull tiger and a she lion. Look closely down on this old one's gray legs and see if there are not tiger spots."

I did perceive some dim markings, but they were more like freckles than the bold jaguar spots.

"An *onza*," the old Indian went on, "always jumps on a dog or a man or anything else that it wants to kill in such a way that it knocks the air, the very life, out of it at one blow. It has power like a flood of water rushing down a cañon."

"You say," I interposed, at the same time offering a cigarette, "that the *onza* is sometimes a cross between a tiger and a lion. At other times what is it?"

The old one with much deliberation picked up a coal of fire in his gnarled hand to light the cigarette. Then he tasted the smoke.

"Mix your tobacco with this cup of coffee," I urged.

"*Caballero*," he at length replied, "you have done a good deed in killing this animal. I am going to tell you something very strange but absolutely true. Something I know. These eyes have seen what I am about to tell. Listen!

"My village is on the Arroyo de Peñasco. It is two days from here. Seventeen years ago there was a witch in that village. She lived alone a little down the arroyo, out from the other houses. She was not so old as you might think, but she was more hideous than any man can imagine. She was as strong as an ox, and big. She ate like a sow, but we never knew where she got her food. It was said that she could enchant deer like a tiger and make them walk into her trap. Maybe she ran them

147

down. She could run very fast, and she tired no more than a coyote trotting towards a circle of buzzards. Her voice was hoarse like that of a bull. She was a *huera* (a woman of light complexion), and all over her body she was as freckled as the egg of a *golondrina*. Her hands and feet were enormous. Nobody knew how bad a witch she was, but all were afraid of her. Sometimes she would with a fresh *tortilla* or a bit of *panoche* (brown sugar moulded) entice some passing child into her house.

"In the same village there lived a man by the name of Ignacio Villagra. He had a wife and three boys. One of them was ten, one eight, and one six. There were some dead children too, but they do not count. These people lived in a house of two rooms. There was no door between the rooms, but each room had a door facing out to the east. There was a *ramada* running along in front of the house. There were no windows.

"One morning early before he got up Ignacio called to his oldest son, Pedro, to go bring in the burros. He wished to make a trip into the mountains that day to bring in two pack-loads of wood. Pedro did not answer. Ignacio called again. No answer. Then Ignacio went around to the room in which his sons slept. Pedro was gone. Pedro always slept next to the door. It was summer time and the door was open. Ignacio thought that perhaps Pedro had already gone for the burros; so he had no worry.

"But the sun got up high, and still there was no Pedro. Another man of the village who was out looking for his own burros found Ignacio's also and brought them in. No Pedro. Then Ignacio gave the cry. His woman was like one *loca*. Everybody went to hunting for Pedro. There was no sign. We hunted till dark.

Then we built fires around on the crests of the mountains so that Pedro might see if he was lost somewhere. We put up crosses.

"In the morning a man said that maybe the witch knew where Pedro was. Ignacio and I and four others went to see her.

"'Oh, my Pedrito,' she cried, 'my Pedrito! Is he lost? He was my only friend in the whole village. My poor little Pedrito!'

"We knew right away then that she had Pedrito hid out somewhere, in a cave perhaps. We tried to get her to tell where the boy was. She would not tell. We wanted to kill her, but if we killed her she could not tell. So we only tortured her. We did not torture her much, though. It took all six of us to hold her. We punched a hot wire through her nose, at the point of it, and through the flaps of her ears. Still she would not tell. She even called on the Holy Virgin to prove that she did not know.

"That night the second son of Ignacio disappeared. There was more hunting through the cañons and calling into the thickets of brush. All was useless. Who can find out the secrets of a witch?

"The next evening soon after dark those men of the village who were not out making signal fires hid ourselves in the brush around the witch's house. We were sure she would come out in the night time to go to the den where she kept the boys. Maybe we could follow her.

"We waited long hours. The stars gave light. About midnight the door of the cabin opened, and the witch stepped out. She stood there a great while, looking, looking, turning her head this way and that way and stretching out her neck like an old turkey who is listening. The coyotes were hushed. All I could hear was my own heart. Everything was still. Then, just like *that*, the witch disappeared. We did not see her go. She just was not there.

"At once we heard a sound over our heads. It was a sound of horror. It went *sh-sh-sh-shoo-oo-oo*. At first it was sharp, swift. It seemed to circle over us. It went up, then down. Then it died away.

"We came closer to each other and waited. I do not wish to deceive, and I cannot tell how long we waited. Again came that *sh-sh-sh-shoo-oo-oo* cutting and swooping through the air, far away and dim at first, and then right over our heads. All at once the witch stood again in front of her house, looking this way and that way and stretching out her neck. She seemed to have come from nowhere. She did not come out of her cabin. She just appeared.

"Well, the next morning we visited her, the six men who had gone before. Still she would not tell. We wanted to kill her, but if we killed her she could not tell. We tortured her a plenty this time. We sawed off, one by one, the little toe of her right foot, then the little toe of her left foot, then one little finger, then the other. We sawed them off with the fiber of the maguey plant, slow, slow, pulling the fiber back and forth. She screamed. It took force to hold her. I was strong then. She swore she had gone nowhere the night before. It did no good to remind her of what we had seen and heard. She cried out to Christ and his Mother and all the saints that she had no knowledge of Pedrito and the other boy.

"We did not know what to do. We were sure she would come now for the third boy, the last one, who was only six years old. Perhaps we could trap her. We worked all day arranging the door to the boys' room so that instead of swinging open on hinges, it would drop like a trap. We had to make a hole up through the roof of the *ramada* and set a trigger. Ignacio wanted to sleep in the bed alone and catch the witch when she came in; Ignacio's woman cried against letting her baby sleep in the room; but we assured them both that in order to bait the witch the boy must be there alone. No harm could come to it, we said, for, once inside, the witch would be trapped and could not get away. Then she would have to confess and reveal the hiding place of the other boys.

"At dark Ignacio got up on top of the house so as to drop the trapdoor should the witch miss the trigger. I was with him. Other men of the village were behind the stack of straw or in the bushes that grew near the house. Still others were where they could watch the witch's cabin as it had been watched the night before.

"How long we waited, Ignacio and I there on top of the house! We did not talk. We looked over the land. We looked at the sky. It seemed to me that the horned moon was going to hook a certain star. How slow it climbed! Then when one horn was not more than a foot away from the star, something came into the room beneath us. We did not see it come. Nobody saw it. We only heard a kind of swish through the air, *sh-sh-sh-shoo-oo-oo*, very swift, and then noises in the room. Ignacio dropped the door. The devil thing was trapped.

"No man cared to go inside the room in the darkness. Yet Ignacio's woman wanted to go in and get her baby. We would not let her. The witch could not carry the little boy away now. It seemed best to wait until daylight before doing anything. Daylight was not far away. We heard scratches. We heard once a grinding of jaws.

The witch might well be angry. No longer now could she call on God and the Holy Virgin to prove her innocence.

"When the first light of the east came, we got ready to handle the evil creature. We had ropes, butcher-knives, machetes, everything that might be necessary. Yet we had no guns. We are a poor people.

"Two men got in front of the trapdoor and raised it. By the life of my mother and the life of God and the life of Mary Most Pure and Joseph, I speak truth. Then what came out the door was not the form of a woman but the animal you have killed. The *onza!* It came out with a leap that knocked both men down. They were sick for a year afterwards. The *onza* never stopped. She ran like a ray of lightning for the cañon brakes."

I believe that old fellow wanted to knock us down with his tale, as the *onza* had knocked his two friends down. He stopped as if he were through.

"But what about the little boy left in the room?" I asked.

"He was not there when we went in to look for him."

"And what became of the witch?"

"The witch?" he repeated, as if not understanding my lack of comprehension. "Listen! When the horn of that moon was hooked around the star that night as I have told you, the men who were keeping watch over the cabin of the witch saw her come out. She limped a little, they said. She stood there looking, looking, just as she did the night I saw her. Then *sh-sh-sh-shoo-oo-oo.* From that hour to this she has never returned."

There seemed no more to say but, knowing well I should not be understood, I remarked, "You must have felt pretty bad for torturing a human being so much when it turned out that an *onza* was to blame."

152

"*Onza*, yes," the old man growled back. "But what more proof could any Christian ask? Look at those four toes missing, the outside one of each foot, on this creature you have killed here. Look too at the holes in those ear flaps. But I must go on. May God guard you!"

"May you go well," I returned, and the explainer of *onzas* was gone.

The tiger hunter sawed on his gourds up and down the Barranca de las Víboras for a week without receiving a response. Then with Inocencio I turned back for Las Cinco Llagas. I shall never cease to regret that bugs destroyed the hide of the *onza*. I still have one of the claws of the beast.

CHAPTER 7

Crosses

As I rode along on the trail back to Las Cinco Llagas, Inocencio was frequently out of sight behind with the pack mule, but once in a while his knowledge of short cuts or my propensity for turning aside to investigate brought him ahead of me. This could be, of course, only in the less broken country.

About ten o'clock in the morning on the last day of the ride homeward we arrived at a fork in the trail. Here Inocencio said, "We came by the road to the right; let us return by the left hand. It is only a little longer."

"I have always liked to come back by another road from the one I went out," I agreed. "I do not know why. Why do you have such a desire?"

He considered a minute. Then he answered, "The rat with only one runway into its den is soon caught by the badger."

I rode on in the lead. Three hours later, while following a thickly bushed *arroyito*, my *mozo*'s intermittent hiss to the mule not audible, I suddenly heard a low but harsh cry, "*Alto!*"

Looking down into the barrel of a thirty-thirty rifle, I halted as ordered. Behind the sights of the barrel gleamed the eyes of White Moustache. He had been well concealed in a clump of brush; now to one side of it he was half kneeling so as to steady his aim.

"You seem to be *norteao, señor*," he said ironically.

In spite of the situation I laughed, for that word *norteao*, more properly *norteado*, has long seemed to me one of the most delectable coinages of the vaquero language. A man "northed" has lost all sense of direction, does not know north from south, although, if a vaquero, he may not admit that he is absolutely lost.

"No, Feliz," I said, raising my voice, "I am well directioned, as my *mozo* back there will tell you."

"Speak your last words low," the ambusher warned. "The time to pay has come, and I am the collector. Do not budge."

If I could delay the parley a few minutes, I thought, I might talk my threatener out of his notion or escape through the arrival of Inocencio. So, pretending not to comprehend the words about debtor and collector, I said, "Very well, you may take all I have here, and if you will wait a moment you may take the mule and his *carga* also."

"The hour of waiting is past. It is the life of a burro and not the load on a mule that is due. Get ready."

"I comprehend your insult," I answered, "but as a last favor tell me on what account my life is due."

"We will not talk further. To deny that you gave

Lupita *torvache*[1] or perhaps some other poison so timed as to kill her after you were well away will not prevail."

Somehow I had not been surprised before. Now I was. "Lupita? Dead?"

"Yes, and in one more second you will be. The reason I did not shoot at first is that I wanted you to know that Feliz Gutiérrez is the one who brings the justice you contracted for."

I could think of but one play. "Feliz," I said, "I wish to die standing on the ground I belong to, not knocked down to it like a buzzard out of a tree. Grant me that favor."

The eyes and finger relaxed slightly, but not the point of the gun. "Dismount then," he said, "and stand one step to the left of your horse. *Pronto.*"

I considered that the chance I had was not more than one against a hundred. I did not carry a six-shooter, but the scabbard in which my rifle rested lightly was on the left hand of the saddle, the stock pointing rearward.

Now my right leg was coming over the cantle, my right hand at the same time reaching, left hand on the saddle horn, and descending body held close to the horse so as to hide the attempted trick. Whether it would have worked will never be known. I heard the singing of a bullet gone wild. I saw the man in front of me give a spasmodic jerk. His hands flew out and he fell over. His *destino* was a knife between the shoulder blades. It went in deep.

The knife was the one that introduced me to Inocencio in camp the day he cut the bull's throat. I had

[1]*Torvache,* a low-growing vine common in many parts of Mexico. It is credited with being more insidious in its effect on both mind and body than *marihuana.*

not seen him approach White Moustache. Now he pulled "The Faithful Lover" out of its "embrace" and wiped it clean on the pants of the dead man.

"The badger as well as the rat seems to know there is more than one runway to the den," I said.

Ignoring the observation, Inocencio held the knife blade out so that the motto graved on it was under my eyes: *For whomsoever this snake bites there is no remedy in the drug store.*

"There is no hair on its tongue," he boasted.

"His claim was," I said, "that I had poisoned a woman."

"Is Lupita dead?"

"Yes, but why should he think I killed her?"

"The knife alone knows what the guts it bites are thinking."

"Then if he did not think I poisoned her, why should he say so?"

"Ask of the knife. It has looked inside the sack. There is more than one way for a man or a woman to be *enyerbado*."

Here Inocencio was playing on a word, for while *herbed* literally means *poisoned*, it also means *put under a spell*. My own deduction was that suspicion and jealousy and failure to gain his own end had twisted the brain of White Moustache into a knot.

"If Lupita did die of poison," Inocencio went on, "it came from another woman. There is no dove but has her gall. Because of respect I said nothing, but I have known well enough there was another thing in Hidalgo besides parrots."

"How did you know?"

"*Pues*," and here Inocencio looked very wise, "it is

not necessary to catch a man in the prickly pear thicket to know that he has been eating *tunas*."

"These are riddles, not answers, Inocencio."

"Perhaps. Nevertheless, as it is said, like a cough, the love of a man for a woman cannot be hid."

"When you use that word love, Inocencio, you use a word that you do not know the meaning of. Perhaps no Mexican man knows it."

"Excuse me, *patrón*. I am but of the *gente* uninstructed. I never looked inside a dictionary."

"Probably the dictionary would not help," I replied.

"I only know," my commentator went on, "that according to nature this man, that man, says, 'I am bound to pluck this flower no matter how many thorns prick my hand.' And then, the flower plucked, he is like the buck that sheds his horns."

"Yes, but while the buck wears them, how proud, how bounding in life he is!"

"You know best, *patrón*. There is no blame for nature. As our fathers said, 'A pair of pretty *chiches* pulls stronger than a yoke of oxen.'"

Here Inocencio put himself in the attitude of a vaquero who with heels braced into the ground and body stiffened back is being pulled by a rope wrapped around his waist.

"What if the man forces his will against the pull?" I asked.

"Why should he? When the fruit is ripe, unless someone pulls it, it will fall anyhow."

"With proverbs you can prove the devil both white and black."

"Yes, the devil is a chameleon."

"As regards fruit, I was going to say," I went on,

158

"that the owner of a garden has a right to what is in it."

"Yes, but there are wild fruits. Remember the *dicho*. 'All meat is to be eaten, all women sampled.' Come, my friend. Molest your mind no further on this matter. The dead to the grave, the alive to affairs."

"Well, how are we going to dispose of this body?"

"We will leave it here. It is beside the road. Others will bury it and put up a cross."

Thus both an incident and a discussion were ended. The only reference but one the saver of my life ever afterwards made to this day's experience was to suggest in the politest way he could that "flies do not enter a closed mouth." At the time he made this suggestion he pronounced also a judgment upon his victim.

"This Feliz was like the young lion," Inocencio said. "The old lion often told his son that the only being in all creation not to be killed was man. 'Always avoid man.' Then the old lion died. The young one became as successful a hunter as his father had been. He grew proud and vain. He was very brave, and one day when he saw a man passing along the road on a horse, instead of crouching low in the brush, he stepped out in full view. The man was a trapper and that very day he set his traps. The next morning when he visited them, he found the lion caught. He raised his gun to shoot.

"'Do me the favor to shoot me in the head and not in the body,' the lion said to him.

"'Why?' the man asked.

"Answered the lion, 'I have a good body. It is my head that is bad. It brought me to this. It knew too much. Shoot it.'

"Thus he fell."

As, riding on, we turned out from a cañon we had

159

followed for an hour to ascend a mesa that would give view to Las Cinco Llagas, the trail passed by two crosses I had seen several times before but not until now noted with any particular interest. I had been told that they marked the spot where an outlaw once held up and killed a traveler and also where *rurales* after capturing the murderer brought him to be executed. The *rurales* were always fond of poetic justice. There was a cross for the guilty and the innocent alike. Looking upon the two mementos, I began to fancy what sort of cross would be put up in the bushes to mark the spot where Feliz came to his destiny, and from that day to this I have never seen a cross beside a Mexican trail without experiencing the same connotation.

The cross may be made of sticks, festooned with rosettes from yucca plants, and planted at the edge of a dirt tank to allure water—or to ward off a devastating cloudburst. It may be of axe-hewn wood bound with rawhide to a solitary cottonwood tree in the oasis-like shade of which pallbearers bringing a corpse down to the *campo santo* have for generations stopped to rest. It may be of stone high on a hill overlooking fields, the sowers of which go each season up to their "cross of prayer" to pray for rain. Away from the trail, the cross may be placed in the tunnel of a mine and at the importunity of the peon miners blessed by a priest, that the ore yield. Or it may be nothing more than a sign in the air made by a poor woman in front of a mud oven before she lights the fire. No matter where I come upon it, it reminds me of that cross I have never seen.

A book could be made out of the stories told by the crosses of the trail. None has roused my imagination more than one I saw while riding across the Sierra

Madre from Durango to the Gulf of California. It was back in a dilapidated grotto of masonry, and before it were a tin can in which a candle had burned out, a withered handful of wild flowers, and two copper two-cent pieces. The story was that here a good man had been murdered by a drunken devil. That was in the last century; yet an occasional traveler with a good heart and a little money leaves a pittance by the cross to buy candles to burn for the dead. Then once in a while a *pasajero* who expects to return collects the coins, buys candles, and on his way back leaves them, lighting one and depositing the others. They will all be used for the purpose for which they were donated.

At the village of Pahuiriáchic on the road west from Chihuahua over which seekers for the Lost Tayopa Mine have for generations traveled and which I too have traveled, there is fixed against the wall of one of the little adobe houses a cross of tin. It marks the spot where the father of a young man who had been rejected by a daughter of the house killed her, so deeply had his blood been insulted.

Two days farther on is the Cueva del Padre, also well named Cave of the Crosses, for here are hundreds of little crosses, some whittled out of pine, some but twigs fashioned by nature, the crossbar on others held by fiber. The walls of the ledge and the rocks about are black with crosses that have been smoked upon them. No *campesino* will pass the site without adding a cross in memory of a priest here killed for his money. He was a German Jesuit named Herman Glandorf but known to the sierras as Padre Gandor. Time and crosses have not decreased his fame. Once, it is told, he pulled a dagger out of his heart and, uninjured, returned it to the villain who had stabbed him; another time he stepped into the swollen river rushing at the base of his cavern home and the waters parted for him to pass.

Farther west on the old Álamos trail rises bleached above a cairn of rocks a cross with a very different story. Here one twilight some *bandidos* who had captured a traveler worth a ransom but who did not want to be bothered with guarding their prisoner buried him in the ground—a hole having been found convenient—up to his neck, hands tied behind him. They all wanted to attend a *baile* at a mining camp not far distant and could not well take the captive along. So they left him thus secured. When they returned in the morning, the body of the buried man had no head. Lobo wolves had gnawed it off. The *bandidos* heaped stones over the remains, already well buried, and fixed a cross in the pile.

On the trail between Zacatecas and Sombrerete there are many crosses—with many stories. Some of them that do not look very old are but replacements of crosses erected centuries ago. In the vicinity of San Martín de la Noria is one that carries with it a striking warning. It is known as La Cruz del Ingrato.

In the latter part of the 16th century there came to Mexico from Spain a coarse, callous brute of a fellow by the name of Santiago Airón. He came as a servant but managed to get some money and then to go adventuring into the Zacatecas mining district. Compassionate fellow countrymen were gracious to him. One day while he was riding with a young Spaniard named Gallegos they came, at a place where the trail pronged, upon a giant cross made of wood painted black, rising out of a great pile of rocks that had been accumulated by travelers. Upon arriving at this sacred wood, the youthful Gallegos uncovered his head, crossed himself, and went on. But Airón was more pious.

He halted, dismounted, cast a stone upon the mound, and then with uncovered head and outstretched arms, prayed a long prayer that terminated with these words: "O Most Holy Cross, grant unto me a mine and I will erect a chapel and dedicate it with a *fiesta* that is proper."

"Well said, Santiago," the youth commented, "but have a care. Behind the cross the devil lurks, you know."

Airón rode on. He and his guide came to the mining camp of San Martín, where he found refuge in the house of a *gambusino*[1] named Juan de San Pedro. When this *gambusino* saw how Airón was obsessed with the idea of finding a mine but how utterly ignorant he was of minerals and rocks, he went out with him one day into the mountains and, by luck or otherwise, discovered a very rich vein. Airón agreed to denounce it in the names of both men. Actually he denounced it in his own. This was in 1591. The mine, called Los Tajos de Airón, proved to be a veritable bonanza and its owner became one of the wealthiest men of Mexico.

Success made Airón even more greedy and avaricious than nature had formed him. He did not erect the promised chapel and dedicate it with proper *fiesta*. He forgot all about prayers. He went on getting more and more money and holding it more and more tightly. He ceased to be merely Santiago Airón, became Don Santiago de Airón, and, marrying a very rich widow in Mexico City, acquired through her Rancho del Peñasco.

In the fall of 1594, while the folk of the Rancho del

[1]An independent miner who picks for high-grade ore or searches for precious metals in slag heaps. His kind often ruin good mines.

Peñasco were holding the *fiestas de los herraderos*, as the rodeo celebration in connection with branding used to be called, their new master arrived, coming from Sombrerete with the most notable personages of that rich *mineral*. The *fiestas* passed, and Don Santiago de Airón set out, accompanied by numerous gentlemen and servants, over the old trail towards his mines at San Martín, whither as a poor serving man he had first gone only three years before.

He had breakfasted richly and drunk deeply. On his high-mettled steed he sat like a conqueror. Leading the van, he spied the cross of black painted wood before which, a poor nobody then, he had so piously knelt and prayed. "*Adiós*, Little Cross," he sang out slyly as he passed it now, without even uncovering his head.

At this very instant his spirited horse leaped and threw him to the earth, breaking his neck and killing him. There against the foot of the great black cross people erected a small white one. It became known as La Cruz del Ingrato—the Cross of the Ingrate. During years that followed, the trails in the Sombrerete country grew to be lined with crosses marking the death dealt by savage Indians. At length they became so numerous that officials ordered them removed in order that travel might seem less frightful. The great black cross and the small white cross at its base were left standing, however. Doubtless they have decayed and been replaced several times during the centuries, but there they can yet be seen and their story still lives.

Crosses, crosses, crosses—on every notable mountain crest that the old trails of the Sierra Madre climb to and on the scant level places in the passes which the trails after weary torture thread, they mark the spots at which "those entitled to wear spurs"—the *gachupines* —allowed their laden Indian slaves to rest. The little burro of the charcoal burner and the mule in the long caravan carrying supplies to the mine know alike that these places of the cross mean a brief halt for rest. They do not know that centuries ago some *padre* blessed the pass or crest, that then muleteers put up a cross supported by stones, and that travelers since that time have upon coming to it added a stone, a stick, any object, to the mound, with a prayer for a good journey. The driver of a pack animal may pick up a rock near some shrine and carry it in his hand all day in order to deposit it on the mound of some cross in which he has particular faith. When that cross falls, he will make another to replace it.

But the trails of the crosses have taken us far from the road to The Five Wounds. To tarry there longer was now unthinkable. I hoped that in bidding my hosts farewell I should not see Dolores. My plan was to ride northward towards the border and then to veer westward across the vast Bolsón de Mapimí, a blank on maps that had enticed me since childhood. Meantime I meant to dispatch a message to my former prospecting partner asking him to meet me in Chihuahua City. He was, I supposed, somewhere in the Sierra Madre; if so, it would be six weeks or two months before he could receive my word and make the rendezvous. I preferred spending this interim anywhere rather than waiting idly in the city.

Fortunately a letter awaiting me at The Five Wounds afforded an opportunity to excuse my hasty departure. As a matter of course, Inocencio was ready to ride with me.

165

CHAPTER
8

Godmother Death

As NOW, far removed in distance and in an expanse of time irrationally elongated by changed ways of life, I remember Las Cinco Llagas, it seems to me that life there was more like a story-book—a story-book filled with as many "pictures and conversations" as Alice of the Wonderland could ever wish for—than a reality. For realities that are outside the range of ordinary experiences, because of their intensified effect upon the senses, seem to be unreal. Death when it comes to one very near us seems unreal; yet it is the reality of realities. And that it was a story-book does not make Las Cinco Llagas any less a reality. "*Nosotros los Mexicanos somos amantes de cuentos*"—"We Mexicans are lovers of stories," a mining engineer who had seen much of the world once said to me.

Often and often I remember Dolores, of the soft voice

166

and—I must always think—the hard vengeance, and
poor dead Lupita so delicious in life; but oftener out of
the story-book there comes to me, I believe, the old
cigarette woman drying and moistening and moistening and drying her shucks, now in the sunshine and now
in the dark windowless rock room of cavern coolness
kept for her in a corner of the monastery that even before she was born had been made into a stable. Once
when by accident I learned how much she craved a
little sugar, I gave her a twenty-centavo piece. That
was the first time she prayed for me the "Prayer to the
Just Judge," but not the last. Sometimes she omitted
some of the details.

"*Jesucristo crucificado* Son, of the Virgin Mary. The
Father calls to the Son, the Holy Spirit responds.
With the mantle of Nuestra Señora de Guadalupe and
with the tunic of Cristo may you and all your family
be enveloped. May you if imprisoned or made captive
be set free. May nor storm, nor fire, nor heathen enemy,
whether Moor, Jew, or Apache, ever touch you. May
you never thirst in the desert, suffer from drouth, feel
the trembling of the earth, or be struck by lightning.
May your horse never fall down a steep mountain-side.
May you be delivered from dangerous roads and
swollen rivers and from the demon and his satellites.
May you never fall into mortal sin or into evil powers
visible or invisible. May your enemies have no eyes to
see you, nor feet to overtake you, nor hands to lay
hold on you, nor tongue to blaspheme you or bear false
witness against you, and should they attempt to wound
you, may their lances be broken, their sabers shattered,
their knives doubled back, and their guns miss fire.
May you be secure from the harshness of the law, from

poisonous serpents, from the guile of traitors, and from sudden death. Mary and Joseph accompany you at all hours. May you be hidden in the wounds of the Holy Ribs. Jesus, the sweet name. Amen!"

This ancient teller of prayers ten times more ancient was frequently a garrulous soul indulging in that utter freedom of speech and philosophy that only extreme age can attain to. She often accused this person and that person of being envious—and certainly to be *envidioso* in Mexico is to indulge in the deadliest of the Seven Deadly Sins—but there was no person whom she accused of this sin more bitingly and vehemently than Lupita's mother, the *curandera*. In short, the old cigarette woman was more jealous, more envious of her than of anybody else in the world.

"Only fools," she railed one day, "would go to her. What is she to set herself up as having all this knowledge concerning life and death! Only fools who are the sons of fools could imagine that she might overpower La Muerte had she all the herbs and *remedios* from here to where the Cruz de Mayo[1] comes up out of the ground. Doctor Matagente [kills-folk] is what she is! It is a barbarity! Not even the godson of Death could cheat her, and as for this old witch of a *curandera*, this ingrate, this disgraced one . . .!"

The *cigarrera's* voice was rising into a steel band. I looked at the string of dirty red muslin tied around her arm above the wrist to keep off rheumatism. My eye caught a segment of the necklace of buck-eye seed she had worn for perhaps decades as a preservative of teeth. She had perhaps two.

[1]The Southern Cross, which appears, not fully emerged, to northern Mexico in May.

"I did not know that Death ever had a godson," I said.

"Why not?" The beldame's voice sank downward toward the level of memories. "It is a *cuento*—a story—come from the old ones who have passed."

It proved to be not a very long *cuento*, but the palsy-voiced *cigarrera* took, it seemed to me, nearly as long to tell it as it takes for a young man in love with life to learn that he himself is not immortal. It seemed to me that she might be Death herself talking. I remember that after she had done and I had been silent a long time, I said, "This seems impossible."

"*No es imposible*," she answered. "The devil knows a great deal because he is the devil but more because he is old."

The thing she told has mulled in me so long and has become so much a part of my own imagination that I should be dishonest did I claim that what I now put down is exactly what I heard. Nevertheless this story of Godmother Death is a true chapter, a chapter of reality, out of the pages of the long, long story-book—with "pictures and conversations"—that I turned through before I rode away from the Hacienda of The Five Wounds forever.

The single-roomed *jacal* in which Pablo, his wife, and four children ate and slept was under the mountain far out from the city. They did not eat much, often not even *tortillas*, and Pablo ate least of all. Had any man hired Pablo he would have been obliged to feed him for a week in order to produce strength for a day's work. But he neither sought the wage of bread nor was sought by it; and as day by day, in sunshine and in shadow, he crouched with *sombrero* on head and head on knees, the life-sense pulsed on in him.

Now it was the Day of the Dead—that day when all of Mexico toasts Death herself and, familiarly, without fear, because she is seen so often, makes her a comrade. In pulque shops men were drinking out of goblets carved into skulls; in humble homes women were setting out, for those who have "ceased to be," the big-loafed "bread of the dead"; in the market booths vendors were eagerly offering toy hearses, jumping-jack skeletons, and doll corpses that leapt out of coffins at the pull of a string. Into the graveyards throngs were carrying the yellow "flower of the dead," there to spend the day burning candles and drinking wine in honor of the silent host beneath the sod, spreading over tombs picnic lunches from which the children would merrily devour sweets cut in the forms of urns, cross-bones, and death's-heads, while balladists sang and peddled broadsides displaying the skull as both clown and king.

And on this morning of the Festival of the Dead Pablo and his wife Concha found themselves the parents of another child. It was their tenth, but five of them were in the *campo santo*—and did not have to be fed. The father and the mother took counsel as to who should be the new one's godmother. It was a boy. They spoke of this woman and of that woman, but neither could arrive at a decision with himself or herself, much less with the other. Only they were agreed that the *madrina* chosen must be just and merciful and, if God were willing, potent.

Then Pablo said: "This day the whole world is astir to do honor to Death. I will go out upon the road towards the city and find a *madrina*."

"Yes, go," Concha said, "and remember that it is a boy. Choose well for justice and mercy and power to help. Perhaps, too, you may find some crumbs of the *pan para los muertos* that I may eat and give milk."

So Pablo went out. He had not traveled far before he was overtaken by a carriage carrying, as he recognized, the wife of the owner of the hacienda on which by sufferance his hut stood. The woman was beautifully dressed, and this morning she shone with the light of charity. She bade her driver halt the carriage.

"Good morning, *señor*," she said in politeness. "Who are you?"

"*Buenos días, señora*," he answered, his hat off. "I am the father of a new born-child, a male."

"Then you are seeking a *madrina?*"

"Yes," he answered, "I am looking for a godmother."

"I will act as *madrina* for your child."

For a moment Pablo hesitated, while the memories of generations went through his mind. Then, "No," he answered, "you have so much that you will not care for more. You are like God. You give to those who already have much; from those who have nothing you take away. While it is in your power to be just, you idly watch the poor man slave all his life, his family starving and the rich oppressor growing richer. No, I thank you, *señora*, but I cannot choose you for a godmother."

The rich woman drove proudly on and Pablo followed in the dust. A long way down the road by a scummy hole of water in a solitary place of rocks he saw another woman, afoot as he was, dressed in dirty rags as he was dressed. While he paused to drink, she arose from her knees, on which she had bent to lap the water.

"*Buenos días, señora*," he said.

"Good morning, *señor*," she responded. "Ave María Purísima of the Refuge."

It was evident that she was the most humble of the folk who call themselves *humilde*, and when she gave the salutation of the Virgin Mary, Pablo gravely gave back, "In grace conceived without original sin."

"And who are you?" she asked.

"I am the poor father of a new born and am seeking for him a godmother."

"Oh," she said, "I am but a beggar woman, but I have eaten of the bread that brings to Christian souls pity and charity. My soul glorifies the Savior. I will stand as *madrina* for your little boy."

Pablo's heart was touched; yet again he hesitated. "But, no," he slowly answered. "You are merciful and you would do what you could, but as this world goes there is no potency in lowliness and poverty. I seek for my son's future and I cannot choose you. My heart gives thanks. Now go with God."

So the two parted. Then coming into a heavy wood, Pablo encountered a third person. She was all wrapped so that not even her lips could be seen, and she moved evenly as if she were used to going where she willed.

"*Buenos días, señora,*" he said.

"Good morning, *señor*," she responded. "*Soy la Muerte.* I am Death, and you are a poor man looking for a godmother to your son. I will be his godmother."

"Dark One," he answered, "I thought I should encounter you on this Day of the Dead. Yet every day is your day. I know you well and you I accept for my son's godmother. I accept because you alone are impartial and treat all equally, the rich and the poor, the young and the old, the high and the low, the ugly and the beautiful, the valiant and the cowardly, the weak and the strong. You take them all with you. When there is no other to relieve wretchedness, you end it. You grant to toiling slaves release and rest. You dry tears and stop hunger. In your ways of justice and mercy you are the only friend of the poor, and you are most powerful of all powers. You, then, I choose as *madrina* for my child."

"Go in peace," Death said. "In season I will come to perform my duties."

Then Pablo went home and told his wife Concha how he had found a godmother just and merciful and potent, and how in season she would come to help them. Then, if not in happiness, in something like peace Concha slept.

True to her promise, the *madrina* came one day to the little *jacal* to visit her *compadres* and take counsel with them concerning her godchild. In his thin face he had shining eyes. His name was Favián. When the *madrina* looked upon him, she said, "With permission I will take this child into the *campo*. I will keep him and care for him and teach him to be a healer. I will instruct him in the ways of life and death."

So the *madrina* took Favián out into the countryside. Under her care he throve and grew. Very early she began teaching him the secrets of all the herbs of the *campo* so that by the time he was of age he knew every *remedio* the land afforded.

When he was eighteen years old, she said to him, "I have taught you the uses of all the plants of the *campo;* no other *curandero* of the land knows so much. Now I am going to make you a gift. Look! This herb is called *la Yerba de la Vida*—the Herb of Life. Only I know

173

where it grows. All the other herbs you can gather for yourself, but only from me can you procure this. If you are obedient and use it according to my instructions, you will be happy. With it you will be able to cure all kinds of sickness in all kinds of people. It will not fail. Yet you must reserve it for extreme cases and often withhold it for the sake of charity. Also this one thing you must always remember. When you see me at the foot of the bed, do not offer *la Yerba de la Vida,* for when I stand thus, I have come to claim my own. Only your bright eyes and the dimming eyes of the one I have come to take will see me, but to you both I will be plain. Now my care as a *madrina* is ended. Go your way."

It was destiny that a strong and comely young man so sage as Favián should soon be in great repute. He went by day and by night into hovels; he answered calls from big houses far distant. When he could not go, patients were brought to him. Always he used the Herb of Life with discretion. He was not mercenary and he was happy in doing good. To the people he was Favián de los Remedios.

Then one day a runner came saying that the Great Cacique of the land lay a-dying, that none of the court doctors could benefit him, and that Favián was called. The messenger added that the desire of the Great Cacique for life was so intense that he had promised the hand of the princess to whoever should heal him.

Favián went at once. In the outer court of the palace he saw only anxiety and grief. The Great Cacique was a good ruler and just. He was sinking fast. Favián was the last hope.

As he was rushing on through the long corridor leading to the dying king's chamber, he met the princess. He did not have to be told who she was; she did not have to be told who he was. She was beautiful like the sky, like flowers after a rain; her skin was as smooth as the grass under sunshine when seen far away, and the curves of her body blended softness into firmness like the swell of waters drawn by an even tide. He was strong and straight, both kindness and power in his features, the lush vigor of youth in every motion of his body.

"Oh, save him for me," she said, the tones of life-giving and of life-hungering in her voice.

"I will save him for myself," Favián said, and he strode on feeling that he could tread down legions.

It was a case for no common herb. As Favián neared the bed, he drew from his wallet the bottle containing the elixir of the Herb of Life.

"A cup," he said to an attendant.

At that instant his eye fell upon the shrouded figure he knew so well standing at the foot of the bed, invisible to others but in silent eloquence looming before him as vivid as the flaming torch of an Indian running in dark night. Only for an instant did Favián pause.

"The air, the air!" he cried. "The Great Cacique is suffocating! Ventilation! Turn the bed around so that the royal one's head will be at the window!"

As quick as the command, the bed was turned—and La Muerte no longer stood at its foot. Death was cheated. The Herb of Life brought recovery.

That evening Godmother Death appeared to Favián, just for a minute. "You have disobeyed me," she said. "The next time the bed will not turn from me. Remember." Then she was gone.

Immediately the Great Cacique prepared to keep his word, and the palace was gay with preparations for the wedding of the princess to the savior of her father.

Now Favián no longer went like a benediction with his *remedios* into the hovels of suffering. The court in which he moved was for the time free from pain and sickness. The actual realm in which he was burgeoning rapt him beyond all things, all thoughts mundane. He had touched the hand of the princess and grown faint, and once when the softness of her breast brushed his arm he was dissolved into ecstasy. He had scented the aroma of her hair, the perfume of her breath. In what must have been but a dream his own lips on her ripe lips tasted the nectar of life that makes youth burst to pour out life itself; then from sheer lightsomeness he darted up among the stars and raced along the edge of the moon. He was the charioteer of Dawn poised upon a peak overlooking the whole earth and ready to set it aglow. One starlit night the two stole away beside the lake; there she danced alone around him, a being translated out of the flesh, and with dew in his eyes he worshiped her and was afraid to touch her.

In the way of lovers they gave each other special names. Out of his knowledge and experience he made one for her—Flower of Life, for the plant exists for the flower and the flower is the quintessence of the herb. And because, as she said, he had made her radiant and because he was the restorer, she called him simply Life.

He needed no sleep. For him all food was dross. He was more exuberant than the white-winged *zenzontle* that in the dawning darts straight up from the highest twig of the highest tree and then pitches straight down, singing, singing, singing. When he walked, his feet hungered to press against the juices of spring grasses and wild red begonias. He gathered petals of roses to strew for her to step upon, and the lightest print of her foot in the sand was too lovely for the elements ever to obliterate. He owned the whole world, but all the roses and jewels and beautiful things in it were not enough for one small gift to her who was above heaven and earth. With a prodigality as easy as an actor's gesture he would have flung away his own life for her; without a qualm he would have crucified all mankind in order to remain alive to love her. Death might beleaguer the world—a world as unreal and as far away as prenatal existence—but without thinking of the matter at all he was conscious of being immortal.

And so for Favián, no longer of the Remedios, the days approaching the bridal morning were flying by. And then without warning, without reason, the sun stood still, the earth ceased to revolve, the air that all human beings must breathe withdrew. The princess was sick, sick unto death.

Not even a horse ever forgets what he has learned. Favián the lover remembered Favián of the Remedies, remembered Godmother Death and her gift.

As he came into the sick room, the face on the pillow lighted. He knelt and took her hand. It was cold.

"Flower of my Life," he said, his voice low under mist, "I will make you well and you will yet be mine."

"Oh, Life," she faltered, her smile still gallant, "but your hand is warm."

There may have been other people in the room, but neither saw them. Then, the mist over his eyes, Favián arose and drew the bottle containing the elixir of the Herb of Life. It had never failed and there was the

177

promise of the Power of Powers that it would never fail.

At this instant Favián heard a gasp. The imploring eyes of the princess were fixed on him, but one finger of her right hand pointed towards the foot of the bed.

La Muerte stood immobile. Only as if to enjoin silence, and at the same time to enforce a finality against all appeal, whether of man or the combined forces of eternity, she slowly raised her hand with the palm held open in front.

But Favián would not be silent. *"La Yerba de la Vida!"* he cried. "Oh, Flower of Life, drink quick!"

Quicker than his cry he had jerked the stopper from the bottle and was thrusting it forward. Then as if wrenched by some unseen force, it slid from his grasp and dashed to a thousand pieces on the tiled floor. When he looked up, the shrouded figure had vanished, and with her all the flowers that had ever blossomed in the world for Favián.

CHAPTER
9

Under the Sign of Ursa Major

W<small>E HAD</small> traveled so far that The Five Wounds had become in remembrance as a foreign country. During the morning my horse grew tenderfooted from having cast a shoe the day before.

"We will get shoes at La Golondrina," Inocencio assured me while I blamed myself for not having put some extra ones in a saddle pocket. "Don Santiago Blanco," he kept saying, "is a man *de confianza*" (a man in whom to put trust) "and of good heart. He knows me well and from a time long past."

At last we got up on a high ridge, followed the irregular mesa for an hour, and then came to the brow of descent. In the valley far below I saw a scanty broken line of trees with leaves turning yellow and knew they were cottonwoods—the desert's sign of water. Beyond one patch of trees, at the foot of a steep mountain mottled with timber, I saw a curl of smoke going up

179

from a cluster of *jacales* that in the distance appeared no larger than so many dog-kennels.

"La Golondrina!"

"Yes," replied Inocencio from his position in the rear, "there you see the ranch of Pedro de Urdemales."

I knew enough of the reputation of Pedro de Urdemales, legendary hero of picaresque deeds and impossible yarns, to catch at the allusion, but said, "I thought the owner of La Golondrina was Santiago Blanco."

"Yes, yes," responded Inocencio, "and he will care for everything, but perhaps Pedro de Urdemales was his godfather just the same."

Had I pressed the subject, I should no doubt have heard much concerning that character who was living in folk-tales centuries before Cervantes put him into a comedy and who is now as familiarly known in Spanish-American countries as ever he was in Spain. To me he is more tiresome than Paul Bunyan. I had no desire to hear how this Pedro de Urdemales sold a pot that could boil without fire, fooled *arrieros* with a tree growing fruit of silver, inveigled an Arab merchant into buying a mule that excreted golden doubloons, or performed any other trick. It suited me to proceed in silence and savor alone the connotations of La Golondrina.

"But we will hardly see swallows this time of year," I remarked, thinking of the meaning of *golondrina*.

"No, they are all gone by now."

"And where have they gone, Inocencio?"

"*Pues, quién sabe?* Some say to Spain; some say to Jerusalem. Who knows? They will come back at the beginning of Lent."[1]

[1]According to an Associated Press report dated March 19, 1935, which cites records kept at the Mission of San Juan Capistrano in California,

The *golondrina* was a pleasant subject to meditate upon, in a land where the name and bird alike are as popular as *la paloma*—even to the point that peon folk sometimes feed boiled swallows to a child slow to talk and rely on a euphorbia named *golondrina* to cure rattlesnake bite. My memory went drifting back to The Five Wounds, where for hours, day after day, I was absolutely contented with doing nothing but watch the *golondrinas* come and go among their mud nests in the roof and as the evening shadows advanced skim the ground in search of insects. The *gente* say that the bird brings good fortune and happiness to the home where it builds. That it fosters contentment I well know—but the most swallows I have ever seen anywhere were in a vast house that has seen nothing but bitter tragedy among the *hacendados* and their women folk inhabiting it.

To me the loveliest and most wafting-away of all Mexican waltzes is the old one called "La Golondrina," a song as well as a melody—a song of home and homesickness and exiled yearning. Two particular memories of it I shall always bear. Once while I was riding on the little mixed train that runs from Torreón to Tlahualilo, I drew four musicians from the second-class compartment of the single passenger car into the first-class section, where there was more room and air. They played waltzes like "La Paloma," "Zacatecas," and "Noche Serena," and then I told them to play "La Golondrina." As they played it, I looked out at the mountains lining the valley up which we were running and at the cottonwood trees along the arroyo paralleling the route; and truly the

swallows have without deviation arrived there on this day, St. Joseph's Day, for the last 68 years. The swallows are said to depart from San Juan Capistrano on October 23, invariably.

mountains and the trees followed the music in rhythm, and time was not, and it seemed to me that I was not, and all at once I understood perfectly, completely how to the music of Orpheus—the music that half-regained Eurydice from iron Pluto, made Tantalus forget for a moment his unending thirst, and stopped the vulture from tearing at the giant's liver—the very trees and rocks grew sensible.

As for the second memory, when I was a boy living on the ranch of my parents down in the brush country of Texas, we used to go once or twice a year to an all-day picnic and barbecue at which a Mexican band played. It always played "La Golondrina" many times, and always on the night ride home and during the night while I was in bed and the next day when I was out among the cattle on the peaceful hills, and for many days and nights thereafter the strains of "La Golondrina" lingered in my senses. Those strains and the memories of those days when in imagination's ear I heard them are often gone from me a long, long way and for a long, long time, but sometimes yet when in the evening I watch the graceful dip of the swallow or catch a note of the lovely melody suggestive of this grace, they come home to me.

As, late in the day, I drew rein in front of the little ranch called La Golondrina, three or four men stepped forth from their loafing positions under the bear-grass thatched roof of the wide and open *ramada* against the cabin. Without stirring from the shed, they had no doubt sighted us coming down the trail long before.

In the democratic manner of *rancheros*, a shade too far down the ladder of property to be called *hacendados*, Don Santiago greeted my *mozo* as an old friend.

"And so you have been in the home of my *compadre* Don Alberto Guajardo," he exclaimed after we had talked a few minutes. "You must stay with me at least three days—longer if you will. The only shoes I have are for mules. Tomorrow I will despatch a man to Múzquiz to get horseshoes. The next day he will return. Come, my friend, into your house.—Pantaleón, see that Inocencio has help in caring for the beasts.—Felipe, get your machete and go at once to the field and cut grass. —Come, come, *señor*, into your house."

As soon as we were within, my host halted in front of me, stood up straight, and, looking me in the eye, spoke these words: "You are now in your house. My name is Santiago Blanco, at your orders. This is my wife."

And Doña María also placed herself at my orders.

The house so freely and with such formal, yet simple, sincerity offered to me was but a *jacal,* a little better built and somewhat more commodious than the four or five other huts stuck around it without plan and inhabited by dependent *parientes* (kinsmen). I regarded my situation and was pleased at the delay.

After drinking coffee, we went out under the shady *ramada* to sit. I was placed in the only chair that could be classed as furniture. Don Santiago sat on a kind of bench hewn out of a mesquite limb that had grown four prongs now serving as legs, crooked but stable. The animals had been led away. The impudent-looking red-headed man of around thirty whom Don Santiago had previously addressed as Pantaleón and two other *parientes* were standing about. All of them wore *guaraches,* the soles of which, cut from old automobile tires or made of rawhide, were strapped to their feet by rawhide thongs. It was but natural that they should take advantage of the break in the monotony of life afforded by my advent to gaze and listen.

"Pantaleón," said Don Santiago as soon as we were well settled, "you take Gregorio there and Anastacio, get the oxen, hitch them to the cart, and go at once to the mouth of the Cañon Centinela and bring in the carcasses of the seven deer I shot there this morning. I hung them in the motte of oak trees at the place where the trail from La Mariposa turns up the cañon. If the meat is not brought in tonight, the bears will surely eat it."

There was silence for a minute. Then Pantaleón, more impudent in manner than in voice, asked, "How many deer, Cousin Santiago, did you say?"

"Seven, and horns so enormous on——"

"Seven at one blow!"

Pantaleón threw these words into the midst of Don Santiago's sentence as suddenly as the stone from the sling of an angry *pastor* knocks in the rib of an errant goat. At the same time Pantaleón and the two other *parientes* fairly doubled up with laughter while Don Santiago indignantly arose from his mesquite *banco*. It seemed to me that I could not possibly restrain myself —but to catch the humor of that "seven with one blow" hurled at the juncture, ridiculous in itself, where Panteleón hurled it, one must know a little story common to the land.

One time, a long time ago, the King of Spain set out disguised to find the most valiant man in all his kingdom. He went from city to city, from town to town, looking, listening, spying, smelling out everywhere for the *valiente*. One evening after dark, while he was walking down a miserable lane, he heard a commotion inside a house at his elbow and then in ringing tones the words, "*Siete con un golpe!*"

"Seven at one blow," softly echoed the king. "Ah, at last I have found the most valiant man in all Spain." And with great joy in his heart he burst into the house. There a little tailor stood exulting over seven flies he was huddling together.[1]

Looking at the louts who had insulted him, Don Santiago stood for a full minute. "*Sinvergüenzas,*"[2] he spoke deliberately, "will you or will you not bring in the carcasses of the deer? Think how much dried meat seven——"

"*Con un golpe,*" jumped in Pantaleón, and again the *parientes* doubled over with laughter.

I looked at Don Santiago, astounded at the calmness with which he contained himself.

"Well?" he queried.

"No, Cousin Santiago," answered Pantaleón. "We cannot move the cart."

"Not move the cart!" Now Don Santiago showed genuine agitation. "Why not?"

"Because," replied Pantaleón, "while you were gone today, killing the seven deer *con un golpe*, a rattlesnake bit the axle and it swelled up so that the wheel does not wish to turn on it."

Don Santiago stood in his majestic gravity a minute longer. "Then let the bears have your meat," he said with contempt and sat down.

[1] So, by derivation, a braggart is a *matasiete*, a kill-seven.

[2] Like "bloody" in England, the term *sinvergüenza* carries a connotation that a literal translation, *shameless one*, in nowise suggests. Men have been killed for calling others *sinvergüenzas*.

At length Doña María and a barefooted *criada* brought a snow-white cotton cloth to spread over the little table under the *ramada* and offered me a basin— the half of a large gourd—of water and a clean towel embroidered with red roosters.

"It is but humble fare we have to offer," apologized Don Santiago as he and I sat down.

"I like the fare of your country," I replied truthfully, "and I am as hungry as a wolf."

"Then all is well," Don Santiago added, "for to hunger there is no hard bread and nothing lacks salt. Therefore, as the Spanish say, scratch and eat."

My appetite did not need further exercise to whet it, but it happened that at this very moment a dog flea caused me to take advantage of the Spanish license.

The long-lingering twilight—"the hour of the deer," as the hunters in the sierras call it—had surrendered to darkness, and the *criada* had laid three lighted pine torches on a well-smoked rock. Frequently during the meal she lifted one of these *ocotes* to better illumine the table. No doubt this candle wood had been brought down from the mountains on a burro.

Course by course, the women served us: a thin soup made out of goat meat and onions; *sopa de arroz* (fried rice flavored with chile and onion); *huevos rancheros* (eggs fried and sauced with a strong concoction of chile and garlic, which would have been better with tomatoes added); *cabrito en su sangre* (kid cooked in its own blood); *frijoles fritos* (beans boiled and then fried); as dessert a slice of *queso de tuna* (a "cheese," or conserve, of prickly pear apples); and, at the end, *café ranchero* (coffee boiled in milk and water and sweetened in the pot with *piloncillo*, the native brown sugar). All the

186

time we were eating, the *criada* and Doña María, carrying hot, freshly cooked *tortillas* in their bare hands, replenished—ten times faster than we could consume them—the stack between us on the table.

"*Buen provecho!*" Don Santiago gravely said when we had finished.

"And may it benefit you also," I returned with thanks. Certainly I had no disposition to complain at the fare, although I did think my host might have improved it by bringing in at least one of the fourteen deer hams left hanging out for the bears to devour.

Back in the shadows the *parientes* had gathered, silent.

"If the bears are so plentiful in these parts," I said, offering cigarettes, first to Doña María, "I will tomorrow morning go out hunting."

"Yes," responded Don Santiago, "they are so plentiful that they are a barbarity. One in particular I wish you would kill. He has damaged me much."

There was a pause of silence. Then Don Santiago shifted himself to look towards the northwest in the direction I was facing.

"See that bright star," he directed, "under the lead ox of the Big Cart."[1]

I looked at the star indicated.

"That star," Don Santiago went on, "almost has its spurs in the top of a bluff which in the winter time breaks the cold *norte* trying to blow away this ranch. It is called Cerro del Gruñidor."

[1] La Carreta Grande, which our ancestors called Charles's Wain and also The Wagon, and which we call The Great Dipper, the "lead ox" being the extreme star in the handle of the dipper. Sometimes Mexicans call the constellation simply El Carro (The Cart).

"But why," I asked, "is it named the Growler?"

"Because," interposed Inocencio, who had heretofore been among the silent ones, but who considered it his prerogative to answer any general question I asked— "*porque es el nombre que le pusieron* (because it is the name they gave it)."

"No," Pantaleón put in, "it is called Gruñidor because the wind up there makes a growling and a grumbling and a rumbling that would terrify *el demonio* himself. The pass over it is called the Pass of the Bad Overcoat, for not even a sheep-skin coat is sufficient when one comes through it against the wind. The wind up there is fiercer than fierceness itself. One time when I was coming through this Paso del Mal Abrigo with a burro loaded with grass, the wind caught him and blew him over the bluff."

"*Bueno*," Don Santiago went on, a patient tone in his voice, "here under this very *ramada* where we sit a kinsman of mine named Tranquilino Molino used to play the accordion every evening and night and often also during the mornings. [Anyone named Tranquil Mill should be a musician!] The accordion belonged to me, and if Tranquilino were playing it after I went to bed, he would leave it on the table here, where no dew could fall on it.

"Well, one morning he came over to play the accordion, and it was gone. We searched everywhere, but we could not find it. The people here are all honest, and nobody could think what had come to pass."

"How *triste* it was without any music!" Pantaleón commented.

"Then about three nights later," Don Santiago continued, "I heard and all the other people of La Golondrina heard the music of an accordion coming down from Cerro del Gruñidor. I could not think who might be playing it. In the morning we went up the mountain but we could find no tracks of any Christian being, only of bears, deer, and other animals. And other nights the accordion sounded. It was a thing very curious. Then the serenades stopped.

"About that time I went to Múzquiz. I had to sell some goat hides and buy provisions. A *mozo* carried the goat hides on a mule. First, however, I must tell you that I have a goat camp two leagues away behind the Cerro del Gruñidor. Sometimes I do not visit it for a week or ten days. It is called Majada Escondida because it is so well hidden. It is a good *majada*—a *jacalito* for the *pastor* to live in, pens made out of rock, and a well to supply water for the little animals."

"And what beautiful little animals!" Pantaleón exclaimed not without diplomacy. "There are more *pintos*, red-and-white and black-and-white, and more black goats, and more yellow goats, and more brindled goats, and blue goats and brown goats and tan goats and more billy goats with long, long beards than in anybody else's herd. How they can climb! What *cabritos* they are! And fight! *Por Dios*, Cousin Santiago, tell how those black billy goats fought!"

"Oh," Don Santiago hesitated, "that is just a joke, a *cosa compuesta*."

"Tell it, tell it anyhow," Pantaleón urged. "What a barbarity!"

Plainly not unpleased, Don Santiago told "the thing put together."

"Why," he said, "one time I went over to the *majada* and on a knoll this side saw two black billy goats fight-

ing. When I found the *pastor*, I told him to get the two
goats and put them in his herd, where they belonged.
Five days later I went again to the *majada* and, passing
the little hill where I had seen the billies fighting, I
looked and saw them still at it. But all that was left
of them was their two tails just brushing through the
air and going at each other. I rode up closer. The tails
were plainly the tails of my billy goats. Not another
thing was left of the animals. Their heads, their horns,
their legs, their bodies—everything was worn away,
vanished. When I asked the *pastor* why he had not
separated the black billy goats and brought them to the
herd, he declared he could not make them quit fighting.
What fighters!"

"*Bravos* to the tail-end!"

"But I will come back to my *historia*," Don Santiago
announced. "*Bueno*, the first man I saw when I got to
Múzquiz was my *pastor*—my own *pastor*—the *pastor* I
thought to be at Majada Escondida tending the flock.

"'What,' I said to him, 'are you doing here?'

"'I,' he answered, 'came to get from the old herb
woman some bark of the wild cherry to cure a pneumonia that I felt approaching me.'

"'But how long have you been here?'

"'*Patrón*,' he answered, 'I came eight and one-half
days ago.'

"'*Por Dios*,' I said, 'what did you do with the goats?'

"'*Pues*,' he said, 'I left them shut up in the pen so
they could not stray off. I intended to return to them
immediately, but God did not will for me to go back so
soon.'

"There I was. There that *pastor pendejo* was. And
—my goats? They must all be dead of thirst and hunger,

190

I thought. I did not even take time to sell the goat hides or buy provisions. I told Don Mariano of Las Quince Letras[1] to send coffee by the *mozo*. I almost killed my horse getting back to La Golondrina. There I caught a fresh one. Spurring him to the *majada*, I melted his tallow.

"When I ascended the last hill, I looked to see if buzzards or crows were flying around over the pen. I saw none. I had a little hope. As I drew near enough to catch a vista over the top of the walls, I thought I saw a goat standing on the trough. Perhaps, I thought, God has remembered me and I can draw water from the well and pour it in the trough and the goats will drink and then they will eat and grow fat again. The trail went down into a low place and I could no longer see over the wall. I rode now at a walk, for, as you know, it is well to let a horse cool slowly at the end of a hard ride. Riding slowly that way, I could hear. My ears were open for the bleat of a goat. I heard no bleat, but I heard the creak made by a rope pulling up water. *Por Dios*, I thought, who can have come to this tail end of the world to water my goats? There is but one trail into Majada Escondida. I had seen no tracks on it.

"Then I came nearer, so near that I could see plainly inside the corral. The goats were alive and some of them were drinking water out of the trough. And, *por Dios* and all things most pure, the one who was drawing water was a bear!

"I sat frozen on my horse and watched him. The goats seemed well contented. They are such stupid animals! The bear kept on drawing water with his hands.

---

[1] "The Fifteen Letters," a favorite name for shops throughout Mexico, the letters of the three words, in Spanish, numbering *quince* (fifteen).

191

He could manage the rope and bucket as well as you or I. Then, all at once, he smelled me. *Wuh!* he said, dropped the rope, and ran through the gate and tore out into the sierras.

"I made examination. By tracks and other signs all was clear. The bear had been herding the goats out of the pen every morning, bringing them in to water in the late afternoon, and then killing one or two for his supper. What other animal would know to fatten his meat? I went to the *jacalito*, where the *pastor* always sleeps. There I found my accordion. I understood now who had played it up on the mountain. What a wretched bear! *Qué barbaridad!*"

"What a barbarity!" echoed in chorus Inocencio, Pantaleón, and the others.

"Certainly in the morning I will hunt this bear," I said.

"If God wills," Don Santiago added.

"*Si Dios lo quiere,*" echoed Inocencio, Pantaleón, and the others.

Again Don Santiago reverted to the subject of horseshoes. "I am going to send to Múzquiz anyhow," he explained. "My son Hilario is to arrive there on the train, and I am sending a horse for him to ride out."

"Yes," put in Pantaleón, "and you will see that Hilario is a true son of his father. He is a colonel in the army."

"Go, go," Don Santiago commanded.

But Pantaleón had no idea of going except in the direction he had started. "Yes, Hilario is a chip of the same tree. His father says so.

"He has two brothers, Juan and Ruperto. When they were all boys, Cousin Santiago one cloudy day called to Juan and said, 'Son, do you see that doe on top of that *picacho?*' The mountain peak he pointed to was four leagues away.

"'No, *papá*, I can not see it,' Juanito answered.

"'Get away from here then,' Cousin Santiago said. 'You are not of my blood.'

"Next he called Ruperto. 'Son,' he said, 'do you see that doe on top of that *picacho?*'

"'No, *papá*, the peak is too far away for me to see into it.'

"'Get away from me, *sinvergüenza*. You are no son of mine.'

"Then he called Hilario. 'Son,' he said, 'do you see that doe on that *picacho?*'

"'No, *papá*, I can not see it, but I can hear the fawn suckling it.'

"'Ah, Hilario,' Don Santiago cried, 'you are my own son. The true blood is in you.' And he gave him an *abrazo* like a bear."

"What memories these *pelados* have!" exclaimed Don Santiago, and he was laughing as much as anybody.

I hoped I should see Hilario.

Although I was fervently solicited to sleep inside, I had my bedroll spread under the *ramada* upon a cot— a bullhide stretched over a wooden frame. On the ground a little way off old Inocencio spread my saddle blanket for a pallet. Before he had wrapped his *sarape* about him to lie down, he came to me with the *novia* (bride, or sweetheart), as he called my rifle.

"They are all good people here," he whispered, "but it is well always for a *caballero* to have his *novia* by his side when he sleeps. He who is prepared is never conquered. May God bless you until morning."

By the time the first rays of the morning sun were beginning to take the sharp chill out of the high November air, every man of the little *rancheria* was standing against the east wall of his *jacal*, warming at the slowly kindling "stove of the poor," each wrapped in a blanket that draped the ground in front of his feet and enswathed his face up to the hat brim. Why the *peones* of the towns and cities have no fires—except to cook by—is explainable, but, despite the customary protest that a warm house gives colds, coughs, and pneumonia, I marveled now, as I have often marveled, at the absence of some sort of fireplace in big houses and hovels alike situated so close to wood that the inhabitants have only to reach out a hand to get it.

While we were eating breakfast, the men of the *jacales* stood on an open mound near at hand looking into the vast world stretching away from them on all sides. They were near enough that I could note their silence and passive immobility. Too lax in figure for statues, they yet appeared a fixed part of the landscape, as much in place as the low-land patches of "squaw corn" on which they live, as much in place as the sunshine that day after day falls upon the mountains and valleys, lulling them into eternal placidity. They seemed to be gazing for something not known, waiting for something never to be. Thus watching, their ancestors stood. The ancestors had a purpose; custom requires none. And so, following the custom of "those who have passed before," the descendants will stand until something yet undreamed of comes out of the immensity and silence to break their vigil.

Don Santiago had already offered me a horse for the hunt, and I knew that during our absence mine would be well cared for. As Inocencio saddled and packed, Pantaleón approached me with a most tristful visage.

"*Patrón*," he said, "you see in what poverty we live here. Cousin Santiago is liberal enough with such as your honor, but imagine to yourself how he rewards us for our services! Like the almanac, he promises much, and then nothing but a wind results. This morning he is despatching the man to Múzquiz. I have a wife so sick that she is dying. It shames me to ask you, but would you as an act of charity give me about *doce reales* with which to send for medicines?"

I gave the "twelve bits" (one and one-half pesos) without hesitation.

"May God pay you," Pantaleón returned, crossing himself.

"I think," said Inocencio a good while after we had left, "that this Pantaleón is one who goes to see the *nopal* [prickly pear] only when it bears *tunas*."

At a gap near the mouth of Centinela Cañon, up which we proposed to camp, we encountered a vivacious old fellow who was a veritable Mexican edition of the Arkansas Traveler.

"Are there any bear in this country?" Inocencio asked him.

"I hope none will eat me," he replied.

"How about water at the spring?"

"It is wet."

"Grass?"

"What cattle have not eaten is still to be mowed."

"Which way are you going?"

"If I don't get lost, I may arrive at the Encantado."

And without a *con permiso* or any other expression of

politeness, the old fellow spurred his rocinante off towards the ranch called Enchanted.

"That *señor*," said Inocencio, "seems to be Don Cacahuate."

Now "Mr. Peanut," as the name translates, is the jokesmith of Mexico. He it was who bought a fine new bridle and a fine new saddle in Laredo and came across the international bridge with the saddle on his back and the bridle in his mouth, "for whatever one wears," as he told the customs officers, "passes duty free." While we shifted the pack on Durazno, I drew Inocencio into telling me something else about Don Cacahuate.

One time he was arrested and put in prison. As always, he had no money, not one *centavo*. In the morning his wife came to see him.

"Bring me some breakfast," he said to her.

"What?"

"Why coffee, of course."

"With what?"

"With milk."

"But I mean with what shall I pay for it?"

"Why, with money."

"Yes, but from where?"

"Why, from the shop where coffee is sold, of course."

Don Cacahuate was such a rascal as a boy that his parents turned him over to some friars to raise. He proved to be so incorrigible that one of them planned to shove him off the bell tower and kill him, but when the friar got up into the tower with young Cacahuate the latter shoved him out. Then another friar put a fighting bull in the cowpen by night and before daylight next morning ordered Cacahuate to go milk. When the young picaroon entered the pen, the bull charged him up a tree. Coming out at daylight to see how satisfactorily the bull had performed his mission, the friar saw the boy in the tree and heard him crying.

"What are you crying for?" he asked.

"I am crying because I dreamed that my father was dying of childbirth."

"That is absurd," said the friar. "Don't you know a man can't have a child?"

"No, a man can have a child as well as a bull can give milk," Don Cacahuate answered.

But I will tell no more Peanut jokes.

I hunted all day without seeing a single fresh bear sign, and the only white-tailed deer that I got a shot at I missed. Inocencio had whetted his appetite for venison, and several times during the evening he referred to the escaped deer.

"Don Federico," he said after we had finished our *gordas* and dried beef roasted on the coals and he had replenished the fire, "I want to tell you something. It is a story about a hunter of deer."

He was squatted, turning alternately the palm and then the back of his right hand to the fire in a manner peculiar to himself, at the same time scrutinizing the hand as if he expected to find in its wrinkles and weather-cleansed encasement of mundane material something mysterious or strangely foreign.

"You know well," I replied, "how I like stories, above all at night like this, told in the open air by the light of a fire."

"One time," Inocencio began without comment, "a hunter who had never been able to kill a deer, although he had hunted often in a good deer country, came upon a big buck asleep. This buck was standing under an open

197

tree and the hunter was so close to him that he could see his side move under the quiet breathing. As the hunter looked at the big buck there so near and so still, he was very happy. At last he was sure of game. And as he drew up his gun, very slowly, to fire, his head filled with plans.

"'I'll take all that meat home to my family,' he said to himself, 'and I'll cure the hide and make moccasins out of it. I'll wear one pair of the *teguas*, and I'll trade two other pairs off for a calf. The calf will grow to be a cow and she will have other calves. While we are having plenty of cheese, one of these calves will grow to be a fine, strong ox. I'll trade him off for a mare. The mare will have a colt, and I'll trade him off for a jack. Then the jack and the mare will bring mules. I'll just raise mules—mules—mules. There'll be one mule at first, then two mules, then three mules, then four, then five, then six, seven, eight.'

"The string of mules filed by in front of the hunter's eyes so that he could not see the big buck asleep. He saw them all loaded with *cargas* and he saw himself as the *conductor* of a whole *recua* of pack mules, *arrieros* helping him. He saw the mules stringing out along the trail to Chihuahua. He could keep himself silent no longer. At the top of his voice he yelled out, 'Hi-lo!'[1]

"The big buck awoke with a jump and was out of shot in the brush before the hunter could aim. As it is said, the Indian, the bird, and the deer are gone when they are gone. He who with his arms engirdles much can squeeze little.

At the conclusion of this apologue there was silence

---

[1] The cry used by *arrieros* driving mules or burros, and also by vaqueros driving cattle. It means, "String out!"

between us for a minute. Then Inocencio seemed to consider that he had perhaps exceeded his license.

"But, no," he amended his lesson, "*la suerte es la buena* (luck destines whatever is good). Besides, the deer has a sensitiveness that makes him more wary than any other animal. He has ears between his toes and on the sides of his legs. The hairs in the ears of his head are stirred by the breathing of a man a rifle-shot away."

I don't know whether it was because of the apologue or because of *suerte*, but the next afternoon our pack mule carried venison to contribute to the kitchen of La Golondrina.

As, near sundown, I rode into the corral, Pantaleón lurched up to my stirrup "as drunk as Judas." I divined at once that the money I had given him was somehow connected with the *mezcal* he had so patently been drinking, and, remembering his sick family, I rated him in downright language.

He drew himself up proudly, removed his coarse straw *sombrero*, and solemnly announced: "*Patrón*, to you he lacks not nor will he lack respect, but so long as there is a distillery Pantaleón Maldonado y Orantes will drink *mezcal*."

Leaving Pantaleón Maldonado y Orantes thus resolved, I turned to meet Don Santiago, whom I saw coming hurriedly from the house. He was all but "destroyed," as the Irish say. He had been disgraced by having his "honored guest" "touched" for money under his very roof. How he had found out about the paltry *reales* I did not learn. It was true, he went on, that Pantaleón was a kinsman, on his wife's side, a family decent enough. But for all that he was nothing

but a *sinvergüenza*, a goat not worth his ears full of
water, a *pordiosero* no better than the *léperos*[1] of the city.
He was the living example of the proverbial genealogy:
"Grandfather *arriero*, father *caballero*, and son *pordiosero*." He was a veritable "blacksmith's dog"—a dog
that lies asleep all day without hearing one beat of his
master's stroke on the anvil, but that at the slightest
tinkle of the butcher knife in the kitchen is alert and
trotting towards it. Absolutely no good could come of
this fellow. Evil spirits attended him. In short, Don
Santiago's wrath mounting up and up, he declared that
he would rather have one of his mare mules foal than
have the shameless one about him.

[1]*Pordiosero*, literally a "for-God's-saker," is a name coined from the
whining cry, "por Dios" (in God's name), with which beggars prefix
their plea. *Lépero* also means beggar, but connotes rascality and the
rabble.

CHAPTER
10

Juan Oso

BUT philosophies, humiliations, and explanations were soon forgotten in the company I found gathered under the *ramada*. First there was Hilario, the colonel. As a respectful son he spoke little before his father; he did not even smoke in his presence. Don Santiago was exuberant with pride, which a few swallows of cognac from a *morral* of bottles brought by Hilario as a present had not diminished. Next there was a goat and fat-cow buyer from Saltillo, presented as Don Julián García. More conspicuous, but lower down in caste, was a gigantic vaquero from the Piedra Blanca ranch to the north. His name was Ismael, and truly, as the angel of the Lord predicted of his name-giver, Ismael was "a wild man dwelling in the wilderness." Before the night was over he took the floor.

Supper was very late coming, and the longer it was put off the more generous Don Santiago grew in paternal pride.

"Now just look at my son Hilario," he finally burst out. "A colonel, and so young! He is going to make a general. He has always been *extraordinario*. While his mother was big and we did not know what day he might be thrown into the world, a rider appeared yelling, 'There the revolutionists come down the cañon.' We had to get out—at once. No time to hunt horses. We mounted what was at hand. The only beast for my wife to ride was a blue mare heavy with foal. She was not Traga-Leguas,[1] but I ordered a man to follow at her heels so that he could help my wife beat her.

"*Bueno*, we went on down the cañon, and I at every bend in the trail calling for my family to spur, to use the quirt, to hurry. At the Puerto de Santa Ana the mare stopped, and right there she dropped her colt. But still my wife had to ride her. 'Come on!' I said. 'I can hear the horses of the revolutionists hoofing the rocks behind us. There is no time to wait for additions.' And so we left the colt and rode on.

"*Bueno*, when we got to the crossing on the Río Sabinas below Las Rucias, my wife said she had to stop and have her baby. There was no *remedio*. We stopped. 'The Comanche that groans will not get to camp,' I warned. She brought forth quick. I cut the cord with a machete that one of my men happened to have, but because I was always keeping my eyes in the direction from which we were flying I cut it off six fingers from the navel. There was no time to be a certified surgeon. There was no time to do anything with the new boy but leave him. Just as he was giving his first squall, I saw dust raised by the *revolucionario* horses. 'Come,

[1] "Swallows-Leagues," the name of a horse in a Spanish folk-tale, "La Rosa Blanca," commonly known to Mexicans.

come!' I yelled. 'The recruits have picked the wrong time to join us.' My wife got back up on the blue mare and again we were following our direction.

"Thus I brought my family to safety, but it was after dark when we rode into Múzquiz. I was grateful to God that the barracks there had plenty of legitimate soldiers to defend us. We went to a house.

"*Bueno,* about daylight I heard the blue mare nickering. I looked out and there she was nosing her colt. In the natural way it had smelled her trail and followed, but its legs were wobbly and it could not follow fast. On this colt's back was the boy we were compelled to leave at the Río Sabinas. He had seen the colt coming by on its way to its dam and in the natural way crawled on so as to get to his dam also. It was beautiful to see with what gusto they both sucked.

"And that boy was Hilario, my own truc son. *El colonel!* Look at him! If you wish proof of what I have told examine his navel. It is the most ample in all the army of the Republic of Mexico."

This detail, however, I had no opportunity to verify. As naturally as Hilario mounted the colt, there followed allusions to my bear hunt, along with questions concerning experiences—or lack of experiences—with that animal.

"Yes," commented Don Santiago, "the bear is a very curious animal, very smart."

Now that a fresh audience was provided, I prepared myself to listen again to the story of the bear and the accordion.

"My father," continued Don Santiago, "was a famous hunter of bears. He lived in the Sierra Madre in Chihuahua and hunted both in that state and in Durango. He hunted not only bears but also deer and ducks and other game. If he did not have cartridges for his gun, he hunted anyhow. One time he went to hunt ducks in a big lake. The ducks on it were as thick as thorns on the *tasajillo* cactus. At the edge of the water he placed over his head a gourd with holes cut in it for the eyes to look through and his mouth to breath through.[1] Wrapped around his waist was a long rawhide reata plaited thin but strong with a big *arriero's* needle[2] fastened to one end. Keeping only his gourd-covered head above water and dragging the reata between his legs, he got out among the ducks. They had no fear of the gourd.

"So he began grabbing them by the feet, jerking them softly under the water, and with the big needle stringing them on the reata. After he had strung a duck he paid no more attention to it but let it drag behind him. He was so busy catching ducks that he did not look back. He caught two hundred or maybe three hundred, he said. Then all of a sudden—figure his surprise!—he felt himself being lifted into the air. He looked and saw that his string of ducks had taken fright at a man approaching on horseback and that they were flying away. They carried him across a prairie to another lake. There he cut the reata and freed himself."

Nobody said anything to this story because Don Santiago did not give anyone time to say anything.

[1]It is a fact that at various places in Mexico the natives disguised under gourds slip into the water among ducks, catch them, kill them under water so that they can make no noise, and put them in sacks that, tied to the waist, drag along.

[2]So called because the *arriero*, muleteer, habitually carries, usually in his hat but often in his hand to use as a goad, such a needle to sew up sacks, jab burros, etc.

"Another time," he went on, "my father was going alone into the sierras to hunt bear. When night came he made a little camp down in a *bajada* and turned his mule loose. This mule was a true mule of the *campo*. She could be turned loose anywhere and she would never go far away. She was little but very strong. Her name was Tabaco, because one time she pitched a sack of Lobo Negro tobacco out of the pocket of her rider. Ah, what a mule she was! Well, my father turned her loose, ate some little *gordas* that he warmed on a little fire, and went to sleep. He had yet a long way to ride, and so, very early, before the Guía had led el Lucero[1] into the sky, he got up.

"He took his reata in hand and stood listening in order to locate the mule. He heard a little sound in the grass and brush and went towards it. When he was near, he bent over to the ground to skylight the animal. He saw a black shape and whirled the reata to lasso it. Then he started to lead the beast towards his saddle, but it would not follow. He wondered what was the matter, for this mule had been trained to lead. He walked towards her to place the rope over her ear; the creature snorted and tried to pull away. One can never tell what a mule will do. Finally he got up to the animal's head. Then he found that he had roped a bear. Because he had left both his machete and his gun at the camp and because the bear was becoming very restless, he had to let it go."

"*Caramba!*" exclaimed Ismael, "but one time——"
Ismael got no further.

---

[1]Preceding the Morning Star, Lucero, called also Estrella del Pastor (Shepherd's Star), is a dimmer star, always fixed with relation to Lucero, that is called la Guía—the Guide.

"So even a good hunter, like our friend here," continued Don Santiago with a complimentary gesture towards me, "may not always get a bear. Another time my father was chasing a bear and shot it while it was running. He saw it stop, seize some grass, and stuff it into the hole made by the bullet. He was taking careful aim to shoot it again when all of a sudden the bear picked up a rock and hurled it. It missed my father, but it hit the horn of his saddle with such force that the rawhide covering was torn off. The bear picked up another rock and my father wisely retreated.

"Don Santiago," I said, "your story brings to mind an account I not long ago heard of a vaquero who roped a very violent bear. This bear seized the rope, quickly drew horse and rider up to him, pulled the man off, mounted, and then rode away with the man dangling over his saddle like a meat goat."

"Do you recall the name of the vaquero?" gravely asked Don Santiago.

"Why," I replied, "he was named Pablo Romero."

"I knew him well," Don Santiago declared. "The encounter was at a pass called Salsipuedes in the Burro Mountains. This vaquero was noted for a very wide and long and red sash that he always wore. One night he very foolishly lay down to sleep near some coals on which he had boiled coffee. A wild bull, attracted by the smell of the smoke, rushed upon him, hooked him between the sash and his body, and went off with him. Thus the bull carried him for eight days. Whenever the bull drank, Pablo Romero lapped water with his hand; when the bull grazed, Pablo Romero reached out and gathered *tunas* to eat, for this happening was in the *tuna* season. This Pablo, however, knew little about bears.

206

"As I was going to tell, the way my father usually hunted was according to the *modo* of the Tarahumare Indians. He carried two knives: one, a dagger, in his belt, and the other, a machete, in his hand. If there were no big trees where he found the bear, he would swiftly wrap his *sarape* about his right arm and wrist and then, as the ferocious one came at him with open mouth, stab down his throat. If the bear slapped the arm extending the dagger, it could not claw through the wrapping. If there were trees, my father would get behind one. Standing up, the bear would try to reach around the trunk after him. Then with the machete my father would chop off the bear's hands.

"He could give a *grito*—more powerful than the yell made by Hidalgo on the night before the Sixteenth of September,[1] more wild than that of the Comanches or of the Tejanos who used to cross our border. This *grito* would make any bear, whatsoever his nature, angry and cause him to come towards my father rather than run away. I know not how, but he had power to draw bears towards him just as a panther stretched out in the grass can by switching its tail draw a filly within leaping distance, or just as a coyote sitting on the ground and looking up at chickens roosting in a tree can attract one to the point of his nose. It was a thing very curious."

"As curious," Inocencio agreed, "as the light which you remember caused the horse of Benito Vela to throw him and then jumped into the saddle itself. That light

---

[1]Mexico's Fourth of July. Hidalgo raised the *grito* a little before midnight of September 15, 1810. Annually, on the anniversary of Hidalgo's shout for liberty, *vivas* for Mexico ring up from plazas all over the republic.

was a thing that could not be put out either by bullets or the holy cross. *Caramba!*"

"Yes," agreed Don Santiago, "I recall how the light rode the horse to death. But that is flour out of another sack."

Here Ismael managed to get in a word.

"I have never hunted bears with a machete," he said. "I used to have a dog that would smell out a bear and keep him in a tree, barking, barking, barking, until I arrived. He was named Tres Orejas, because one time a bear split his right ear in two from base to tip and then he had three ear-flaps. One morning I was going up into the Piedra Blanca mountain to help kill some wild cows that could neither be driven nor led down. We were drying the meat and bringing it down on mules to sell. Tres Orejas went along with us.

"Just as we got up on the mesa I heard him bark. I started after him, but a minute later we struck five wild cows and a *toro orejano*.[1] There was nothing to do but go after the cattle. We killed them as well as some others, and that afternoon I could not find Tres Orejas. He did not come to camp. When we got back to the Piedra Blanca ranch four days later, Tres Orejas was not there. *Bueno*, about six months after this I was again on top of the mountain, and right in a cañon that cuts through it I found Tres Orejas. He was sitting on his hind legs with his tongue sticking out and his nose pointing into a pine tree. I looked up in the tree and there was a bear. The bear and the dog were both dead. They were just dried-up skeletons! No buzzard, no crow, nothing had bothered their skins, and they were both as natural as life."

[1] A bull "eared," unmarked; a maverick.

Utterly ignoring the interruption, Don Santiago resumed his narration: "At La——," but the fat-cow buyer was ahead of him. He had a most unvarying tone of voice and was altogether *muy serio*.

"There are," he announced, "many instances of the dog's faithfulness." At this point a cur happened to be smelling about his feet in quest of a crumb, and the fat-cow buyer gave it a severe kick. "A very noble animal indeed, and——"

"Also he is sometimes very greedy, as you, Don Santiago, have no doubt observed," Inocencio interposed, at the same time glancing towards Ismael and the fat-cow buyer. "One time a dog with a bone in its mouth was walking a pine log that made a bridge across a river. When he was halfway over, he met another dog carrying also a bone in his mouth. He jumped on this other dog and as a result he not only lost his own bone but was knocked over into the swift current below and drowned."

It would never have occurred to Inocencio that his interruption might afford a target for his own fable.

"You, Don Santiago," he concluded, "were on the trail of a bear until the dogs went to barking."

"They were not my dogs," Don Santiago answered.

"No," and again Inocencio freed his mind. "Whoever wears the *guarache* knows where it galls."

"As I was saying," the narrator got going again, "at La Quiparita there was a very famous bear. He had a white star in his breast and was therefore called Lucero. The trail from Chihuahua to Sonora crosses La Quiparita, and here this bear used to catch people and eat them."

"Certainly he would not kill a woman and eat her," Ismael remarked.

"*Pues*, the meat of a heifer is more tender, more savory than that of a bull," the cow buyer from the city spoke authoritatively.

"How is that?" Inocencio contradicted, "when everybody knows that the older the rooster the more savory the soup."

The cow buyer must have known that when the *gente* go to the sign of the red flag, which means that meat is for sale at the place flying it, they prefer bull meat to veal. Nevertheless, he persisted with his argument.

"And if a nice Christian heifer came along with just enough fat on her to make her bones round and soft and not so much as to shake loosely on her *nalgitas*, why should not the bear eat her?"

"Don't make me think of such a thing," Ismael almost exploded. "The bear always has another purpose for Christian heifers."

"Yes, the purpose of a vaquero from Piedra Blanca," Inocencio settled the matter, probably not intending his remark to be the undiluted compliment that Ismael accepted.

Don Santiago went on: "No bullet ever seemed to hurt this bear—not even a bullet with a cross cut on it. Then after Lucero had molested travelers for many years, my father went out to kill him with the machete. He found the bear without trouble, and jumped behind a pine tree. The bear came on. But this Lucero bear was so quick that his arm dodged the machete stroke. Then he slapped my father down and bit him cruelly. At the slap my father lost his machete. He knew nothing else to do now but appear dead, like a coyote that has been caught. Only God knows why, but after the bear considered my father dead, instead of making a meal as was his custom, he started off. My father raised himself up ever so little; the bear saw him, wheeled, and came back to cuff him some more. There was no great distance between the life left in my father and death, but for five hours he played dead. Every once in a while the bear would smell at his mouth and nose. At last he left."

"*Pues*, Don Santiago," roared out Ismael, the vaquero, "you have not told the most wonderful thing of all about the bear."

"What is that?"

"It is his way of stealing young women and keeping them."

"I am not telling lies," answered Don Santiago.

Ismael was on his feet, laughing, the pine torches laid on the rock lighting up his tousled black mane, his black burly lips, and his thick, gnarled frame. He had the floor, and for more than an hour he stood, sat, leaped, crept, whirled, poised motionless, now casting his giant *sombrero* to the ground, now hanging it on the back of his head, now with legs spread wide apart running his hands through his matted thatch of horse-tail hair, his voice as coarse and stout and sensual as the features of his pock-marked face. After the tale that he thus poured out is forgotten, I shall remember him as the most brutally fierce talker I have ever listened to. He began with one of the ancient rhymes that story-tellers in his land so often start with.

> "*The drunkard drinks wine*
> *And the boy eats bread.*
> *If this tale's a lie,*
> *It's not out of my head.*"

211

And this is the tale that he told:

One time a young woman named Consuelo belonging to a family who lived alone in the sierras went to the spring to get an *olla* of water. After she had filled the *olla* and was raising it, she felt her waist embraced. She tried to break away but was powerless. She was strong. She had strong, clean legs and hips. She had strong arms and neck. Her back was straight, her chest ample. She looked to see what strength held her. It was a bear.

He took her to his cave. They were more than two days reaching it, the bear sometimes carrying her in his arms, sometimes on his back, sometimes letting her walk by his side. When he could, he traveled in water, so as to hide his tracks. But even if people had followed him and caught up with him, they could have killed this bear only with a blade of Toledo or Oaxaca. Such a bear is bewitched, *encantado;* bullets cannot harm him. Only the best steel can reach his vitals.

The cave was away up in a cañon, distant from any trail but the trail of deer, and down in the cañon under it trickled the waters from a *chupadera,* or seep-spring, in a place too rough for any cow or horse or man ever to visit it. About the *chupadera* and down the moist cañon bed grew wild cherries, *tejocotes, capulines,* and other fruit-bearing trees. It was late summer, when berries are ripe, but in the morning Consuelo needed more than berries to satisfy her hunger. The bear watched her pick for a while; then he took her back into the cave, rolled up into the entrance a great boulder that for all her strength and desperation she could not budge, and went away. When he came back hours later, he brought a freshly killed fawn. She understood that it

was for her to eat. As her people were little better than
barbarians, she knew how to eat the liver raw. She pulled
off the skin and hung pieces of the meat to dry and be
cooked by the sun.

Thus the bear and the young woman lived together.
Sometimes the bear would shut her up in the cave and
go a long distance off and bring back ears of corn from
the fields down under the mountains. In time he allowed her to go with him to gather food. He well knew
where the scarlet rich berries of the *madroño* grew; he
took her to the best patches of black *brazil* berries and
the orange-red *granjeno* berries. He delivered to her
pieces of dripping honeycomb clawed from crevices in
the rocks. The bear is more like a man than any other
animal. He can walk upright; he has hands to use; he
eats the same food that *cristianos* eat; his brain is quick
to understand. No, it is not impossible that a bear and
a *cristiana* could live together.

Consuelo became used to the bear. Whenever he went
away from her, he always left her in the cave with the
boulder to guard it. She made bags of deerskin and
brought in fruits to dry; she dried meat to keep. She
ground up corn on rocks, and, though for a long time
she had no fire to make *tortillas*, the dry powdered corn
mixed with powdered meat and dried berries made a
food that kept her strong and well.

The late winter months and the spring months were
the hardest for Consuelo, and for the bear too, for then
the earth yields little food, except game and a few
roots and the early flowers of the yuccas. Sometimes
the bear was sluggish for days at a time, but in this
country the animal does not sleep all winter as it does
in the north. Bears do not understand fire, but when

Consuelo, after she had been a prisoner for many months, started a flame by friction of sotol stalks, her master forced her to make the fire inside the cave. Perhaps he understood the signal that smoke makes. She cooked the blooms of dagger and *palma* by placing them with water in a bag of deerskin and putting hot rocks in the water to make it boil. With a knife made of flint and the help of the strong arms and claws of the bear, she cut the meaty parts of sotol and maguey and brought them in to roast.

Before a year passed Consuelo began to suffer pains. She had the bear take her down into a flat, and there she gathered the potato-like roots of the broad-leafed *mula* weed, which looks so much like a beet. She boiled these roots in the water heated with rocks and drank the tea. One evening she drank a great deal of the *te de mula;* the next morning a child was suckling her breasts.

From his waist down this child was bear and from his waist up he was man. The old bear brought in more food than ever. The boy grew and the hair came out thick on his legs and hips. He had a good head and from his mother learned early to talk. He was very astute, very cunning, very much alive in the brain. While he was yet a toddling, his mother taught him to shoot with a bow and arrow. No longer now did the bear keep her a prisoner in the cave.

The years unrolled. When the boy was six, he was bigger than most boys are at sixteen. One day while the old bear was gone far away on a hunting trip, the boy asked his mother where her home used to be before she came to live with the bear. She told him.

"Let's go see people," he said.

"Oh, I am afraid to leave," she answered.

"Do not be afraid," he said. "If the bear tries to stop us, I will kill him. Besides, if we leave while he is gone, he can never find us."

Consuelo was ashamed to go among people; yet she was eager. At last she consented. Before setting out, she took some skins and put them on her son and fastened them with thorns and sewed them with deer tendons so that he was dressed. She was particular to cover him well from the waist down. Her own dress was of skins, and both of them wore *guaraches* made of hide.

They had to travel a long time before they came to people. Some did not believe the story Consuelo told of her life with the bear, but when they saw the boy they had to believe it. Yet when he was clothed like a Christian and had shoes on his feet, nobody could see the hair on his legs or note his other features of a bear. Then his mother took him to the *cura* and had him christened. The priest named him Juan Oso—John Bear.

The *cura* was a very rich man, and when he perceived how astute and alive in the brain Juan Oso was, he took a great interest in him. He put him in a school to learn to read and write. Juan Oso learned as fast as a mare can trail her colt by smelling its tracks on the ground. But his mates found out about his hairy legs, and one day one of them, a big bully, jerked his pants down so as to expose him. Juan Oso was as strong as an ox. With one blow he knocked his tormentor dead. There was no more school for Juan Oso.

Some more years passed and now Juan Oso was bigger than any other man in the world. He stayed about the ranches, but sometimes he would go alone into the sierras and be away for weeks and months. He was very restless. One day he went to the *cura*, who was also his godfather, and said to him: "*Padre*, I wish to travel."

"Very well," replied the *curita*. "Tell me what you need for your travels and I will provide everything."

"I need but two things," Juan Oso answered. "A walking-cane and a pair of burros loaded with money."

"I can have a *mozo* load the money on the burros at once," said the *cura*, for he was very, very rich, "but it will take some time for me to have a fine cane inlaid with woods and bone and ornamented with a head of gold. For that is the kind of cane you shall go provided with."

"No, no," cried Juan Oso. "I do not want any fancy inlaid work and I do not want a cane with a gold head. All I want is a cane made out of pure iron, and I want it to weigh two tons."

"Very well," said the rich *curita*, and he gave orders to the blacksmiths to make the walking-cane of iron and to make it exactly two tons in weight. It was finished and given to Juan Oso. Swinging it gayly, he set out, followed by two burros with sound backs tightly loaded with gold and silver.

At first Juan Oso visited the cities, and there he made the coins flow like a river. His fine *charro* suit and his *sombrero* were embroidered with silver. He had a saddle inlaid with silver. He bought out saloons so that he could treat his friends, and gay girls swarmed around him as thick as horseflies on a sand flat in summer time. Within a year all the money was gone, and Juan Oso had nothing left but his giant hands, his bear legs, and a good machete for which he had traded the iron walking-cane.

Then Juan Oso went alone into the sierras. He would not starve. Like his father, he could rob bee trees. Like his mother, he could grind the mesquite beans into *mesquitemal*. As in his childhood, he could kill meat with an arrow. He wove a rope out of the fiber of *lechuguilla*, and with this he waylaid a mountain sheep, lassoed her, milked her, and made cheese of the milk.

One day while Juan Oso was out in the sierras he saw a lone man running as fast as an antelope. He stopped the man. "Why are you running so?" he asked.

"I am running," the man replied, "because God made me a *corredor*—a runner. I run from one mountain peak to another, down one slope, across a valley, and up bluffs to the next *cumbre*. I never tire. I am the fastest *corredor* in the world."

"But how is it that you possess such ability?" Juan Oso asked.

"Oh," the *corredor* answered, "when I was a baby my mother gave me the milk of a pet doe. As I grew up, I ate no meat but deer meat, and every night I rubbed the tallow of a fat buck into my legs. That is why I now run as swift as the deer."

"Why, then," Juan Oso said, "come with me. I can't pay you gold or silver, for all my money is gone, but I can lead you to where deer range in herds like goats."

So the *corredor* went with Juan Oso. He often ran down deer. The two had plenty of meat.

After Juan Oso and the *corredor* had been together a number of days, they saw a man asleep down in a deep valley, a *carabina* by his side. As they neared him, the sleeper awoke and grabbed the rifle.

"Don't shoot," shouted Juan Oso. "My name is Juan Oso, a friend. Who are you?"

"I," replied the man, "am a *cazador*—a hunter. I can shoot the eagle in the air, the buck leaping through the brush; even without touching its head I can cut off with a bullet the red tongue of a lizard darting out to catch a gnat. I can shoot farther away than other men can see. I can kill game such a long distance off that I have no strength to run and get it."

Just then Juan Oso saw a buck running slantwise up a mountainside half a mile distant. "Look!" he cried. "Shoot it!"

The *cazador* shot, the buck fell, and the *corredor*, like a second bullet, sped away to bring in the carcass. A few minutes later he returned with the deer hanging over his shoulder.

"You and I would make a fine pair," said the *cazador*. "You could run about starting up the game, I could shoot, and then you could bring it in."

"*Sí, señor*," said Juan Oso. "Join us and we will all live together. But tell me, how did you acquire such eyesight?"

"I will tell you," the *cazador* said. "When I was old enough to hunger for something sweet to eat, my father commanded that I should never taste the brown *piloncillo* made from sugar cane. He commanded that the only sweet thing I taste be honey. Then he forbade even honey until I taught my eye to follow the bee to the crevice in the cañon cliffs.

"On a certain cliff three hundred feet from the ground there was as entrance to a bee-house a hole only large enough for one bee to enter at a time. This hole was in the shadow of a rock that projected over it. According to the custom of these little animals, a sentinel bee stood all day long, drawing back to allow honey-

gatherers to enter and ready to challenge any thief who
wanted to go in empty and fill himself. Using pine poles
notched into ladders and clinging to some narrow ledges,
my father climbed to this portal of the bee-house. By
his orders I must not watch. Up there he captured the
sentinel bee and painted his wings. When he came down,
he ordered me to stand out in the cañon below the hole
and describe the color of the sentinel. I could see the
little fellow plainly; I said he had red wings. This was
true. My father had painted the wings with red ochre.
After this I had plenty of honey. Thus my sight was
trained. I had a bow and arrow; and when pine logs were
burning, I practiced shooting at the little up-flying cin-
ders until I could hit them by night as well as by day."

So Juan Oso and his two followers went on. Fifteen
days later they came to a man who was pulling up a tree.

"Who are you?" demanded Juan Oso, as he admired
the strength of the man.

"I am an *arrancador*" (one-who-pulls-up), answered
the man. "I can pull up only little trees now. My people
are poor, with nothing to eat. I have gone away from
them to root like an armadillo. I pull up bushes and eat
the insects at their roots. If I had stronger meat, I could
pull up the biggest oaks that grow."

"But how did you learn this?" asked Juan Oso.

"*Señor*," replied the *arrancador*, "I learned from the
little but fierce *jabalina* [peccary] that uproots the *viz-
naga* cactus in order to eat the meat under its thorns."

"Come with us," said Juan Oso. "My hunter and my
runner provide so much meat that you will soon be root-
ing up a forest."

So the *arrancador* joined Juan Oso and ate all the
meat he wanted. But after a while the travelers came to

a vast desert country spread out between barren mountains that grew only such bitter growth as the *gobernador* (greasewood) and that gave forth not one spring of water. The ground was white with alkali. Perhaps this country was what people now call the Bolsón de Mapimí. Juan Oso and his followers were staggering from thirst and they were almost blind from the glare of the hot, bleached ground. They were crossing an arroyo full of white rocks when Juan Oso stumbled upon a man stretched out on his stomach inhaling deep, deep breaths.

"Who are you," asked Juan Oso, "and what are you doing?"

"I am," the man answered, "one who sucks water out of springs and lakes and rivers and causes it to flow to me. I can change the course of a great river. I wish I could draw food to myself as I draw water, but I cannot."

"We have food for armies," Juan Oso answered, "but we are dying for a drink of water. *Por Dios*, go on sucking the air and bring water down this arroyo."

The man continued sucking air. Before long the thirsty ones heard a rumble. Then they saw a tide of water sweeping down. It was clear and not muddy as is water after a rain. They drank and drank and they filled their gourds. There was so much water and it was so delicious that they bathed in it, and they were very contented.

"But where did you acquire such skill in sucking?" Juan Oso asked.

"I acquired it," the great sucker-in answered, "from my experience as a *tlachiquero*. In my country the maguey plants grow as tall as cathedrals. To get the honey-water for *pulque* out of them, I used to suck not through just one long gourd but through many gourds spliced together. I could stand in one place and suck the honey-water through a canal of gourds as long as an irrigation ditch. Thus as a *tlachiquero* I learned to draw in."

The sucker-in laughed and went on with Juan Oso and the others, singing:

> *"Know you that pulque*
> *Is liquor divine.*
> *The angels in heaven*
> *Prefer it to wine."*

They went on and on until they came in sight of a forest of towers. Not for a great while now had Juan Oso been in a city. He decided to enter this one in a royal manner. He went ahead. Behind him came the hunter, gun ready. Behind the hunter but often prancing out first on one side and then the other, came the *corredor* with a giant buck dangling from his shoulders. Behind him came the *arrancador*, who just at the edge of the city pulled up a mighty cottonwood tree and went along holding it as an umbrella. Last in the line came the man who could suck in rivers; he was not trying to suck in rivers now but he was breathing deep and making a rumbling sound, and his cheeks puffing out and sinking in looked more curious than the gills of a whale.[1]

Such a spectacle as Juan Oso and his procession made naturally aroused curiosity. The whole city stirred it-

[1] It is possible that the narrator, Ismael of the Piedra Blanca, never saw a whale.

self in wonder and alarm. A general and a regiment of soldiers galloped up and halted the parade, making Juan Oso and his men prisoners.

"Who are you?" asked the king of the city when Juan Oso was led before him.

"I am Juan Oso, a peaceable man."

"No, you are not peaceable," yelled the king. "Do not try to contradict me. You have alarmed my people and disturbed the peace more than an army of revolutionists would have done. You and your men must die."

"Is there no recourse?" Juan Oso asked.

"Yes, there is one recourse. Yonder is an extensive forest, the trees thick and high, the ground underneath them covered with brush. If you can clear that land for fields by this hour tomorrow, your lives are saved." The king laughed and turned away.

Closely guarded, Juan Oso and his men went to the forest. Immediately the *arrancador* began pulling up trees. Pines, cedars, oaks, he yanked each tree out with one pull and cast it back over his shoulders. Juan Oso himself pitched the trees into great piles. The hunter, the runner, and the sucker-in-of-rivers burned them. That night the city was as bright as day from the light of the bonfires. The people were more alarmed than ever. By daylight the ground where the forest had been was as clean as the floor of an *era* (a threshing pit).

Now this king was a tyrant, and he was afraid of such forces. "I promised to save your lives," he said to Juan Oso. "I keep my word; at the same time my wisdom says to keep you prisoners."

"Is there no recourse?" asked Juan Oso.

"Yes, there is one recourse. On the other side of the mountain from here a bold river rushes down into a waste of lands. If you can change that river so that its waters will irrigate the new fields, you shall go free."

Then Juan Oso with his men, all heavily guarded, went out to a dry arroyo bordering the vast plain they had cleared. The man who could suck in rivers lay down and began to inhale. He inhaled with such force that roofs were pulled off some of the fine houses in the city. After a while the people heard a rumbling sound; then those who were not afraid to look saw a wonderful stream of water rushing down the creek.

The morning after this Juan Oso and his men again appeared before the king.

"I have saved your lives, I have promised you your freedom," said the king. "But before I give you a passport to go out of my kingdom, one other service you must do me. Among the crags of yonder high mountain lives an eagle that daily for a hundred years has swooped down, taloning lambs, colts, and even now and then a child to carry to its nest. This nest is on a pinnacle so straight-up and lofty that no man can scale it. Whether at rest in its eyry or in flight, the eagle is safe from all marksmen. Bring this enemy to me dead or alive, and you shall go freely and safely where you will."

The hunter was already scanning the crag. At the very moment he looked, the eagle, appearing no larger than a bat, began rising and circling above its nest. The hunter raised his gun. The eagle fell dead—on top of the peak. Now the *corredor* sped. A wonderful thing the people saw. This *corredor* could run up the perpendicular wall of a bluff as easily as on level ground. He was like the bird carpenter. Within half an hour the giant wings of the eagle were spread above the doors of the king's palace.

The king was delighted. He had burros loaded with all kinds of wines and foods for Juan Oso and his men, gave them *mozos* to serve them, and invited them to stay in his kingdom as long as they wished. Juan Oso decided to go out into a range of sierras west of the city, where water and game and timber were abundant, and camp.

After his first morning's hunt he returned at noon to find the camp all torn up and the *corredor* lying on the ground bruised and bleeding.

"What has happened?" asked Juan Oso.

"While I was cooking the venison," the *corredor* answered, "a black man, a positive giant, seized me and beat me. Then he tore up the camp and dashed into the cañon."

"That was surely the devil," said Juan Oso. "He will come back tomorrow."

So the next day Juan Oso stayed in camp. At noon, just at the time Juan Oso was turning some deer ribs on a stick over the coals, the black devil sprang upon him. Juan Oso whirled, grabbed his machete, and with one lick cut the devil's head in two and sliced off his right ear. This ear he put in his pocket. Meantime the black devil's body was flopping around like a chicken with its head cut off, and instantly it flopped over the rocks into a hole so deep that the bottom could not be seen.

Strange sounds, some hoarse, some soft, began to be heard from the hole. The next morning before daylight Juan Oso sent the *corredor* to the city to bring back the longest rope made. The *corredor* brought two enormous coils. Juan Oso spliced the two ropes. Then he tied one end around the *corredor* and prepared to let him down. It was understood that one jerk on the rope would mean to lower away and two jerks would mean to haul up.

Before the first coil of rope had been played out, Juan Oso felt the signal to haul up. When the *corredor* appeared at the brim of the hole, he admitted that he had not reached bottom. He was just afraid to go any deeper. One by one Juan Oso tried lowering his other men. The darkness, the strange noises, and the awful depth caused each one to signal to be raised before he reached bottom.

Then in a great rage Juan Oso tied the rope around his own heavy body and ordered all four of his followers to lower him. Down, down he went, the length of the first rope, then past the splice, then down more and more of the second rope. The men above felt only signals to lower away. Finally the jerks ceased. Juan Oso was at the bottom.

Off to one side he distinguished the crying of soft voices. He went straight to the sounds. There he found four beautiful young women. They told how the black devil had stolen them and carried them to the bottom of the well. Juan Oso was happy to be the rescuer. He led the four beautiful young women to the end of the rope, tied it to one of them, and gave the signal to pull. Steadily the rope went up, and then after a long while it came down again. Thus each of the four was delivered from the black devil's den.

When the rope came down the last time, Juan Oso tied it around his own waist and signaled to pull. There was no answering haul. He jerked harder; he yelled, he roared. Only echoes came back to him. He did not know what could be wrong. As a matter of fact, the *corredor*, the *cazador*, the *arrancador*, and the man who could suck in rivers had each carried off one of the four beautiful young women without regard to the fate of Juan Oso. They had left the rope hitched to a boulder.

Hours passed. Juan Oso ceased to yell and roar. Then he felt hunger. He took steel and flint and punk out of his pocket and struck a light. The cavern floor was strewn with all kinds of debris. Juan Oso built a fire. Then he pulled the black devil's ear out of his pocket and put it on the fire to roast. Just as it began to cook, he heard a hoarse voice groan out, "Don't burn me, don't burn me."

Juan Oso had forgot all about the black devil. He lighted an *ocote*, ran about, and in a crevice found the groaning devil, his head cut open, his right ear cut off. Such a thing gave Juan Oso the *corajes*.[1] He grabbed the black devil and with a mighty swing hurled him up out of the well. But the black devil continued to moan, "Don't burn me, don't burn me." The moan seemed to Juan Oso to come from miles away. The hideous sounds were unpleasant to him. He took the black devil's ear off the fire and put it back in his pocket.

Now an idea came to Juan Oso. He jerked the rope again. This time he did not expect response. He was testing the rope to see if it were well tied. It appeared to be fast. Juan Oso began pulling himself up hand over hand. He pulled himself out of the hole.

He went straight to the city. He found the population in great rejoicing over the rescue of the four beautiful young women. Their marriages with Juan Oso's followers were already being celebrated. His own fortune was better than a dream. The king was so pleased that he gave Juan Oso the princess to marry.

At this point in the narrative, which I may not have quoted exactly in every instance, for it is hard to remem-

[1]Something like "a fit of the spleen" but more serious.

ber so many words, Ismael explained that Juan Oso had never before been in love.

"Who knows why? Yet perhaps for this he was so strong. Now he made love to his betrothed, and he sang her a song that the *gente* on the frontier still sing. It goes thus."

At the first three notes a burro near by set up a prolonged braying. I believe that nobody present, however, except myself regarded the harmony. It is impossible to put down the burro's song, and as Ismael's was not so good, I shall not quote it.

"And Juan Oso lived in a palace with chandeliers as brilliant as those of a cathedral. He kept the black devil's ear in his pocket, for without it the black devil would be forever powerless. In time children were born to Juan Oso and his wife, and not one of them had bear's feet or bear's hair or any other feature of the bear. And Juan Oso lived *muy contento* all the rest of his life."

As he finished this story, Ismael of the Piedra Blanca showed his swart face and his white fangs in a laugh that would have fitted well either the black devil or Juan Oso. In the manner that he had begun, he concluded with a rhymed convention out of antiquity:

> "*I went down one lane*
> *And came up tother.*
> *Basket full of holes—*
> *Now tell me another.*"

But Don Santiago was in no mood for "another." Before we went to bed that night he called me to one side.

"As all sensible people know," he said, "it is necessary to make time pass agreeably. But this man Ismael is a *sinvergüenza*. He has no regard for the truth. He is just an *hablador*.[1] Your route is the same as his, but I advise you to travel alone and to have absolutely nothing to do with him. He ruins everything I say."

In after times I had for a *mozo* in the Sierra Madre a civilized Yaqui Indian, Cruz by name, who told me a long story about another giant half-bear and half-man named Policano; also of a young woman rescued by *arrieros* from a cave in which a bear had sealed her up. Later on at the abandoned mining camp of Los Lamentos in Chihuahua I met a native who had inherited from his forefathers the *historia* of a bear's kidnaping in that region a *señorita* on the eve of her wedding and keeping her for a week before the rich *hacendado* who was her father, the frantic lover, and other ranch people found her imprisoned at the end of a box cañon, where the bear had been bringing her roasting ears and stolen *tortillas*. But I never expect to find such another place for bears as La Golondrina.

The next morning I delayed purposely in setting out, though delays in getting away from any Mexican ranch are prolonged. Primarily, perhaps, I wanted to respect the earnest desire that I not travel with a man who "ruined everything" my host said. And anyhow I liked lingering there and by thus lingering to show my appreciation of the rare, yet customary, hospitality I had met.

During the time of trifling about I had occasion to speak to Doña María apart from her husband. More diffident than I need have been about offering pay for

---

[1] While *hablador* may be translated merely as *talker*, the word carries the connotation, at times, not only of idle but of false speech.

the entertainment I had received, I told her that I had
learned how the wife of her kinsman Pantaleón was sick
and that I wished to leave money to buy medicines.

"It is true that Concepción is sick," Doña María
answered, "but no medicine can help her."

"How do you know?"

"She is *desalmada*."

"She is *un-souled?*"

"Yes, she is a woman who has lost her soul."

"I do not understand," I answered, "how that can
be."

"But yes, she has lost her soul," Doña María repeated. "She lost it more than five years ago. That does
not keep her from bearing children and grinding on the
metate, but there is no cure that medicine can give."

"In the name of the Holy Virgin," I requested, "tell
me how Concepción lost her soul."

"You must know two things," Doña María explained.
"In the first place, when one goes to sleep in a house, it
is well to place near the bed an *olla* of water so that if
the soul wanders out of the body it can drink. It is also
well to keep the door shut so that the soul will not stray
far off. In the second place, when a person has a nightmare, the soul is away from his body and he must not
be awakened suddenly. That is nearly as bad as killing
him in his sleep. The soul leaves only during sleep and
it must return during sleep. It cannot get back to its
home after the person to whom it belongs is awake.

"*Bueno*, five years ago last summer it was very hot
and all the people slept with their doors open. During
the night Concepción had a nightmare and cried out.
Pantaleón awoke her quick, like that. God is punishing
him for his foolishness. The soul of Concepción was

away and it could not get back. Also there was no water in the room. Concepción has not had a nightmare since. Perhaps if she had one and struggled long enough in her sleep, her soul might come back into her. Medicines can do no good. *Lástima de Dios.*"

"Yes, the pity of God."

And so I said good-by to La Golondrina.

"*Adiós.* A happy journey!" the *parientes* one and all wished me.

"May you go with God!" Doña María said.

"If God so grants," I responded.

"May you go well!" Don Santiago said as he gave me the embrace. "Blessed will be the eyes that see you return here." Then as I moved off, having bent his elbows so that the tips of his fingers were on his breast, he opened his arms with a great gesture, thus to show me that his heart remained and would always remain open.

After I had ridden twenty minutes, I turned in the saddle for a last look at La Golondrina in the valley below. The only life I could make out was a curl of smoke and four or five diminutive figures, motionless, standing on the bare mound, not so much watching as waiting.

CHAPTER
11

Bolsón de Mapimí

NORTHERN Coahuila, through which we were now traveling, is a better grazing country than that we had set out from. Here a majority of the haciendas, many of them owned by Texans, Englishmen, and other foreigners, are fenced. A severe drouth had been and still was upon the country; had our animals not been desert-bred they could not have persisted. It was not feasible to carry rations of grain to last more than two or three days, and it was difficult to buy corn at the few habitations. Of grass there were only the roots and a few dead spikes protected by thorned brush.

One late afternoon while we were crossing an American hacienda partly watered by wells and windmills and known as Ojo Apache, I saw, several hundred yards from the trail, three men with axes chopping in a wide expanse of sotol. More than a hundred cattle were loosely bunched around them to eat the food that was being unlocked. Sotol is a species of low-growing yucca, the leaves saw-toothed. Out of it is distilled a fiery liquor called also *sotol*, and Apache Indians used to eat the roasted hearts of it; some Mexicans still do on occasion. These hearts, from which the tough, serrated leaves spring out like the scales of the artichoke, will nourish stock, but they are so well defended that no animal can get to them unless the plant is chopped open.

"Inocencio," I said, "let us ride over and ask the men where the nearest water is and also for some chopped sotol for our animals." Then, in sheer idleness, I added, "How can we tell which is the most responsible man?"

"There is a way," Inocencio responded.

"Tell me."

"Watch. He who pulls the *gamuza* most is the owner."

"None of these men are owners, you know well."

"Yes, but the principle is the same."

"Nor do I see any buckskin."

"I am going to explain. One time a man and his son were traveling when they saw two individuals working with a deer's skin and making it into *gamuza*. 'Which is the owner?' the son asked. 'He who pulls the *gamuza* most,' answered the father. It is just a saying with us."

Approaching a squat, thin-waisted man, his skin as dry and weathered as his sandal-exposed toes, who seemed to be "pulling the *gamuza*" a little harder than either of his fellows, I greeted him and asked, "How are you?"

"*Pues, señor*," he answered, speaking with great vigor, decisiveness, and animation, accompanying every word with pantomimic gesture, "the whole *caballada* is trotted down."

He could have said nothing to express more fully the badness of things.

"Why, what is the matter?" I asked.

"*Pues, señor*, look about you. Plant and animal are alike withered, dying. No rain to make grass for nearly two years. We people still have corn and *frijoles* to eat, but how can we sprout a green leaf when nature suffers so?"

"It is very bad," I answered. "I feel much."

He lowered his voice. "And what do you know of this new business of Ojo Apache?"

When a man travels on horseback through a big land, he learns intimate details about every owner and range. I knew that the owner of Ojo Apache had ten years before foully cheated his partner out of the land, and I knew too that now by the trick of an ambitious general his holdings had been "embargoed." The cheated partner was a dear friend of my father's; I rejoiced that the cheater was being paid his dues.

I answered, "I know nothing of the matter. As the saying has it, '*Lo del agua al agua.*'" This is a phrase hard to interpret. It means that what is got out of the water goes back into the water. The chance was too good for Inocencio, who had come up but had said nothing beyond the customary greeting.

"That is it," he interjected. "A certain milkman of *guaraches* crossed a river every morning carrying milk to the town, and always when he got to this river in the *mañanitas*, while the light was still obscure, he stopped and scooped water into the can."

"Ah-ha," agreed the *sotolero*, making the motion of scooping water with his hand.

"*Bueno,*" Inocencio went on, "thus he gained and

after a while he had money to buy a pair of shoes. He did not put them on his feet but started out carrying them to his house. He intended to use them for *fiestas* and special occasions like that.

"When he came to the river this day, it was up. But he went on in, riding back on the burro's hips, the milk cans in front of him. Now the water began to float the cans and the *burrito* was struggling to swim and the milkman found himself very busy. He had not hands enough. His shoes were swept away and out of sight. Then on the other side he stopped and looked where his shoes had gone. '*Lo del agua al agua*,' he said."

"Well said," the *sotolero* exclaimed. "*Muy bien dicho*."

"Yes," Inocencio added, "Dios forgets sometimes, but not forever." I had told him the history of the scoundrelly owner of the Ojo Apache.

Noticing a large, very fat red steer among the poor cattle, I asked how the animal came to be in such prime condition.

"That ox," the sotol-chopper answered, coming a step nearer my horse and lowering his voice without weakening its timbre, as if he were going to impart a matter of profound privacy, "appears to have some *secreto* of sustaining himself that he will not make known to the other cattle. Every morning he comes up to where they are chewing like slaves in order to keep their skeletons standing up. He comes alone from God knows where and salutes them like some hidalgo that will give only his cane to a peon to shake. He takes a little sotol to be polite and never says one word, not one word, as to how he keeps so fat."

All during this speech the speaker was working his

hands, fingers, arms, shoulders, head, and facial features to indicate the approach, the salutation, the lofty hauteur and inscrutable sapience of the red steer.

"Yet the other cattle appear not to be jealous of him," I remarked.

"No, they are not *políticos.*"

I now turned to the matter that had brought me to the man for whom "the horses were all trotted down." Indicating the location of a well to be beyond an intervening hill, he said that he and his fellows had their camp there. They had already cut enough sotol to do the cattle for the day and now they would "with entire *gusto*" split open two sacks of hearts for my beasts.

The *sotolero* now informed me that his name was Juan de Dios, "at your orders." Riding towards the well, I looked forward to further talk with him as much as to seeing our beasts enjoy a good meal of sotol.

"Like hope," Inocencio remarked, "it will not fatten but it will maintain."

While chewing a core of the sotol myself after supper, in order to relieve the taste of over-strong goat meat, I remarked that a blind man who had lost his sense of taste might imagine it some sort of artichoke. I really thought it more resembled celery, but I should have been at a loss to define celery; wild artichokes were known.

"He who eats artichokes and kisses an old woman," Inocencio came in pat with a saying I suppose he had some time heard in the sierras but that here seemed absurdly foreign, "neither eats nor kisses."

I was thinking of the desert ahead of us. "Could a man dying of thirst," I asked Juan de Dios, "be helped by this plant?"

"Perhaps," he answered. "Certainly more than by eating the heart of the *lechuguilla*."

The daggered *lechuguilla* is as bitter as green persimmon. "Did anybody ever try it for thirst?" I asked.

"I did. One time."

I waited.

"God saved me, not the *lechuguilla*."

Juan de Dios now with fervid energy began sticking bits of twigs into the ground. Near them he put the backs of his hands against the earth, holding up his gnarled fingers to indicate stubble.

"The land up there to the northwest where you are riding," he went on, "is like that—just tables and slopes of *lechuguilla* daggers. But in the land also grows the *guayule*. In the year one thousand nine hundred and seven I was gathering *guayule* to be sold to the factory of rubber. We had our camp at a big tank. There was no other water for a long, long distance. Each day we had to go farther and farther out from the tank to find the *guayule*. I was gathering it by myself. I went out in the morning with my *tortillas* for dinner, a bottle of water, and an old knife. It was in the time of the *canícula*"—the dog days of July and August— "and it was so hot that the rattlesnake crawled only at night.

"One day I went afoot because my burro was too lame. I would gather the *guayule* into piles and later carry it in. I went far out. *Bueno*, by noon I had drunk all the water. The sun in the sky danced up and down like a crackling frying in grease. The thirst came, but I had to keep on gathering *guayule* in order to buy *frijoles* and corn for my family. There was no *remedio* for this. I pulled until nearly dark, and then I started back to the tank. The thirst of the body was like that of the ground under a dead broomweed.

"And then—I do not know how—perhaps it was the thirst—I found myself lost. There was no moon. There was no trail. And *lechuguilla* everywhere. I cut out the heart of one to chew. The bitter juice made the thirst thirstier. I kept on, but I did not know where I was going. Sometimes I would stop to listen, to consider; then I would go on.

"Know you, *señor*," and here the voice of Juan de Dios lowered into that tone of confidence I had already noted in him, "a man who lives all the time out sees some strange things come to pass. *Bueno*, according to the stars it was two hours past midnight when I sat down on top of a hill to rest. I did not know what to do. I am *puro hombre de campo;* yet I was lost.

"While I was sitting there, the moon, sick and thin, came up over my shoulder. And then right out in front of me, perhaps twenty feet away, I saw a *león*, a *pantera*. He was just sitting on his haunches, still, his face towards me. I could see the white of his breast.

"I did not wish to try to fight with this animal. I arose and started away from him. At once he made some jumps and galloped around in front of me. There he sat again, silent, not moving, just gazing."

Juan de Dios slunk his shoulders and held the palms of his hands outward in front of his body to simulate the posture of the panther.

"And now fear made thirst die. I gave a shout and leaped towards the north. Quickly the *león* gave some jumps and again was in front of me, just sitting there silent as if he were going to say a prayer. *Por Dios*, I could not comprehend this. Then God seemed to give

237

me valor and I stood up straight and I said to myself, 'This animal is not offering to attack me. He is not waving his tail and stretching out his body in preparation to leap. It seems that he is not my enemy. Therefore he may be my friend.'

"I took one step towards the animal. He arose, but in a gentle manner like a dog. I took another step. He turned and started off. Another step and he was retreating slowly but with his head turned back as if to advise me to follow. I went on, following the adviser. He went this way and that way, twisting through the *lechuguilla* and the chaparral. Then in about half an hour we entered a trail. I did not know where the trail went to or where it came from. It was well beaten, but I knew not which direction of it to take. I followed the *león*. He went on and on.

"In the summer time the light comes very early. Not long after *el primer gallo*[1] my guide stopped, looked at me, and then stepped out into the chaparral. Now I saw just ahead in an open place a *jacal*. I advanced. In front of the *jacal* was a little wagon with two barrels of water in it. They had been hauled from a hole three leagues away. Thus the lion, *como un amigo de los hombres*, saved my life."

"Thanks be to God," said Inocencio.

"Had the lion been hungry, would he have acted as 'the friend of men'?" I asked.

"Probably in that case I should not now be here to tell of him," the *sotolero* replied. "And had it been a female lion—the worse."

"The lioness, then, is never friendly to man?"

"Never. The female never favors *cristianos*."

[1]The time for "the first cock" to crow—before dawn.

Following this, the talk took a direction that I do not wish to record. It was as barren as the ground between the clumps of sotol.

After the men had left early the next morning to begin their day of sotol cutting, I asked Inocencio what he thought of the lion as a friend to man.

Pausing with a saddle blanket in his hand, he answered, "Thus they say *el león* sometimes succors people. It is hard for one man to tell what is in the head of another, much more to tell what is within the head of an animal. Without doubt the creatures have their civilization, but what it is the *cristiano* cannot say. As the proverb teaches, 'Only the spoon knows what is inside the pot.'"

That the pack saddle might get on the mule, I did not prolong the discussion.

For days that stretched into weeks we rode. After corkscrewing up cañons lined with cedar, traversing arid and unstocked mesas merely patched with grass, and threading passes over mountains fringed with pine and piñon, we left all fence lines and came by degrees out upon that vast and vaguely defined desert known as the Bolsón de Mapimí, on some old maps called Tierra de Muerte—Land of Death—which extends from the Río Bravo southward through western Coahuila and eastern Chihuahua to Mapimí in Durango, projects itself into Zacatecas and San Luis Potosí, and includes other vaguely defined *páramos* nominated Llano de los Gigantes, Llano de los Cristianos, and Llano de los Lipanes.

Immense and mysterious, appallingly barren and yet productive of a fantastic life, maddeningly monotonous except to one who can "read infinity in a grain of sand,"

239

terrifying but enthralling, the Bolsón de Mapimí stretches out an irregular elevated basin hemmed around by low naked mountains that infringe upon and crumple it and are always in sight. These shed the sparse rainfall into arroyos that are bone dry a few hours after a rain and that, without coming to a terminus, sink into the parched solitude. According to geologists, some of the basins that make up the great Bolsón were in æons past lakes of water. It is as if a vast ocean had been petrified and desiccated to remain forever silent, sterile, desolate. A traveler through this region is fortunate to reach water of any kind once a day and he must tack his course to do that. The patches of dry, coarse, wire-like *sabaneta* grass or the equally tough *toboso* or the fibrous *chino* are always far from any watering. Generally we camped with no water except that carried in canteens, often half-drained before grass and time of day allowed us to halt. Occasionally we stopped at a lone *ranchería* of poverty.

The nights grew freezing cold; the days remained blazing hot, the penetrating wind of darkness turning by mid-morning into a scorching blast. The sun usurped and flooded without filling the immense vacuity of sky. The intense light, reflected and redoubled by the ashen soil upon which it beat, was blinding. The powdered alkaline dust raised by the feet of our horses was swept into the nostrils of both man and beast. The gait was weary.

After having for eighty years been beat upon by this sun of the Mexican mesas, well might the great Porfirio Diaz, as he waited in alien Paris for time to put an end to his long, long career, wishing the while for "*algo de Oaxaca*"—some thing from his native state—say of the

240

gray ball over the Champs Élysées, "it is only *un sol pintado*." And this is the desert out over which that other exile, the silent and doomed old warrior Victoriano Huerta, used to watch the processional of stars as he stood in front of his cribbed cottage at El Paso and mumbled of *"mi país."* "Would," he said, "that the desert between Mexico and the United States had remained *desierto* and that the friars had never brought donkeys from Spain."

And so we rode. If not in time, then in distance covered, the *jornadas* had to be short, for with pack mule and without grain or other forage travelers cannot rush barrenness that stretches away and away into other barrenness. It was as if I had never known any other land, any other life, any other beings but Inocencio, the mule, and the two horses. The foothills were covered with black rock, not volcanic, I am told, appearing to have been spewed out of a furnace. Now and then we came to sand dunes on which grew gray switch mesquite and gray *chamiso*, their roots affording fuel.

It was the grayest land I have ever seen. The *candelilla* (from which wax to make candles, *candelas*, is extracted) is gray; the *guayule* rubber plant is gray; an abundant weed called *mariola*, resembling the *guayule*, is gray. The *agrito*, so green in Texas, every leaf of it a three- or a five- or a seven-spined thorn, is gray. *Palmas*, Spanish daggers, and sotol are all gray, the stalks below the crown of needle-pointed leaves often bleached white; and in the season of bloom their gigantic clusters of flowers on towering stalks—the "candles of the Saviour," as the *gente* call them—are milk white. Gray too grows the stubble of daggers called *lechuguilla*. The *nopal* is gray; the cholla-like *cardensi*, in its thorny

241

tentacles innumerable nests of the small gray birds called "the old ones," is gray. A gray deer stands invisible, except to desert eyes, against a gray yucca; the jackrabbit has a gray rump; the deadly rattlesnake and the harmless "hog-snout" are alike the color of the land. On unending stretches of greasewood and *hojasén* and on willows and *pinacates* growing along the dry waterdrains paved with billions of rounded white and gray rocks, the gray bark inclines to blackness. Far away sometimes a valley appears green; that green is an expanse of the grotesque *ocotillo*, each stalk studded with thorns protecting its miniature stemless leaves, the points of the stalks in time of rain becoming a blaze of inaccessible scarlet. All one afternoon I rode through a plain of big *palmas*, yuccas, aflutter with thousands and tens of thousands of silent migratory bluebirds.

Moving seemingly as slow as the desert terrapin, day after day, through the gray and immense solitude of the Bolsón de Mapimí, his ego subdued by the elemental vastness until it seems to be of no more consequence than that of the most humble of all land-crawlers and to have become a mere atom in illimitability, a man grows to feel that no human drama ever was enacted, ever could be enacted, upon such an unrelieved and empty stage. Yet here also human history has written itself, though without a Livy to picture its page and generally without leaving any more impression upon the unresponsive and immutably bleak earth than the evanescent *huellas en el cielo*—"tracks in the sky." Somehow, I know not why, the long, lone cry of a Bolsón coyote in the night suggests human destinies as eloquently as the broken arches of the Coliseum ever spoke to Byron. By day the omnilucent glare of the sun

242

palpitates an Iliad of vanished races, vanished centuries, and vanished ways of human life.

Under that sun long, long ago the *conquistadores* rode north this way to gather slaves for their mines. They rode back, and behind them, too fierce to ever be enslaved, the Comanches beat out a highway. West of the Pecos in Texas, on the two great paralleling cordilleras of Mexico and over the broken plateau that lies between them, it usually rains in the summer, the average rainfall varying greatly according to the lay of the land. By September the grass is ripe and the holes are full of water. And so to old people in northern Mexico the September moon is still "the moon of the Comanches," though the Comanches themselves called it "the Mexican moon," for it was under this moon that they annually swooped down.

Astride half-wild horses captured from the mustang herds of the plains or from the *caballadas* of Mexican ranches raided the season before, they rode on stirrupless pads of sheepskin or buffalo hide, their bits and bridle reins alike of rawhide. Their arms were mostly bows and arrows, the bows of Osage orange, the arrows of *vara dulce, palo duro,* or other tough growth. The arrows were carried in a quiver of wildcat hide slung from the shoulder. Each warrior was provided with a lance of ashwood and a *chimal,* or shield, of dried buffalo bull hide. Some of them carried Bowie knives or machetes from Mexico. Here and there one was armed with an old blunderbuss *escopeta.* Thus equipped, in the time of the Comanche moon they rode down the Comanche War Trail, which from their range on the Llano Estacado to the depths of the Bolsón de Mapimí half a thousand miles southward stretched as plain as a chalk mark.

Once across the Río Bravo, these Cossacks of the desert scattered, some to push up the Río Conchos to the very walls of Chihuahua City; some to harass the ranches of far-away Durango; some to veer east and raid haciendas in Coahuila, where—in the region of Saltillo at least—cattle went unbranded for years because there were no horses on which to work them. The Comanches raided even into the states of Zacatecas, San Luis Potosí, and Aguas Calientes. Boys, girls, young women, and horses were their object—the children to be raised as true Comanches, the young women to serve as squaws, and horses—never enough horses—to ride, the symbol of power and glory and riches of all the Plains Indians.

Before the bitter *nortes* of winter blew down, the Comanche Trail was again vivid with life northward bound. On some of the captured horses were the lashed captives. About the belts of the captors that drove them dangled scalps taken from kinsmen of the captives. The dust from the hoofs of horses—horses—horses—rose in clouds; behind the rearmost plunderers, after they had left waste land behind them, rolled clouds of smoke from grass fires set to impede pursuers. Now and then bands deflected from the trail to shun avengers. But there was no way to cover or hide the great Comanche War Trail itself. It was worn deep by the hoofs of countless travelers over generations of time and was lined with the whited bones of horses. In Texas it has been plowed up, tramped over, cemented under. Trains and automobiles annually carry across it thousands of English-speaking people who are not aware that it ever existed. But across the Bolsón de Mapimí and below it and in the land fringing upon it the raiders who beat out the

Comanche Trail ride vividly yet in memory, and the moon under which Bajo del Sol and the cohorts following him and his mother used to terrify *todo el mundo*—all the world—is still *la luna de los Comanches.*

Bajo del Sol was so named because he feared nothing "under the sun." His mother was so old that she had to tie her lower jaw to the top of her head with a thong in order to keep it from flopping against her throat and breast. But long after she put her jaw in a sling she continued to ride the Comanche War Trail and to direct the forays of the braves. Against this ravaging the central government did nothing. Far removed from the center where politicians lied and generals fought to possess the spoils of office, haciendas and ranches comprising an empire were by a few hundred naked savages kept shuddering with terror.

The only *remedio* was a bounty on scalps. A hundred years ago the governor of Chihuahua issued a *Proyecto de Guerra,* stipulating that 100 pesos would be paid for the scalps of warriors and 50 pesos for the scalps of squaws. Then into the Bolsón and into the sierras rode Kirker and Glanton and other scalp hunters, some of them from Texas. A scalp was a scalp to them, and when their perfidy in murdering innocent natives for the bounty was discovered, they had to flee. About the same time Weyman, lately of the "Texas Navy," was exchanging Apache scalps for cash in Durango. In New Mexico the bounty was on ears instead of scalps, and the "two great curiosities" noted by the naturalist Wislizenus in the Governor's Palace at Santa Fé were "windows of glass and festoons of Indian ears." For half a century the price of scalps rose and fell, and not all the raiders who rode down the War Trail lived to ride back. When in 1846 the Englishman Ruxton, as he tells in his extraordinarily interesting *Adventures in Mexico*, reached Chihuahua City, he saw "dangling over the portals" of the cathedral "the grim scalps of one hundred and seventy Apaches who had lately been treacherously and inhumanly butchered by the Indian hunters in the pay of the state." Twenty-eight years later Santleben, noted freighter of the Chihuahua Trail, saw on the plaza in front of the cathedral a procession of conquerors, accompanied by bands of music, displaying scalps on poles. On an unpublished map I have, dated 1851, "Unknown Region Except to Hunters of Indians" is scrawled across the Bolsón de Mapimí.

The Apaches did not wish to kill all the *rancheros*. They wanted some to remain to grow stock for them, and they ironically called the Mexican inhabitants of the region their shepherds.

All uninhabited spaces are silent, but often it seemed to me that these of northern Mexico are more silent than any others I have ever known. Like the natives, the land seems to remember to be silent. In southern Mexico the folk remember Cortés and Cuauhtémoc and the Malinche as of yesterday; in northern Mexico they remember the raiding Lipanes, Apaches, and Comanches as of last night. One time in the Sierra Madre of Sonora a *mestizo* whispered to me in front of a cave: "Look at those bundles of shucks; Geronimo and his Apaches left them there." He seemed to feel that Geronimo might be lurking behind us. In Coahuila, Chihuahua, Nuevo León, and Durango I have many times had pointed out to me a corral in which horses were guarded against the Comanches, a spring that the Apaches used as a rendezvous, a pass through which

they swept their booty of captives and horses, or some
other feature commemorative of the savage invaders.
"He will make a fine man if the Apaches do not bind
him to a cactus," is a saying yet to be heard, reminiscent
of the time when the "tigers of the desert" stripped
Mexicans and bound them naked against thorns.

Riding, in Coahuila, on the high ridge overlooking
the broken wastes of the Cañon Espada on one side and
the Cañon San Agustín on the other, I thought to myself, "Surely some savage sentinel used this promontory
for signaling." Then I saw the ring of stained stones
from which with a blanket the gusts of smoke were sent
up.

"Yes," said Inocencio. "Smoke snuffs going up one
by one from such a high point as this mean to prepare
against the enemy; his tracks have already been seen.
A little smoke sent up from the side of a mountain is for
the purpose of locating friends, and the answer to it from
a similar place means to come in peace. Fires out on the
prairie mean that the people making them want to talk
with their enemies."

Once, on the Mesa de Ramadero, between the great
Sierra Potosí and the town of Galeana in Nuevo León,
I saw beside the trail an enormous *palma real*, a species
of yucca. It looks as old as the *ahuehuetes* of Montezuma
under the heights of Chapultepec and in its way is as
distinguished as they or as the hoary *anácahuita* remembered in legend as the "Tree of the Padre" at Múzquiz,
or as the Tree of Crosses, all its thorns and all its
branches growing in crucifix form, at Querétaro. Using
two ropes to measure it and then later measuring the
ropes, I found that at its base this *palma real* is 15.89
meters in circumference, and a yard higher up, at the

point where the trunk flares into a straight line, 8.2 meters in circumference. Hacked into the trunk are steps by which for generations folk have climbed to gather the *palma* blossoms, which they cook as a vegetable, and the ripe fruit, called dates, which they eat raw and make into a kind of candy. But what struck me as most extraordinary about this giant, aside from age and size, were the carvings on its bole—carvings similar to red and black pictographs often seen in caves used by Indians, with Christian crosses added.

While the Cossacks of the desert yet rode their wild ways, gigantic Mexican carts beat out another trail, in part following the Comanche Trail—for trails must go by water—across the Bolsón de Mapimí. It became known to history as the Chihuahua Trail. Not an ounce of metal in their ponderous frames, every timber held in place by rawhide or peg, their wooden wheels seven feet in diameter screeching on wooden axles except when "greased" with succulent pads of the *nopal*, the mighty *carretas* lumbered along from the mining camps of Parral, through Chihuahua City, across the Bolsón, across the Río Bravo, through San Antonio, and on to Indianola on the Mexican Gulf—a distance of over 1200 miles. They carried silver, in bullion and in minted pesos, beans, salt, cotton, horseshoes, hides. To note only one dry stretch, the Mexican bulls, yoked by horns as ponderous almost as the cart axles, pulled their loads

across the 90 waterless miles from Julimes to Chupadera
—a mere "suck spring"—and then on 60 more waterless
miles to the Paso de la Mula.

In time mighty freight wagons, each drawn by ten
and twelve Mexican mules and driven by Mexican
freighters, supplanted the ox carts on the trail, but not
in the country. And the Comanches still rode. The
wagons trailed in trains, camping two or three times between waterings, at every stop going into the corral
formation which makes of wagons a fort. In the darkness of the night the *caporal* would blow his whistle and
each of the more than a hundred mules enclosed in the
corral would go to his proper wagon, or if one were re-
calcitrant it would be immediately *sensed* by its driver—
for the faculty thus employed in darkness to catch without delay a dark mule out of a numerous *mulada*
amounted to more than *sight*—and led into place.
Within half an hour the train would be moving.

And then the wagons went the way of the *carretas*,
and the Comanche Trail and the Chihuahua Trail became but traces in history, and the Bolsón de Mapimí
became more silent and more deserted, emptier and
vaster in its solitude than ever before. For the vanish-
ments of life—life existing only in memory—but inten-
sify the emptiness of a vacancy once occupied. It is true
that for military purposes a railroad now runs to Chihuahua City from Presidio del Norte, where the freight
trail used to cross the Río Grande—and an engine pulls
a half-dozen cars over this track once each way every
week. True also one may travel by rail—once in a while
—a hundred miles from Escalón eastward to Sierra
Mojada in the heart of the desert, but riding thus he will
pass only one or two wells of water; then he may keep

249

on traveling east for more than another hundred miles and of habitations see merely the huts of section hands whose women draw water from a reservoir behind the engine.

The last stir of human life upon the Bolsón de Mapimí was during the Mexican Revolution that began in 1910. In the early winter of 1913 old Don Luis Terrazas, his scores of descendants, and half a hundred other rich Chihuahua families fled up the Chihuahua Trail for the safety that lay north of the Río Grande. They fled from Pancho Villa. Terrazas owned, some say, seven million acres of land in the state, some say fourteen million. He owned a large portion of the largest state in the republic of Mexico, and a considerable part of this land lies within the Mapimí desert. Don Luis was the state. On the hegira he took with him 5,000,000 pesos in specie —so they say—and left 600,000 secreted in or under the pillars of his bank. American mining camps of the Parral district sent along half a million in gold and silver bullion. There were over 3,000 of the refugees. There were peon women on foot carrying chickens and babies. There were fine carriages drawn by fine mules with outriders. There were single vaqueros and trains of wagons; there were ox carts and loose longhorned cows. There were disconnected strings of pack mules and burros—and whatever the stuff in their cargoes, whether the pesos of Terrazas or the golden combs and jeweled earrings of a Spanish jeweler, no animal crossing the Bolsón de Mapimí carried anything more precious than a gourd of water. The trail was marked with carcasses. In the mountains of the Big Bend on the Texas side men yet look for treasure that Orozco and other refugees are supposed to have secreted there.

Four years later Pancho Villa, retreating from Carranzistas, set out from the ancient mining town of Mapimí with 1,200 men; when four days later he reached Los Jacales to the west, he had only 900 men and many less than that number of horses. During the four days neither man nor beast had come to water, for the sparse *aguajes* to right and left were guarded by the enemy. The men singed prickly pear for their horses; they ate prickly pear themselves. But prickly pear is sparse where the Bolsón is worst. Had the men and horses alike not belonged to the desert, few indeed could have thus traversed it.

No longer does the Bolsón, as a chronicler of the *conquistadores* wrote, referring to the Lipan Indians, "disgorge nations barbarous and cruel," but unchanged and unchangeable it brands—when it does not burn the very vitals out of them—the swart folk who exist upon it with a brand not recordable in the script of letters or figures.

They do exist. Despite what has been said of solitude, there are *ranchos*. Before the Revolution these lands sustained hardy Mexican cattle that could go for days and even weeks without drinking, in seasons deriving what water they got from thorned prickly pear and the stalks and flowers of the varied yucca and agave growth, at other times walking for leagues from the rare watering places to the mountain *rincones* and low *playas* affording grass. On the Mesa de los Fresnos, a beautifully timbered, high, rough, well-grassed but unwatered region lying east of the Bolsón proper, General Treviño of the vast Hacienda La Babia once—so an honest man who had served him as a *caporal* told me—ordered 5,000 head of his Mexican cattle turned loose. "Yes, they lived and they increased. No, for months at a time they had no water."

Here in this land a colt will follow its mother ten miles to water; when it is grown it is only a pony, but it will never need shoes of iron and it "belongs to the race that dies before tiring." It will carry a vaquero two or three days between drinks. Deer, antelopes, and certain other animals that thrive on the range do not drink water at all. And the animals, the gray brush, and the men are all of one breed. A vaquero with the toothache will pour worm medicine into the cavity. If that does not "cure" —kill the nerve, he will have four men hold him down while a fifth inserts a red-hot wire end into the hole. When a Pancho Villa gathers his "leathered ones" from the deserts and sierras of this North Country, the world may well shudder.

A part of the country we were traversing Inocencio knew only in a general way, but neither he nor any other *campesino* I ever met had a clear conception of distances.

"How far is it to the Jaboncillos?" I asked of a man whose beard and hair might have been woven into more raiment than the tatters about his body comprised. ("Long hair, short brains," was the subsequent comment of my *mozo*.)

"*Señor*," he replied, "I do not wish to deceive you, but for me, on this burro, it is two *cigarros* and a little piece of another."

I saw that the shuck in which he was rolling a cigarette was unusually long, and I wondered how much time he took to smoke it and how long after it was smoked away he waited to roll another.

At the Jaboncillos, where we watered our stock and filled canteens, Inocencio declared that although he had never traveled our trail to the Piedrita, he knew it must be "a little far," probably six or seven leagues. A man who was putting oak bark in a barrel containing water for the purpose of tanning a deerhide declared, however, that it was really *cerca*, "near."

We rode three hours and camped. The next morning, after having ridden until nearly noon, we met a *campesino*. He stopped, according to the custom of the country, on my left side, and, each of us reaching across his horse, shook hands.

"What is the news?" I asked.

"But no," he replied, "*todo es pacífico*."

Then in answer to the same question, I replied that where I came from "all was pacific" also.

He took me for a peddler and asked if I had in the pack any sugar, coffee, and thirty-thirty cartridges to sell. I gave him a cigarette and inquired about the distance to Piedrita.

"*Pues*, just follow your direction," he answered. "*Es muy cerquita ahora*—it is very near now."

Along late in the afternoon, our beasts flagging from heat, thirst, and the alkali dust, two peons driving a single burro loaded with sticks entered the trail ahead of us. As we overtook the pedestrians, the one on my side saluted in the old-fashioned way.

"How far is it, my friend," I asked, "to the Piedrita?"

"Keep on following your direction," he replied, at the same time gesturing for a light from my cigarette. "It is just over those hills and is *muy cerquiti-ti-ti-ti-ta*."

When at last we arrived at the Piedrita, there was only enough light left in the sky to reveal the greenish scum on the pygmy hole of water that supplied the ranch, man and beast.

"Your leagues are long ones," I said to Inocencio.

"*Sí, señor*," he replied, "*son leguas de hombre*—they are man-sized leagues."

It is not that the *campesino* wishes to deceive. In the first place, distance, like time, is to him a hazy abstraction. In the second place, he knows that whoever travels wishes to arrive; so, by nature sympathetic and accommodating, he leads the traveler, if not to believe, then to hope that his destination is near. From the same motive to please, a vaquero from an outlying range will report to the manager of a hacienda that a sprinkle is a rain, and any laborer on the most arid land can any day find many signs to indicate a wet season. There is a little story current on both sides of the Río Grande to illustrate this peon desire to be accommodating.

Two hunters were going out into an unfamiliar country to hunt. At the place where they camped they met an old-time vaquero.

"Are there any deer in this vicinity?" they asked him.

"Deer!" he exclaimed. "Yes, yes, *muchos, muchísimos* (many, very many). And fat—and what antlers!"

"How about antelopes?"

"Antelopes, oh yes. On those plains behind yonder mountain."

"*Jabalinas?*"

"Certainly there are *jabalinas*. They run in such bunches that it is well to beware of them, for they are fierce. The brush is popping with their teeth."

"Turkeys?"

"You will hear concerts of them in the morning."

"Quail?"

"Such bunches that sometimes the sun is clouded with their flight."

254

"And bear?"

"Just go to those oak mottes on the side of the mountain, and you will see how they are fattening on acorns. Yes, there are more on the other side of the mountain than here."

"What about elephants?"

"*Elefantes?*" The ancient informant paused, scratched his head a minute, repeated the question, paused again, and then raced out his words: "Yes, *elefantes* there are, yes, yes. However, I do not wish to deceive you. I must tell you the truth. They are well hidden and you will have to hunt for them."

"Look at those tracks in the sky," Inocencio called to me one afternoon, at the same time gesturing towards some crows circling ahead of us. "They say there has been a kill at the Chupadera del Indio. Perhaps we shall find a camp there."

We did find fresh signs of a camp right at the *chupadera*, which, supplied by rains of the preceding summer, was barely trickling out of the rocks. The crows were interested in the remains of a deer. On one of the boulders I saw a half-dozen curious symbols that had been picked into it a long time ago. I asked Inocencio what they signified.

"They do not," he answered, "signify treasure, as the ignorant think. They are of the Indios."

Some of them were to be found in the list of signs or symbols that my friend Don Alberto Guajardo learned from the Kickapoo Indians as a boy and that he later copied down for me.

"We go so slow," I said to Inocencio.

"Yes," he replied, "but, as you know, of more value a dropping of water that endures than a stream that

255

dries up. Grain by grain the dove fills her craw."

The sun, throbbing out of a sky of brass, was still high; the end of the day's ride was still seemingly as far away as glasses tinkling with ice in some shaded room of cool air that existed only in a haze; the rough grease-wood mesa crawled away under the glare of heat-devils to naked mounds of gray and red—when upon reaching the crest of one of these mounds I saw coming along the trail towards me a mule carrying a woman, behind her on foot a man with a guitar. Doubtless she walked sometimes.

We all stopped for salutations, and each set of travel-ers found that with the other all was "*silencio.*" I asked the man where he was from. From Durango. I did not query as to why he was so very far from home. He had a firm, unsmiling face of subdued but astonishingly vi-brant reddish-brown complexion, and clear across the left side showed a long, clean scar of other years. Sharp moustaches hid whatever his mouth indicated. He was not afraid to look one in the eyes but he did not so look. He moved with the effortless alacrity of a cat. Both he and the woman were immaculately clean. She was maybe twenty years old but looked much fresher than most women of her class attached at that age; she was as firm in physique as he and about her there was something at once daring and modest. He was about forty-two years old.

After we had all drunk water out of my canteen and the man and I had smoked a cigarette each, I suggested a song. It took him some time to tune up. The young woman stood beside him, in one hand a kind of metallic triangle against which she kept time by striking it with a hardwood rod. From the moment he began picking his guitar she kept her eyes absolutely glued on his face,

whether because she worshiped him or in order to keep time with him I could not tell; yet it was clear that she worshiped his very breath. Occasionally at some note in his voice a glow of happiness would shine through her features.

I cannot describe the liberating and refreshing effect the opening bars of the song had upon me. The song was one of the several popular *corridos* about Villa. At the end of the first verse I yelled, "Viva Pancho Villa!" and then the troubadour sang on "as if his song could have no ending." There were between thirty-five and forty verses to it—all about the "terror of the North," "the man who laughs and kills," "a prophet like Mahomet," "this Bonaparte of the sierras," sitting on his "sorrel horse, pistol in hand, teeth gleaming," the "feline pupils of his eyes dilating," shouting, "We are born to die," the "very god of his Dorados," "rude but great of heart," making "formidable explosions of steam engines," dynamiting bridges, amid *"una gran confusión"* burning caboose and passenger cars, now sacking Torreón, now in the town of Columbus leaving "as a little remembrance only sixteen dead gringos." But alas for *"pobre* Pancho Villa." In Parral traitors and ingrates waylaid and murdered him.

> *"Vuela, vuela, palomita,*
> *párate en aquella orilla,*
> *avísales á los gringos*
> *que murió Francisco Villa."*
>
> (*Fly away, fly away, little dove,*
> *But stop there just ahead,*
> *And advise the valiant gringos*
> *That Villa at last is dead.*)

While the singer sang, I, almost as intent on his and his companion's faces as she was on his alone, glanced at my round little mule Durazno. His ears were working back and forth in a kind of time and now and then he was twitching his lips. I could not decide which of us, Durazno, the woman-girl, or I myself was most appreciative of the balladry. I did not offer to pay for it for two reasons: first, there are some things that money does not pay for, and secondly I had a "gratification" to present. I told the troubadour that if he would accompany me back to the next water, singing on the road, I would compensate him. He agreed, transferred their few belongings from his mule to mine, seated his wife behind the saddle, and then mounted himself. Riding thus, he could play as well as sing. Now the desert was no longer dreary, and all afternoon Durazno's pleasure continued as a benediction. The *campesinos* say truly that "with singing the road grows shorter."

It was dark before we saw a light and knew that we were nearing La Joya—The Jewel—a lonely mud hut on the side of a naked hill at the base of which, however, there was a spring. We pulled saddles off against the wall of the house. The occupant, a poor renter, had his corn spread out on the bare ground in front of the *adobe*. He was glad to sell some but at the request to let me have some fodder he flinched. What I saw was all he had on hand, he explained. I told Inocencio to make the transaction.

"No matter how high the pullets roost," he quoted, "they'll come down for corn." He did not have to use a handful of "corn" to bring the fodder down.

The renter invited us in to share his house, but as it was occupied not only by his own family but by that of

259

another man who stood about, hardly thick enough for the wind to blow away, and as it consisted of but a single room, I declined. The walls, however, broke the wind. While Inocencio was watering the beasts and I was trying to build a fire out of twigs, the only fuel in the whole country, the woman of the house brought forth a stack of *tortillas*. I thought of one of those sayings about themselves the *gente pobre* have:

Where one can eat there is enough for two,
Where two can eat there is enough for three,
Where three can eat there is enough for four, etc.

The cold and the tediousness of riding so long a jaded horse had cramped my legs and my walk must have betrayed the fact. I heard the woman say something out of wrapped mouth to her husband. Then in a soft musical voice she asked me if I had rheumatism. I told her that I had something like it. Thereupon she suggested that I sleep with her *pelón* dog—the hairless dog, once quite common in northern Mexico and Texas but now rare. I had heard all my life how this dog's body absorbs pain out of a rheumatic lying against it, but this was the first time I had ever had an opportunity to test the efficacy of the *remedio*. Yet I hesitated. Then the woman assured me that, although she sometimes rented the dog, she was offering it to me free. Still I hesitated. I was to know that the dog was clean, she said, for after it had lain against any *reumático* whatsoever she always washed it. She said that the dog liked to sleep with people wrapped up in a blanket but that a hole must be left for its nose to breathe through. I finally swore that I had never had rheumatism and that it was too cold anyway to leave an opening in my blanket.

That night the *músico* sang ballads about Heraclio Bernal, who gave five hundred pesos to a poor family in the sierras, who killed ten *gachupines* in the mountains of Durango and ordered their skins tanned for boot leather, and who even when dead and in his coffin made all the mounted police and soldiers shake with fear. The *músico* sang about nearly all the other famous *bandidos* of his *país*. In fact, *tragedias* of desperate deeds and men made up most of his repertoire. It was the old, old story of the *valiente* on horseback. During a lull after a second ballad concerned with Pancho Villa, the little thin man of the house volunteered to his host, not to me, that Villa, "before he died," could never be put down because he had power to transform himself. One of Villa's own men had told him that on a certain field this general, hard-pressed, got down, slashed open the belly of a dead horse lying by, turned himself into an ant, and crawled into the cavity, there to await the going away of the enemy. Then he emerged and was his proper self again.

The next day Inocencio began recalling to me for the fortieth time the peace and prosperity of the land under Don Porfirio. I have known many old "Porfiristas," and now as I think of the matter they have all been quiet, honorable, kindly men. Inocencio was one of them.

CHAPTER

12

The Man of Goats

ON THE afternoon of the day before Christmas I sighted a *pastor* grazing a small-sized flock of goats alongside the trail in the direction we were traveling. Wrapped in his gray blanket, walking so slowly that he hardly seemed to walk at all, his eyes commercing with the ground, he looked like some holy hermit of the Middle Ages. As we drew even with him, he showed no curiosity or desire to communicate with his fellow beings. It was not until I had shouted to him a second time that he responded. Then while he saluted with his hat he looked away towards a half-dozen errant goats and with hissing maledictions threw a curved stick at them. It ricocheted along the ground to within a few feet of its target, but was deflected by a boulder.

"Why don't you use a sling?" I asked.

"Because," he replied, "after the stones I cast with

262

it had knocked out the eye of a nanny and broken the leg of a kid, my master forbade me to use it."

"Then you have a sling?"

For answer the shepherd reached under his blanket and pulled out a dead quail of the scaled variety—the *tostón*.

"It will never sing *tostón, tostón* again," he said solemnly, imitating the bird's cry.[1]

"Then the feast of *nochebuena* is assured," I remarked.

"The bird is yours, *señor*, and would there were two of them."

"Nevertheless," Inocencio interposed, "a sparrow in the hand is worth more than a vulture on the wing."

As I looked at this goat-herder more narrowly, he appeared cleaner than most of his kind I have known. There was a light in his eye. The snags in the legs of his blue denim breeches made by thorns of the "wait-a-little-while"[2] and other brush had been sewed up with strings from the Spanish dagger. The edges of his coarse gray blanket were all frazzled, but it was an honest blanket.

Then the man of goats informed me that "your little *jacal* is at your orders no more than a little way" on down the trail, beside a brush pen and a tank of water made by a dam across an arroyo. And, yes, the water was "very sweet." Riding on, I found it polluted by

---

[1] A *tostón* is a fifty-cent piece, and often the male bird does seem to say, very rapidly, that word. In fact, he speaks this Mexican locution—it is not Spanish—so perfectly that I always prefer calling his kind *Mexican* rather than *blue* quail.

[2] The catclaw, called in some parts of Mexico *uña de gato;* in other parts *gatuña;* and again *tantito* (a little while), abbreviated from *espérate un tantito* (wait a little while).

263

goats but drinkable, especially in the form of coffee or of tea made out of the *poleo* weed. A thicket of scrub mesquite made a good windbreak. I did not even look inside the thatched *jacalito*. As usual, there was no grass about the watering place. I directed Inocencio to take Durazno and the horses off about a mile and loose-hobble them. While he was doing this, the strong ammoniac odor emanating from the goat droppings all about the premises caused me to wonder if there might not be something to the Mexican belief that goats kept in a house will prevent the inhabitants from taking consumption.

Well before dark the *pastor* shut his herd up in the brush corral. He accepted gratefully my invitation to eat with us, and before long I discovered that he was more diffident than indifferent to human society. In reality he was starving for company, and having been fortified by some "little swallows" of *tequila*, many swallows of coffee, which he generously sweetened, an abundance of food, and a five-centavo packet of cigarettes, he became *muy compañero*. When I like a man, my nature goes out to him and warms him. Also it has been a constant observation of mine that goat-herders, commonly called ignorant, make much better company than scholarly Doctors of Philosophy. On this night and the next day and the next night, I dare say Toribio, for so the *pastor* had been christened, unlocked himself more freely than he had ever unlocked himself before and found more within himself to unlock than he had ever dreamed of possessing. "Here you are," he said once while we were talking, "stretched out on the ground before the fire as *corriente*—as common—as we are. Why should I not be free with you?"

He was not above fifty years in age. In contrast to the raucous voices that men of his occupation often develop from shouting to goats and listening to their metallic bleating, his was very soft. Not all his life had been spent out with them. As a boy he had lived in the great quadrangle of the hacienda La Babia, owned by General Treviño. Once he had a job in the quicksilver mines on the Río Grande and bought all the tobacco he wanted, but the *tunas* were very poor in that region; so about the time of the Revolution he left it, too homesick for the prickly pear apples of his own *país* to remain away from them longer. About every ten days his master brought him *frijoles*, salt, and ground corn to bake mixed with water, salt, and goat tallow, in a skillet—but no tobacco or coffee. The master also allowed him to kill a goat now and then for meat and tallow. Sometimes he lived at the ranch and herded out from it. During the biannual season of goat-kidding he had company.

In his camp he had a comical rooster and four comical little hens. One of them, minus tail-feathers that a coyote had pulled out, laid an egg every day, he said, and he presented me for my breakfast the last egg she had deposited. The fowls roosted in a coop of poles elevated on four posts.

With them was a female *paisano*, or road-runner, that Toribio had raised as a pet. He expected to get a cross between her and the game rooster that would result in a supreme fighting cock, high-leaping, quick, long-spurred, and fierce.

"Did you actually ever see a cross between a game chicken and one of these chaparral birds?" I asked.

"Why not?"

Now, although I have heard of such crosses and also

of other contra-biological crosses between chickens and *chachalacas* (Mexican grouse of the hot country), between sheep and hogs, between deer and goats, between *jabali* (peccary) and hogs, and even between dogs and human beings, I have never been able to see one. Perhaps it is because of their high regard for mules that the Mexican folk believe so strongly in phenomenal crossbreeds.

"What will you do with the fine game cock you are going to raise?" I asked.

"During Holy Week I shall be free, and then I shall take my wages and go to the *fiestas* at Sierra Mojada. Men have won as much as five hundred pesos on a *gallo*."

"Yes," I replied, "they have also lost all they had."

"It is according to the will of God."

"Certainly," put in Inocencio, "one cannot tell. 'Which *gallo* will win?' a gamester once asked the devil.

"'*Quién sabe?*' the devil answered. 'The two of them have knives.'"

Hardly more than an hour after dark the rooster crowed a squeaky, screechy, weak crow.

"Ah, how my little *gallo* loves to sing!" Toribio exclaimed. "Look you how early in the night he has begun. Perhaps a norther is coming."

Involuntarily, after the manner of men dependent upon the weather, we all looked into the sky. I arose to stretch my legs and to get a view away from the firelight.

"The Little Goats"—another name for the Pleiades, or Seven Sisters—"appear dim," Toribio announced.

"Don Federico," Inocencio asked me, "how many of the Little Goats are there?"

"I cannot count them," I said. "There are said to be

266

seven, but the astronomers claim they number many hundreds."

"There were seven before the Revolution," he returned. "Since then there are only six."

As all our eyes were turned to the once seven Cabrillas, a star of unusual brilliance shot across space. "May God guide it!" two voices murmured, to forfend its hitting the earth in disaster.

Again the *gallo* exulted with his piping voice.

"But you must listen to him when it is growing morning," Toribio said. He laughed to himself a soft, almost inaudible laugh. Then he ran to the chicken roost, caught the *gallo* by the body, and brought him to the fire. The fowl blinked a few times and summoned all his strength for another crow.

"*Gallo* of my bowels!" Toribio exulted, more to himself than to us.

"The fierce fighting cock sings even while held." Inocencio's pleasure in his own irony was plain.

"This one should sing especially well tonight," I commented.

"Yes, he will sing, '*Cristo nació! Cristo nació!*' (Christ is born!) Had Inocencio been a scholar he might have compiled a dictionary of animal polyglot; in that case, however, he would not have known what the *animalitos* say. "But out here," he went on, "we cannot attend any *Misa de Gallo*."[1]

"A long time ago," and I knew from the tone of his voice that the man of goats was remembering a story, "so the old ones tell, there was here in this country, but farther to the west in the mountains, a village of Indians that used to send runners out very early every morning

[1] Literally, Cock's Mass; Midnight Mass.

to bring in the sun. These morning-makers were young men. They would start out of the village about the time the Star of the Pastor was coming up and run to the east. Then they would run back to the village singing. Then they would run to the east again and back, and thus keep on running and singing until at last the sun came up and began following them home. Every morning, every morning of the world, they must trail out; thus those who had passed before had done.

"Finally a stranger came to the village to spend the night. He was a man very clever and cunning and astute. I suspect he was a Spaniard. Before the first light he heard the *mañaneros* singing, and he went out of his *jacal* and saw them running.

"Why do you run and sing so in the morning?" he asked of them after the sun was up.

"'Oh,' they answered, 'we are the morning-makers. We run and sing to bring the sun. If we did not run to the east and welcome it and coax it, it would never get here. We have to bring in the sun every little morning in the world.'

"This sharp stranger laughed at the Indians. 'There is no use of all this bother,' he said. 'I have a little animal that brings in the sun better than all you morning-makers can bring it.'

"'And what is this little animal?' they asked the sharp stranger.

"'It is the one who sang to Saint Peter,' he answered. 'It is called the *gallo*.'

"The Indians all wanted to see and hear this *gallo*. So the sharp stranger told them that if they would show him a vein of silver, he would present them with the little animal and then they would never again have to get up so early and run for the sun. They agreed to show the vein of silver if the *gallo* was as good as represented. Then the stranger went off. In about a month he came back with the *gallo*.

"That night only the children slept. All sat up to watch the *gallo* bring in the sun. About ten o'clock he crowed. Then about midnight. Then at three o'clock, then again at four. The Guide Star was leading the Star of the Pastor up into the sky, and now the morning-makers were becoming very restless. For what if they did not bring in the sun? and what if the *gallo* could not bring it in? and what if there were no sun? But the cunning stranger held the runners back with promises and assurances. He swore that if the *gallo* did not bring the sun, his own life was in their hands. Then the *gallo* crowed very loud and the first light came into the east. There was the sun.

"This was a marvelous thing. Showing him with both hands—willingly—the Indians led the cunning stranger to a very rich vein of silver. After that the *mañaneros* did not have to get up early any more. All they had to do was to listen to the *gallo* and go back to sleep. Since then there have always been *gallos* in the country and the sun has always risen after their calls in the morning. Nobody in the world loves the *gallo* more than we people who have descended from the Indians."

"Yes," Inocencio pronounced judgment, "I am sure the cunning stranger was a Spaniard, and this *cuento* proves very well the truth of the old saying that a Spaniard against a native-born is like a hawk against a chicken."

A sporadic gust of wind blew a whirl of dust composed

largely of powdered goat droppings into our midst, and I sneezed.

"Jesús!" said Inocencio.[1]

"Jesús!" iterated Toribio.

"Thanks," I said. "The weather is going to change."

"That ring around the moon so signifies," the *pastor* gestured.

"There are always signs and signs," I deprecated, "but tell me frankly which of all the animals is most astute in forecasting the weather?"

"Perhaps the coyote," answered Toribio. "*Quién sabe?*"

"Perhaps," agreed Inocencio.

"But you know," I led on, "how the burro predicted the storm better than the campful of *científicos* with all their instruments."

"That is a *cuento* that has lost its jest," Inocencio said. "Still, with his head and his tail both, the burro has sagacity."

"Yes," Toribio agreed, "the burro is a sage. His *cruzada*"—the stripe on his withers crossing that down his back—"is a sign. Yet the coyote—he was once the dog of the devil."

"I did not know that," I answered. "What is the history?"

"*Es una cosa de pastor,*" he replied.

"Yes, so is Christmas a matter pertaining to *pastores*, and so is the oldest play regularly acted in America."

A man may appreciate a compliment without alto-

---

[1] This form of exclamation—the abbreviation of a prayer—following a sneeze is said to have originated in Spain centuries ago during a deadly pestilence—probably influenza—the victims of which were seized with violent fits of sneezing.

gether comprehending it. Anyhow, the story accounting for the sagacity of the coyote came forth.

In the beginning of the world before man was here, Dios had a great flock of sheep that he herded himself. At the same time el Diablo had a great flock of goats that he herded. Their camping grounds were in the same valley close to each other, and every day each *pastor* had to take his flock over a mountain pass and down into a cañon for water. To help him with the sheep God had some shepherd dogs, such as we have now; the devil had for his shepherds some coyotes. These coyotes were well trained, always ready. The voice of their master was law to them. They never molested the goats, but protected them. Now, because goats are more hardy than sheep and have more *ánimo*, they nearly always strung in to the water ahead of the sheep.

One day the great Dios said to el Diablo: "This earth was not made for you; it was not even made for me. It was made for Christians called men. I am going to bring them here so that they can have flocks and cultivate the ground and live content. I want to buy out your goats and give them to men."

"No," said el Diablo, "I am very contented here and have no will to dispossess myself."

"But," said Dios, "these men and you cannot get along on the same range. We must come to an agreement in some way."

"Very well then," el Diablo replied, and he had a cunning grin on his face. "I will make a proposition by which either I will get out and leave to you the whole range with all my goats and your sheep, or you will get out and leave me the range with your sheep as well as my goats."

271

"All right," said Dios. "Every individual for his own saint and every spider for his own web. What do you propose?"

"Thus," replied el Diablo. "In the morning we will start for the water in the cañon at the same time, each with his herd and his dogs, and the one who gets there first will have both the sheep and goats."

"I agree," said Dios.

And to make the agreement binding each crossed himself and each took a hair from the beard of the other and kept it.

"Of course," said Dios, "with the tail goes the ewe. As a result, if you win, you will have my shepherd dogs to guard the sheep, and if I win I will have your shepherd coyotes to guard the goats."

"No, I cannot say about that," responded el Diablo. "These coyotes have heads of their own. They obey me, but I speak not for them. They answer others for themselves. If you win the goats, you will have to ask the coyotes if they will change masters."

"*Ándale!*" Inocencio put in at this point. "Now we are going to see how the devil walks free after midnight."

Early next morning, while the two flocks were coming out of the corrals and pointing towards the mountain pass, Dios caused a very heavy fog to descend. It was so thick that neither of the *pastores* could see the lead animal of his flock. Nevertheless the sheep kept going straight for the pass. But it is the nature of goats not to travel in a fog or mist, and now they did nothing but mill around. El Diablo cursed them and the coyote shepherds sat on their tails and howled as if it were going to rain. An hour later when Dios got into the saddle of the mountain he caused the fog to lift. He

272

looked back, and there el Diablo with his goats was still at the corral. Dios saw them start in a trot, but long before they reached the summit, he had his sheep watered and grazing on the grass beside the little river.

When el Diablo arrived he was exploding with *corajes* like a firecracker Judas on the Saturday of Glory. But he had lost and he immediately gave possession of the goats.

"I want the coyote shepherds too," said Dios.

"I told you," said el Diablo, "that I could not guarantee them. Speak to them yourself."

Then el Diablo gave a whistle that brought the coyotes towards the two *pastores*. They came slinking up, moving as easily as shadows of buzzards on green mesquite grass and looking out of their yellow eyes in that evasive way they have to this time, so that the eye of no man can catch their gaze any more than his hand can grasp the wings of a cloud. Then they sat on their rumps in half a circle.

"My coyotes," spoke el Diablo, "this Señor Dios has by a trick won all the herd of goats, and I must abandon the range. He wants you to remain as shepherds with him."

"No," said the coyotes, "we have but one master and that is el Diablo."

Then said Dios, "It is not I you will be serving. The owners of the flocks will be men living in these lands. I am going to put men on earth and they will be masters of all. Those creatures like the sheep and the goats and the good shepherd dogs that serve men and obey will be cared for. Those that do not serve and obey will be regarded as enemies and will have the hand of all men against them. Remember this before you decide."

273

But, no, the coyotes would not listen to reason, and when el Diablo left the goats, they went away too. Instead of remaining as guardians, they became the most depredating beasts of prey the goats know. And the men whom Dios put on earth saw that these coyotes were enemies, and they have always pursued them and killed them.

"Next to God," the *pastor* concluded, "the coyote is the most astute animal in all the world."

"Yes, he is as cunning as an eagle with his shoes off," Inocencio agreed.

"He is more sage than the fox on the *llano*," the *pastor* continued. "When he sings on the hill in the morning after the sun is up instead of down in the valley before daylight, he is speaking of the rain to come."

"That is a belief and nothing more," Inocencio now disagreed. "The coyote howls when he is empty and he howls when he is full, and he is a liar at all times. As for these *cuentos* about the coyote, there are as many as an ox has hairs. Nevertheless, as has been said, he is very sagacious. I knew a householder whose chickens slept in some mesquites inside a corral of solid adobe walls. The gate opening into it was solid and it was always kept shut. There was a hole, a very small hole, in the wall even with the ground, and through it the chickens went in and out.

"Well, one night a coyote got through the hole. He always has a hungry nose. As is well known, this animal can sit under a chicken roost and point his nose up and flash his eyes and after a while the chicken will fall into his teeth. In the same manner he can run round and round barking under wild turkeys in a tree and thus cause them to become drunk and fall out.

"*Bueno*, when the householder went out in the morning to look at his chickens, of three of them he found nothing but the feathers. Then he ordered a *criado* to put a rock in the hole every night so that the coyote could not again enter. The *criado* put the rock every night for a long while, but one night he forgot it.

"The morning following, the householder went out as usual to inspect all his little animals. There in the corral the ground was covered with feathers, with chickens without any heads, and with heads without any chickens. It was a barbarity. And there over in a corner was the assassin swelled up like the heated bladder of a hog. His legs were sticking straight out, his mouth was open, and all else was in the manner of an animal that is well dead from having been herbed. It was in the time of summer and the hide was of no value. The man thought, 'This coyote filled his stomach so full he could not pass out through the little hole in the wall and then he died from something wrong in his system.'

"He called a boy to drag the creature away. The boy came and gave the body some kicks and tied a rope on its hind legs and went dragging it over rocks and gullies and through little thorn bushes. He dragged it something like a hundred *pasos*. The man was standing watching him all the while. Then the boy stopped. 'Take it farther still,' the man yelled to him, 'so that it will not stink to us.' Then the boy went on a distance farther. He took the rope off the legs and gave the body some more kicks and started back to the house.

"The man was still watching. When the boy was halfway back, the man saw the coyote raise up his ears and then his head. All was safe. He leaped to his feet

275

and galloped off into the brush. The coyote can play dead better than a 'possum. He is *muy astuto, muy diablo.*"

Whether the stimulating effect of ammonia ultimately becomes soporific or not, I cannot say; I know that in Toribio's goat camp I slept more soundly than a dead coyote. In good time the scrannel-voiced *gallo* properly inducted the sun to the eastern edge of its race course.

"I hope you slept with *gusto.*" Inocencio expressed himself according to his matutinal wont.

"With much *gusto,*" I replied, "but it seems to me that I have the taste of goats on my tongue."

"*Naturalmente,*" he replied with a humor that often left me uncertain as to how far it was conscious. "As our fathers taught us, he who sleeps on a *petate*[1] may expect to get up belching straw."

My special breakfast of a spitted Mexican quail basted with goat tallow and one egg *a caballo*—that is to say "on horseback," or "fried in water"—took the taste away.

And now Toribio directed me to look at the gathering "sheep in the sky" overhead and at "that *vaca* in the northwest." I saw the "sheep"—a mackerel sky—and a truly dark "cow" was banking in the northwest. Moreover, Toribio called my attention to the fact that some coyotes were "singing" on the hills. "And look," he exclaimed, "at my goats, how they are jumping about and sneezing. Goats always know about the weather."

In short, I had better not travel, for the cold *norte* was going to blow the world inside out, the rain descend

[1] A mat woven of the fiber of yucca leaves or reeds.

in torrents, and God only knew what other phenomena of the elements break loose.

"*Bueno*," Inocencio commented, while he scoured a tin plate with ashes, "he who gets wet in the morning has leisure in which to dry himself."

However, I hastened to inform my company-loving *pastor* friend that while I was not afraid of the wind, which was imminent, and while I could not think it would rain at this season of the year unless the old Indian sign appeared, "Black all around and pouring down in the middle," I had resolved not to spend Christmas Day traveling as if it were any other day but stay in his camp and respect it like a Christian.

In fact, the norther brought no rain, but as it bolted onward—hurling in its van a solid wall of cloud, fringe-lashed and of inky blackness, somehow gathered out of the welkin of aridity, at the same time sucking up and driving before it curtains, whirls, gulfs of dust and sand —it appeared ominous enough to make any sentient soul upon the vast desert, the Bolsón de Mapimí, over which it was sweeping, conscious of the utterness of unrelieved solitude. For many minutes before it arrived we could mark its rushing race towards us, and as it drew nearer, its roar was like that of some hurricane-driven surf about to break over the shore line of a continent and devour it. The low sun in the southeast turned to that redness which in Spanish is called Blood of Christ. The sky held colors of yellow and saffron and orange and gold—all dust. This was not the "wind of eternity" which Thomas de Quincey heard soughing through the chamber of death. It was the wind that blew between the poles when the earth was void and before God had set the planets in their spheres.

While it was yet a long way off, Toribio ran to his *jacalito* and brought out on his shoulders a kind of waterproof cape thatched from the fibrous leaves of the yucca commonly called beargrass. Then he seized my butcher knife and fell upon his knees, making signs in the air as if to "cut" the storm cloud, at the same time calling out, "In the shadow of San Pedro, O Hermit of the Pastores," and reciting over and over this prayer:

> "*O Holy Mother of San Juan,*
> *With infinite power thine,*
> *Deliver me from this bad hour,*
> *The guilt of which is not mine.*"

He dashed to the ash pile, gathered ashes, strewed them upon the ground in the form of two great crosses, side by side. Then he stood and kneeled between these crosses while he "cut" the air and prayed. I saw Inocencio, too, cross himself. Then I could see nothing, although I heard my old *mozo's* invocation, "Praised be the sweet names of Jesus, Mary, and Joseph."

But the end of the world had not come. Within an hour the ten thousand lashing whips of the air were laid, the brunt of the sandstorm was past, and the wind became but a steadily diminishing gale. The air was sharply cold, though. Of course the wretched *jacal* had no chimney, but a fire built in a nook of the brush made it as comfortable as any room. I noted the perfected art with which my companions shifted the ends of their *jorongos*, or blankets, draped about them so as to get the heat underneath without drawing up smoke. I threw into the fire what few *pastores* would burn—a branch of the "accursed *junco*," the leafless "all-thorn"

278

bush—"accursed" because, according to the belief of
the bleak land in which it grows, it afforded *the* crown
of thorns, and "now the butcher bird is the only bird
that will alight on it."

About ten o'clock Toribio announced that he was
going to turn his goats out and let the dog care for
them. Tomorrow, though, he said, the raw hard *mata
cabras*—"kills goats"—would blow from the southeast
and he would have to keep his eye on every poor
nanny. I went to the corral with him to pick out a kid,
which he said he had "license" to sell, and for the
roasted flesh of which I felt a strong "exposition." Also
I craved a *macho*—a "mule,"—which consists of the
fatty intestines of a goat or sheep looped and tied into
a knot and roasted on coals. The "animal manna"—
fat and lean "blending into one ambrosian result"—
which Charles Lamb found in pig crackling, never sur-
passed the *macho* ineffably delicate in its deliciousness
that Inocencio turned for the apex of my Christmas
dinner there by the goat herder's camp.

I observed that some of the goats had pieces of black
rope tied around their necks and that several others
were wearing coyote skulls on rope collars. The black
collars had been "cured" in some sort of preparation
supposed to repel the ever-preying coyotes. The skulls
would make them wary too, but they had probably
been tied around the animals' necks in the beginning
to heal them of screw worms.

When the herd was turned out, a blue-colored nanny,
bleating lustily, rushed headlong for the *jacal*, and there,
continuing to bleat and turning round and round, waited
for the *pastor* to come. He gave her some bits of cold,
hard *tortilla* to eat and then milked her, all the while

talking to her. This was his pet, Sancha by name. In idleness, for I was familiar with the tradition of goat-sucking among *pastor* folk, I asked him why he bothered with a cup.

"The milk will be good with the coffee," he answered.

Then a little later, when we were back at the fire and alone, for Inocencio had gone to see about the horses, I took up the subject again.

"*Señor*," he said after a while, "we *pastores* are very ignorant, very simple. I will tell you something. When I was only a few days old I was left an orphan. Some poor people took me. They had nothing to give me but goat milk. That was enough. When I was just a few months old, they turned me over to a gentle nanny in exchange for her little kids, which they ate. She gave plenty of milk and before long she was so well-trained that when I cried she would come and bring her teats within reach of my hands and mouth. If I slept late in the morning, she would nose me to be sucked. She licked me with her tongue as if I were her own kid. When she went dry, another goat was found for me.

"Of course I learned to eat *frijoles* and *tortillas*, but after I became old enough to follow the goats in company with the dog, often I did not get enough to eat. My people were very poor. Then I would suck whatever goat had plenty of milk. An old *castrao* (a castrated male goat) in this bunch was my special friend. On hot days I would get sleepy and lie down anywhere. When I awoke, that *castrao* would be lying down on one side of me and the dog on the other; but perhaps my herd would not be in sight. I could not tell where they had gone. Coyotes do not molest much in the heat of the day, else the dog could not have stayed with me. Then

280

I would mount the back of the *castrao*, the dog would put his nose to the ground and trot ahead, and thus I would find the animals."

The blue-colored Sancha continued to sniff and nibble around the camp until I told Toribio that if he did not chunk her away she might become permanently motionless.

"I do not think any more of her," he said, complying, "than the brother in the *cuento* thought of his pet goat."

"How was that?"

"One time," he answered, accepting a fresh packet of cigarettes, "there was a man who had a flock of goats and two sons. He died, leaving to the first born a mare, two rooms of the house, and four fig trees; to the other he willed one room of the house, a burro, and two fig trees. The goats he left to be divided between them equally. The younger of the sons was the *pastor* and he did all the work. The other was always riding around, dancing at the *bailes*, racing his mare, and playing monte.

"Now, this *pastor* had a pet among the goats, a *pinto* named Sancho, and he thought more of him than he did of his own stomach. The *pinto* liked the *pastor*'s company better than that of the other goats and was always with him or the dogs. He even slept with the *pastor*, and he tried to scratch his fleas in the manner of the dogs. He did not consider himself a goat at all.

"After a while the *pastor* became tired of doing all the work, and one day he said to his brother, '*Hermano*, let us divide the goats.'

"'Why not?' the older brother replied. 'But, *hermanito*, how shall we divide them?'

"'Well,' the *pastor* answered, 'we will divide them

according to the manner of our ancestors. I will go into the house out of the way. You will go into the corrals and cut the bunch into two parts.'

"'Just so,' said the elder brother. 'Then we will take the knuckle bone of a goat and throw dice with it to see which has first choice.'

"'No,' the younger brother objected, 'after you have made the division, I will come out and choose for myself whichever part I like best. That is the old way and it is the just way.'

"'Yes,' the older brother agreed, 'it is the old way and it is the just way.'

"'Then the *pastor* went into the house and the older brother went to the corrals. He put all the goats into one pen. Then he put Sancho into a separate pen. Then he picked out the best goat there was and put him into another pen. Then he picked out the runtiest little goat there was, a broken-legged, gotch-eared thing, and put it with Sancho. Then he picked out another beautiful goat and put it with the first choice. So he went on putting into one pen all the fat, young healthy goats and the most fertile, thrifty nannies, and in the other with Sancho all the cripples and all the poor and all the nannies with udders spoiled by the *cinturón*[1] and those with bad teeth and others too old to live through the next winter, and everything else that was worthless. At last the goats were all divided, exactly the same number in each pen.

"Then he called, '*Hermanito*, I am ready. Come and choose.'

---

[1]The *cinturón* is a kind of beetle known by "people of reason" to be harmless but believed by *pastores* to be devilishly fond of biting goat udders and thus causing ulcers.

"The *pastor* brother came out. He looked in one pen and he saw all the fine goats. He looked in the other and there he saw Sancho, who was calling to him. He saw also the creatures with Sancho. For a long time he looked at first one pen and then the other.

"At last he spoke. 'Sancho,' he said, 'I love you a great deal, but you are in the wrong company for me. I will take the other pen.'

"Thus the big brother showed that he did not understand all there is to know about *pastores*."

When along in the afternoon the dog brought the goats all safely in, I asked Toribio how he had succeeded in making this helper so efficient.

"As always," he merely replied.

However, since people do not know the "always" method of training Mexican shepherd dogs, I shall explain it. In the first place, they are almost never of a shepherd breed, but mongrels. This one of Toribio's was of a sable hue running into saffron, somewhat the color of a Mexican swallow, and hence called Golondrina. On his forehead he bore the scar of a burn in the shape of a cross, showing that he had been cured of a rattlesnake bite. He could outgrin a Cheshire cat but would allow no human hand to touch him.

To make a true *pastor* dog, the Mexican takes a pup before its eyes are well opened and delivers him to a nanny goat from which her new-born kids have been removed. At first she must be held and forced to allow the puppy to suck. Gradually she adopts the pup and it devotedly adopts her. Sometimes his sharp claws pressed against her udder hurt, but she docilely submits. In time he can follow her with the herd, and often he learns to steal milk from other nannies. He grows up thinking he is a goat, but at the same time asserting his canine antagonism for coyotes and other predatory animals. He not only protects the goats but learns to keep them together and to direct their course. He seldom barks, going about his business very quietly.

After all, the range of a *pastor's* talk cannot be very wide, however intensive on some subjects his knowledge may be—on brush as a forage, on the weather, always the weather, on goat psychology, and the ways of *pastor* dogs. Yet now and then the fullness of a *pastor's* knowledge in this restricted field reminds one of the old admonition to "beware the man of one book."

Toribio asked if I knew how to tell which months of the year have more than thirty days. Then he instructed me in the manner familiar to Mexican children. The left hand is closed, and, beginning on the knuckle of the little finger, the months are counted off, the long ones falling always *up* on the knuckle joints and the short ones *down* in the depressions between the knuckles. Thus, January is up on the knuckle of the little finger; February is down in the depression next it; March is on the second knuckle, April in a depression, May on the third knuckle, June in a depression, July on the knuckle of the index finger; now, going back to the knuckle of the little finger—for the thumb does not come into the count—for the long month of August, the up-and-down system continues patly until December terminates on the knuckle of the middle finger.

Like many other shepherds of the fields and like some *rancheros*, Toribio could compute by the *epacta* (epact) the phases of the moon months ahead; but his mastery of the *cabañuelas*—a method of prognosticating the weather for a whole year by observing and averaging that of the 31 days of January—is not so common. Properly, the *cabañuelas* comprise only the first 24 days of January; the next 6 days are the *pastores;* then the last day, January 31, is the *canícula*, although for other purposes the *días de canícula* (dog days) come in July and August. A diagram is necessary.

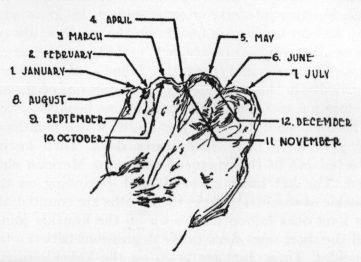

4. APRIL
3. MARCH
2. FEBRUARY
1. JANUARY
8. AUGUST
9. SEPTEMBER
10. OCTOBER
5. MAY
6. JUNE
7. JULY
12. DECEMBER
11. NOVEMBER

Two by two, as may be seen, the first 24 days of January are linked into twelve units representing the twelve months of the year. To exemplify, the averaged weather of the 2nd and 23rd days of January prognosticates the prevailing weather of the 2nd month of the year, February; that of the 3rd and 22nd days determines the weather of the 3rd month of the year, and so on.

But such averaging is not fine enough. In addition to the prognostications supplied by the *cabañuelas* must be taken into account the weather of *los pastores.* The 6 days comprising the *pastores* are divided each into quarters, making a total of 24 quarter-days. In the same

285

manner that the 24-day units of *las cabañuelas* are linked, so are the 24 quarter-day units of the *pastores* linked. Now the prognostication for February will be based on the averaged weather not only of the 2nd and

23rd-day units of *las cabañuelas* but also of the 2nd and 23rd quarter-day units of *los pastores*.

But still not enough elements have entered into the calculation. To be absolutely accurate in prognosticating, one must take into consideration the *canícula*— the last day of January. As the 24-day units of the *cabañuelas* and also as the 24 quarter-day units of the *pastores* are paired and employed, so the 24-hour units of *la canícula* must be taken into consideration and the weather of each pair of hours averaged with the weather of each of the corresponding pairs of days and quarter-days.

Compared with the simple old English folk method of taking the first twelve days of January to prognosticate roughly the weather of the twelve corresponding months of the year, the *cabañuelas* appear very complicated.

I do not know any exhibition of memory more wonderful than that of a *pastor* at kidding time. There may be many hundreds of nannies in a bunch, all white and all about the same age, looking to an unpracticed eye as much alike as so many grains of corn. Five or six hundred of them, perhaps more, will drop kids within sixty hours, a majority giving birth to twins. At first these nannies recognize their offspring only through smell. As soon as one has dropped her kids, the *pastor* or one of his helpers stakes them by means of a cord, one end of which is tied to a foot and the other end to a peg, right at the spot where they were born. They must not rub against other kids and thus mix scents. During the day the nannies are herded out; when they arrive at the *majada* in the late afternoon, many of them cannot locate their kids. The *pastores*, though, know each nanny by sight, by the sound of her voice, or by something hardly definable; they remember where this or that nanny's kids are staked and take her to them. Every day the cords have to be changed on the feet of the kids to prevent sores. During the three or four days while the nannies are kidding, the *pastores* sleep hardly at all.

The time of goat gestation being known—five months less five days—and the lecherous habits and potency of the billy goats being invariably dependable—one of them is capable of serving fifty or more nannies within twenty-four hours of time—the billy goats are placed with the nannies on a date so that the kidding will come in the light of the moon. Any *pastor* can tell what phase the moon will be in five months hence. There are usually two crops of kids a year. It is curious to see at castration time a *pastor* pulling out the little testicles of the male kids with his teeth. He sterilizes old billy goats by deftly twisting, without any incision, their testicles up in their flanks, there to atrophy.

For the *pastor* to know goats, dogs, and weather is not enough. He must know the brush. For instance, he knows that the *coyotillo* bush will, if they graze upon it, give his goats the creeps. Again he knows that although the red berries and the green leaves on the *guayacán* are alike harmless, yet the limbs of the bush grow a stubby thorn that pricks the snouts of goats grazing on it and causes sores; he knows too that the *guayacán* is about the last of the bushes just before spring to shed its leaves and that when all other brush is leafless, goats will hunt this. So he must herd them away from it; however, if despite him they get sore noses from eating on it, he directs them so that they cannot possibly get the "milk" of *golondrina* weed in the sores, for then the sores would become very bad. Many a *pastor* can give lessons in folk botany to the wisest old woman herbalist.

Despite his stock of curious lore, the Mexican goatherder will always be considered as possessing the lowest form of human intelligence recognizable outside of

insane asylums and as following the most contemptible
occupation known to civilization. I write not to contradict notions. The things and methods to which the
name of *pastor* is commonly applied show how essentially he belongs to the soil. A loop cast in the shape of
a figure 8 so that it catches an animal by the head and
front feet is called *mangana de pastor;* a certain simple
but secure hitch for fastening a pack on a mule is called
amarrado (tie-knot) *de pastor*. The Morning Star is the
Star of the Pastor. The fattest goat in the flock—the
goat that any shepherd would be likely to pick for his
own eating—is the *cabra de pastor*. Meat cooked over
the coals is roasted *al pastor*. An unusually large *gorda*—
a corn-cake filled with beans, meat, rice, or some other
ingredient—is a *gorda de pastor*. In the north country,
bread—usually of corn meal, water, and salt, with sometimes tallow—mixed in the skillet in which it is cooked
is *pan de pastor*. If one lies down by the campfire, particularly on the side that the smoke comes towards, he
is on the *lado* (side) *del pastor*.

Nearly anything of the *campo* is likely to be *al* or
de pastor; a tuft of grass or some leafy branches laid
to put meat and bread upon is a *mantel* (tablecloth)
de pastor; moss used to wipe clean a machete blade, a
dish, or one's mouth becomes a *servilleta* (napkin) *de
pastor*. A certain weed (Acalypha phleoides Cav.) the
solution of which is used to cure wounds and boils is
the *yerba del pastor*. Another weed (Turnera diffusa
Willd.), widely known as an aphrodisiac, is the *pastor-
cita*, or herb of the *pastora*. Again pin-grass, or alfilaria
(Erodium cicutarium), said to have been imported from
Europe but now naturalized over much of Mexico and
the Southwest and used as a *remedio* for sore throats,

is known as the *pastor's* needle. In short, anything or anyone rude, primitive, is *muy pastor*, and to say of a person that with him it is "One peso in hand, one goat counted out" implies that, like Bobo Pastor in old Spanish comedy, he cannot compute beyond one and one. Nevertheless, it is granted that "every one in his own business is king"—and, just as not all who whistle are *arrieros*, "only the *pastor* can trim the goat's head correctly" and *tatemar* it (cook it in the ground) exactly right.

As on the second morning we were preparing to set out, I asked Toribio how it was that, loving company so well, he could live so much time in isolation.

"I like to live in silence," he answered. Then he added, "Come here, please, for a little minute."

I followed him a short distance, and there on a flat limestone he pointed out, carved into the soft rock, the design for playing the game of "The Coyote and the Goats." It is an old, old game that has gone by many names. I have seen the geometric lines over which it is played carved in the steps to the bell tower of a church by Lake Chapala, in the shadow of bluffs over water where the women of Guanaceví in Durango state come to wash clothes, on the mud-baked *patio* of a *jacal* deep in the jungles of Sinaloa, in the insect-tracked sands under the feet of a deserted dead man hanging from the limb of a huisache tree against the fringe of a treeless desert in Zacatecas, and finally in front of the cottage of a Basque shepherd amid the Pyrenees of Spain. In this game twelve "goats" try to pen the "coyote," which meantime tries to "eat them up." Children play the game with pebbles; I like best to play it with red *frijoles* for the goats and a single pebble for the coyote.

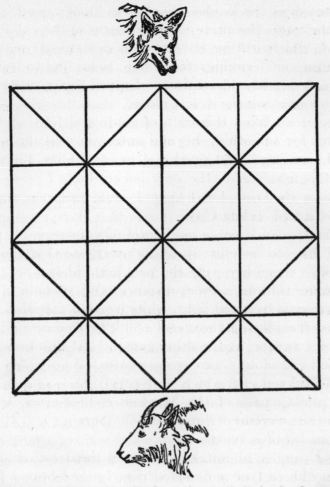

For more than "a little minute" I looked at the design to which Toribio pointed.

"If I am lonesome," he explained, "I can play *solitario*."

About the stones were numerous charred ends of sotol and Spanish dagger stalks, showing how the solitary player had lighted his evening game. His "coyote" was a small rock gleaming with "fool's gold"; his "goats" were the agate-hard red beans of the mountain laurel, which will lie for years on dry ground without sprouting or decaying, and which, according to legend, originated from blood-drops dripped by a wounded warrior crossing the desert alone.

Because I liked this man of goats and felt indebted to him for something beyond entertainment, even beyond a willingness to give his all in hospitality, I handed him "as a *recuerdo*" the only pocket knife I possessed. It was a good one, but I knew I could soon procure another in Chihuahua City.

"And as an humble testimony of your servant, take this," he said in reply, speaking quietly so that Inocencio, who was busy with the packing, did not hear. At the same time he drew from his clothes a chain of ten links carved from the light, white wood of the *jaboncillo*, or desert willow. At one end a link hooked around the tail of a coyote; at the other end the last link grew out of the head of another coyote, whose tail projected into a graceful spike on which were carved the eagle, snake, and prickly pear of the Mexican coat-of-arms. I still keep the souvenir—along with the onza's claw. It is a curious bit of carving.

As I went to mount, this *pastor* of the desert held my stirrup like a true *mozo del estribo*, for had he not been at the Hacienda la Babia when it was the court of a principality? Then he seized my left hand, the hand on his side, and put his ugly lips to it.

I see him now as I first saw him and again as I last saw him when I turned from the cutting *mata cabras* that was blowing from the southeast for a parting glance. He was moving off slow, slow so slow that he hardly seemed to move at all, behind the goats, wrapped in blanket of gray, a gourd of water slung over his left shoulder, a curved stick in his right hand, his eyes on the ground, for all the centuries the image of some holy hermit of the Middle Ages.

I saw Inocencio glance also. Then I heard—words spoken as much to himself as to me probably, "The goat has an instinct for the brush. . . . He who was born to be a gourd will never become a *jícara*"—a half gourd used as a dipper or other vessel, and in the past often beautifully lacquered.

"I hear you, Inocencio," I said. "In your own idiom, is it the huisache's fault that it was born on the prairie?"

There was silence for a while. Then the philosopher spoke: "True, master, and if being poor were a blot, my own skin would be *pinto* all over. They say that for the poor in this world Justice rides a burro and the Judge goes afoot."

At this I showed Inocencio the carved chain and coyotes.

Without much interest beyond that motivated by politeness, he granted, "It seems that also the *pastor* has his intelligence. As the *mozo* said to his master after he got the loaded burro across the *barranca*, 'Every king to his own kingdom.'"

CHAPTER 13

Adiós

Came the last supper on the desert. Inocencio made the *pan de pastor* out of cornmeal and I fried the remainder of a venison ham. A can of water boiled with a chunk of *piloncillo* turned into savory syrup. Raw onions balanced the diet. *Gracias a Dios* for solid food and an appetite to enjoy it.

Inocencio put the *"novia"* by my side under the cover and said, "Until morning," and I answered back, "If God so wishes." Then, as pulling the tarpaulin over my head, I shut out the vision of the Little Goats and the Three Marys going across the sky and with the munching of horses in my ears began accumulating the warmth that brings sleep, I felt regret that the morrow's night would find us at Sierra Mojada, whence a train runs to Chihuahua City.

There the good old man who had served me so well and I must part, he to go back, I to go on. And there we did part, not without ceremonies and not without counsels. He had always heard, he said, that the *gente* in the Sierra Madre of Chihuahua were "shameless ones" and now that I was going among them I could not have too much care and alertness, for "the fish that sleeps is swept away by the current." I did not remind the counselor of what he knew well, that the Sierra Madre of Chihuahua was already trodden ground to me.

In this village of dead mines we had found a *mesón* at the intersection of the streets placarded as "16 de Septiembre" and "Venustiano Carranza y No Reelección." I was spending the last half hour of the day's sunlight sitting in the corral for the pleasure of watching my beasts enjoy their corn, which was poured on some sacks, while Inocencio guarded the hogs and chickens away. "Thus the eyes of the master fatten the horse," he said facilely.

"Perhaps," he added, "it is your wish that I seek a buyer for the animals, as you cannot take them with you."

"We will settle that in the morning," I replied.

"If God lends life."

The disposition of Durazno and the horses was already settled in my mind, but I said nothing further on the subject.

"And now, my master and my friend," Inocencio went on, "because you have been frank with me and because you will understand and because after God you are next with me, I am going to tell you something that has a truth in it. Perhaps you will recall it when you go among strangers and will, as we say, remember to put on your *guaraches* before treading thorny ground.

You are instructed; I am ignorant. Yet I am well burned with the years, and as it is truly said, 'The *tuna* that has been pecked is the one that knows best about birds.' Faces we see, hearts no. A man among foreign ones cannot be too distrustful."

No Laertes could other than assent to such a deferential Polonius. It was evident that the old man had been preening himself for something special.

"*Bueno*," he continued, "one time a young *charro* who wished to travel into the world was presented by his father with a fine *palomino* horse that trod nothing but the pure air, his mane of silk curling into waves at every step, his ears alert every minute, and his bottom as deep as his *ánimo* was high; also with a new saddle, the horn inlaid with a hundred pieces of lucent woods and the leather parts ornamented with little alligators, a silver-plated bridle, spurs that rang like bells, a beautiful Saltillo *sarape* that water could not go through and as bright as the rainbow, *sombrero* embroidered all over with horseshoes and eagles, *chaparreras* on which the silver weighed as much as the leather, an eight-ply reata in which the rawhide strands were plaited as smoothly as the strains of a waltz, a thirty-thirty rifle of radiant blue—everything new, beautiful, and *muy fino*. He was fitted out like a twenty-four.

"So he went riding away looking at his shadow and singing for another reason than to scare away sorrows. And within himself this young man was as bright and sound as he was without. He had no tail for anybody to step upon, and he wore his hat *a media cabeza*.[1]

[1]When a man can wear his hat *a media cabeza*, pushed back on his head, he has nothing to hide; he looks the world in the face with clean conscience, with pride; he is independent and owes nobody anything. The

Only he was without experience and expected to find the bounty of God wrapped in a *tortilla*.

"Then at a gate in the mountains overlooking a valley of fields, the young *charro* met an old man driving a burro loaded with roasting ears. As to fatness, this burro looked like the horse that died just as he was learning how not to eat.

"'*Buenos días*,' the *charro* said.

"'*Buenos días, caballero*, and how do you find yourself?'

"'Well, well. Three rocks and one tick.'

"'Thanks be to God,' the old man said. 'And my heart, that is a fine outfit you have. Would you let me look at your lovely new rifle in its beautifully stamped scabbard?'

"'Why not?' the young man answered. 'With pleasure,' and he pulled the bright thirty-thirty out of its scabbard and passed it to the old one.

"The old one took it by the stock, threw a cartridge out of the magazine into the barrel, and pointed the gun straight at the owner, full-cocked. 'Now,' he said, 'step right over there to my burro, get six ears of corn, and eat them.'

"'That is a good joke,' said the *charro*. 'I ate *elotes* for breakfast just about an hour ago. I am fond of them, but I could not contain any more right now. Barrel full and heart content. Thank you for your offer just the same.'

"'The burro is the one who will thank me,' the old man growled, 'for lightening his load. You'll find that you can eat, for every growing youth has a lobo in his belly. I am not playing.'

expression sums up in itself everything of spiritedness, pride, and honor that a man can be possessed of.

"'Nor I either,' the *charro* said. 'Take your music to another house.'

Now he was angry and he reached to get back his gun, but the old one's finger was on the trigger.

"'Move yourself,' he said. 'Here there'll be no long track between the word and the act. Eat those ears of corn and eat them quick. Eat them raw, and if you wait a minute longer you'll have to eat the shucks! Go in a trot! Hurry! Be sudden!'

"When a closed-head declares that his horse mule is a mare mule, nobody can argue with him. So the *charro* gnawed the grains of corn off six cobs and swallowed them down into his already well-filled stomach. They nearly choked him. Then the old man removed the cartridge from the barrel of the rifle and in a very agreeable way handed it back to its owner.

"'Let this be a lesson to you,' he said, 'not to trust everybody you meet. Perhaps now you'll not offer your arm again to be twisted. *Adiós*.'"

Had Inocencio been a man of guile, he would certainly have ended his exordium at this point. Maybe he couldn't stop before he had told out the whole story, as it had descended to him and as he had embroidered it. Anyhow he made no pause.

"'Not so fast, my uncle,' the young man called. 'Your burro still has too heavy a load.' Then he gave a jerk to the lever of his rifle, threw a cartridge into the barrel, and aimed right at the heart of the old man. 'Now,' he said, 'I'm going to give you a sop of your own chocolate. You eat six *elotes*. Pick big ones.'

"'Now,' the old man cackled, 'you are making a good comedy. Nevertheless, I have just come from the field, where we had a fire and roasted so many *elotes* that after we had eaten I had to give three of them to my burro. How he likes toasted corn!'

"'It is the other burro's time to eat again,' the *charro* said. 'And instead of six ears, just for your delay you'll eat eight. The cart belongs to you. Pull it.'

"The old one saw that the other meant business and, considering that it is better to say, 'Here a hen ran' than 'Here a cock died,' he mashed his gums on the corn and at last had it all down.

"When he was through, the *charro* put his gun back in the scabbard but kept his hand on it. Before he gave his *palomino* the spur, he said, 'Let this be a lesson to you not to be offering advice to everybody you meet. As sure as you spit against the sky, the spittle will fall back in your face.'"

"I doubt," I said, "if the advice did the old man much good."

"The old man, no," Inocencio conceded. "He was too near finished, and anyhow an egg-sucking dog will keep on sucking eggs even though they burn his mouth. It is well said that he who is not handsome at twenty, strong at thirty, rich at forty, and wise at fifty will never be handsome, strong, rich, or wise."

"Inocencio, do you think I shall ever be wise?"

"*Pues*," and he did not smile, "you are strong."

The next morning early he brought a brazier made out of a tin can to warm my room and then respectfully withdrew while I should dress. He knew that I preferred drinking coffee after I arose rather than in bed. After he had brought it, he with a little embarrassment tinging his pleasure laid the scabbard containing "The Faithful Lover" upon my bed. I was to keep it as a *recuerdo* of one who wished always to serve me.

"Perhaps," he said, "it will have more memories for you than for me. I learned a long time ago that the dead do not snore."

After breakfast, having settled with him, I told him that Durazno and the saddle horses were his. In the one passenger coach of the train he arranged my saddle bags, the sack containing personal effects, the scabbarded rifle, and "The Faithful Lover," also in a scabbard, all with more shiftings and fittings than he would have taken in arranging a *carga* of assortments on a mule the first morning of travel. As yet no one was seated near us. Then he spoke.

"As our fathers taught us," he said, "what the eyes do not see, the heart does not feel. But this is not always true. Until my eyes are closed with dust I shall feel for you. Excuse all my poor services, but remember that if ever I can serve you, after God only you are first. You go. God preserve always the vigor of your body and the health of your soul."

I had purposely left "The Faithful Lover" exposed among the articles carried by hand rather than pack it up in the bed roll, which with saddle and some cooking utensils were in the baggage car. As Inocencio stood now, neither of us saying anything, I saw him eying the knife. Presently he picked it up and in a low voice asked me to follow him. He led to an unobserved spot behind the little station. There he unsheathed the knife, which was polished bright and newly sharpened, and with it cut a small vein in his left wrist. He wiped the knife clean, put it back in its scabbard, placed the scabbard in my left hand, and then with a finger took his own blood and marked a cross in the palm of my free hand.

"This sign is more than words," he said. "*Soy el suyo. I am yours.*"

Then he gave me the *abrazo.*

I stood on the rear platform of the lurching car until a curve cut off view of the station. As long as I looked I saw a little old man, who could be stately though, and who had muscles that never tired, an enormous straw hat on the ground beside him, making the gesture of the open heart towards me, touching his breast with the fingers of his hand and then extending his arms and holding them stretched out wide apart. I remembered a sentence from some writer of Mexico I have read:

"Just as all plant life springs from the soil, so from it come also the souls of men."